A Perfect Square

isobel blackthorn

ODYSSEY
BOOKS

Published by Odyssey Books in 2016

www.odysseybooks.com.au

A catalogue record for this
book is available from the
NATIONAL
LIBRARY   National Library of Australia
OF AUSTRALIA

ISBN: 978-1-922200-45-7 (pbk)
ISBN: 978-1-922200-50-1 (ebook)

For Dr Lesley Kuhn and Elizabeth Blackthorn, without whom *A Perfect Square* would never have been written.

Part One

Construction

Number

That twelve signified completion was not in dispute. They both knew the symbology. Setting aside the Imams, Apostles and Tribes, of concern to each of them, mother and daughter in turn, were the twelve signs of the zodiac and the twelve notes in the chromatic scale. Yet all things ended at twelve and Harriet felt ill-disposed towards the containment the number implied. As if through it the cosmos had reached its limit of emanation and, duly sated, foreclosed on thirteen, a number doomed to exist forevermore as a mere twelve-plus-one.

Her gaze slid from the pianola to her lap, a soothing dark green, and she found she was able, momentarily at least, to liberate herself from her musings. For Harriet Brassington-Smythe was apt to read much into life when there was not much to be read. Happenstance would lodge in her imagination, resonant with significances. She saw rainbows of colour when there was nothing for others but grisaille. Her mission, for she was that zealous, was to make manifest through her art this unique perception, as if she, one of but a special few, were privy to nature's inner secrets. It was not an altogether ill-founded zealousness; the one time she ignored the colours of her perception she found herself, nay the flesh of her flesh, in immense danger, and when at last she did tune in and saw the sharp glitter of black iridescences, she was so alarmed she gathered up her necessities, the tools of her trade and her daughter, and took flight.

That had been a long time before and far better forgotten, and to that end she had never spoken of the event to her daughter.

Harriet was in the prime of her life and in excellent form. Her long sculpted face, untroubled by the vicissitudes of ageing, had grown into its virtues, with large eyes the blacker side of brown, and a mouth at once pert and proud, the lower lip protruding a little beyond its counterpart, capable of a moue as much as an extravagant smile. The whole visage set off by a mane of wavy black hair that shone in the sunlight without a flicker of silver to be seen. She was a woman of grandiosity, bedecked as she liked to be in a calf-length dress of vintage twenties. She had taken on the dowager look, her presence imposing, perhaps off-putting to all but the most courageous.

Over the years she had attracted few lovers and ever since her one passion curdled she had remained single. She led a secluded life, one that provided fertile and slightly acidic soil for her eccentricity to flourish like an azalea. Yet quirkiness was a quality she reserved for her friends, the two women with whom she shared much of her time, hardy perennials Rosalind Spears and Phoebe Ashworth. Together they were three stalwarts, for decades remaining in the same garden bed set against the same stone wall of personal tradition, enjoying the comforts of moisture and shade.

She was suddenly uncomfortably hot. After a quick glance in the direction of the pianola, she stood. It had been an unusually warm late winter's day and at last a cool breeze blew in through the front windows. She drew the curtains further aside, curtains of luxurious sanguine velvet, gorgeous to touch, curtains her daughter had said in one of her vinegary moments were more likely to be found in the boudoir of a courtesan.

The garden was admirable at that time of year: long and wide and south facing, and shaded on the high side by a stand of mountain ash, with a half-moon raised bed that coursed much of the garden's width retained by a low bluestone wall. Her gaze lingered here and there over the ajugas, columbines, penstemons and erigeron daisies, at last settling on the delicate leaves of the weeping Japanese maple, and the hellebores and euphorbias at its base. A wide drive of crushed limestone wound its way from door to carport and thence to gate, skirting the wall where the raised bed was widest. To either side of the gate, two rhododendrons provided privacy and, together with a row of tree ferns, dogwoods and camellias, formed a dark backdrop. At times she felt like liberating the garden from that herbage screen, throwing the space open to The Crescent, but her privacy mattered more. A handful of youngsters had gathered outside the garden of next-door-but-one and she could hear their laughter. It wouldn't be long before they were gone, but she pulled the windows to the mullion, fastened the handles and moved aside. She wasn't normally bothered by juvenile activity, any more than she was given to gazing out her front window, yet she wanted to shut out distractions, even as she shut in the dissonance—dissonance at once familiar and disappointing.

Her daughter had taken possession of the other end of the room, ambulating the space between the pianola and the fireplace like a cougar in a cage.

Ginny was nothing like her mother. A tall and willowy woman, with hands narrow and long, as were her feet. From an early age her hands appeared destined for the keys, her feet to slosh about in too-wide shoes, manufacturers assuming that long feet were also always wide. Feet aside, she was the image of her maternal grandmother. She had the same fine mousy hair and wan pallor, the same small and round mouth that formed an 'o' when she parted her lips, and the same grey eyes that looked through to the back of you with innocence and suspicion. Grey, accented by her choice of grey slacks and matching grey shirt, the only colour about her person that ghastly paisley-print jacket, a relic from the paisley period of her teenage years.

It was a bizarre spectacle, watching her grey squirrel of a

daughter, more quarry than predator, more suited to a birch wood than a rocky range, prowl back and forth across the Kashan rug. She had not been an assertive child and there was a time Harriet had worried her biddable nature would be a disadvantage in a competitive world, but as a teenager Ginny had acquired a measure of defiance, a sure sign of an independent will.

The symbol she had chosen for this defiance was paisley. Whatever she wore, dress, skirt, trousers or shirt, it had to be paisley.

Harriet was steadfast in the belief that Ginny wore the design not because she liked it, but to cause her mother distress. William Morris, Harriet may have endured, at least he was contemporaneous with her era, but there was something so Seventies in the look. The *Seventies*, that accursed decade when the hippies took hold of the occult and turned it into fairy floss.

And there her daughter was in her paisley jacket, pacing back and forth. If she kept that up she would wear a track in the Kashan rug. With every circuit the mirror that took up much of the far wall captured her reflection, doubling the impact. It was fast becoming a sensory overload and Harriet felt relieved to find herself a good distance away.

The dining and living rooms had been combined years before Harriet inherited the house, along with the means to reside comfortably in it, the result a spacious high-ceilinged room with walls of exposed clinker brick. Evidence of its former design was a heavy beam spanning the width of the room and supported at each end by a stout post. The floorboards were the original oak, for Harriet would not countenance floor covering as pedestrian as carpet. The fireplace at Harriet's end of the room had been removed to make way for bookshelves. Shelves she had filled with volumes on art and art history, mostly confined to the 1920s: Surrealism, the Dadaists, Art Deco, Expressionism, the Cubists, and Pure Abstraction. There were books on individual artists, books on movements, and books on technique. The shelves sagged in the middle beneath the weight.

Facing each other across a low mahogany table, two sofas, upholstered in a sanguine hue a shade lighter than the curtains and festooned with gold cushions, bore witness to Harriet's affection for comfort. Beyond the oak beam, the remaining fireplace was set in a wide clinker brick chimneybreast that tapered in steps to the ceiling. Beneath the mahogany mantelpiece, the arc of bricks that defined the hearth wore the soot of many fires.

On the far side of the fireplace was the entrance to the kitchen, accessed through a vintage glass-beaded curtain. Black, diamond-cut and varying in size, the glass beads were arranged to form several undulations, the curtain's scalloped fringe not quite brushing the floor. The curtain was Harriet's most treasured piece, lending her living quarters an air of authenticity. But alas reinforcing in Ginny's eyes the stamp of the bordello.

Harriet's expressionist artworks, hung with a keen eye for balance, adorned every expanse of wall. There was not a thing to be out of place in the room, no knickknacks, mementoes, objet d'art, or pot plants, the room uncluttered save for two tiffany lamps, each centred upon an occasional table that filled an otherwise empty corner, an antique pedestal ashtray that was never used, an old record player housed in its own teak veneer cabinet, and a carriage clock on the mantelpiece bookended by photographs of Kandinsky and Klee in ornate oval frames. Absent from the arrangement was a photo of Ginny, Harriet having long before decided she was not sentimental when it came to her daughter.

Harriet left the window and ambled around the back of a sofa, running a hand lightly along the upholstery as she went, before sitting and leaning back, ankles crossed, one hand dangling from the armrest, as if in repose she would take command of her side of the room.

Ginny paused in her perambulations, shot a cool stare in Harriet's direction then, as if following her mother's lead, took up the pianola stool, going so far as to open the instrument's lid and run a single hand down the keys.

The glissando intruded on the silence.

Ginny pressed a run of notes in slow succession. 'Not twelve then,' she said without shifting her gaze from the keys.

'Not twelve.'

She played the notes again, her composure thoughtful. Perhaps she would run through the scales or play something from memory for there was no sheet music on the ledge. Harriet watched in anticipation. That she showed an interest in the pianola, however half hearted, was, Harriet hoped, evidence of recovery.

Three weeks earlier Ginny had pulled into the driveway in her small hatchback. She alighted with a quick scan of the garden, paused at the sight of her mother crouched by a window box dead-heading pansies, then she heaved from the boot a heavy-looking suitcase and her keyboard and stand lashed to a trolley, and lugged them to the front door. She seemed forlorn and Harriet's heart did a squeeze. She knew straightaway that Ginny had left her weasel boyfriend and hoped this time it was for good.

For three years she had endured their relationship, suffered whenever she pictured his faux muso appearance, a mismatch uniform of drainpipes and unkempt suit jacket, woollen scarf and sunglasses. The despicable Garth, who Harriet had from the first considered talentless, played a perpetual circuit of dead-end gigs, his showy singer-songwriter pretentions little short of delusional. She could never fathom what Ginny saw in him.

She dusted off her hands and followed her daughter inside.

Ginny parked the trolley and her suitcase in the hall and entered the living room.

'Tea?' Harriet asked.

'Why not,' Ginny said and flopped down on a sofa.

The glass beads tinkled as Harriet parted the curtain. She slipped through, releasing her hand slowly to let the beads settle. She set about making the tea, the fragrant leaves swirling in the pot a mockery of the motherly obligation that swirled about in her heart.

She returned with a tray and set it down on the coffee table. 'You can stay as long as you like,' she said, hoping that would stretch to no more than three nights.

She sat on the other sofa and poured, passing Ginny her tea.

'I've lost my job,' Ginny said, directing her comment more at the cup in her hand.

'At the Derwent?' Harriet said, hoping to keep her tone natural.

'I can't make ends meet in North Melbourne without it.' Her voice was faint and small.

She had relinquished her lofty ambitions at least, or so it seemed. All through her doctoral studies Ginny had craved an academic position. After much fretting over her prospects, upon completing her thesis she had managed to acquire a twice-weekly residency at the Derwent Hotel. It was only a stop gap, she said, while she waited for something tertiary to come up. She would scowl at the music industry, the paucity of opportunities it afforded when she had had to go all the way through university and gain a doctorate to get the sort of gig she could have managed in her first year. Harriet never mentioned that her unmet aspirations might have had a little to do with her attitude, not to mention the low-life company she kept.

'They can't just fire you,' she said, worried that Ginny's return home would prove more permanent than she might have liked.

'They can and they have. The job was casual. I am, as they say, a dime a dozen. Besides, they had every right. You know their reputation. All these years I've been dressing up like a Gucci doll for that swanky joint and then Garth walks in and it's ruined.'

'Looking like a bum?'

'Oh Mum.' She paused, shooting Harriet a reproachful look before lowering her gaze. 'Well yes, with his guitar in hand. He came right up to where I was performing and knelt on one knee and played his latest song to me. I was halfway through "Moonlight Sonata". He was so drunk he lost his balance and fell at my feet. Then security came and dragged him away.'

'But you did nothing wrong.'

'By association. I would have disowned him but as they steered him off he launched into a loud lament about how much he loved me and would see me back at home.'

'Oh dear.'

'Not oh dear,' Ginny said, at last lifting her face. 'It's totally understandable that I'm fired. The hotel couldn't risk him turning up again.'

Harriet gave her an awkward smile. It was an inevitable ending; Garth had been a drag on Ginny from the start. Even the circumstances of their meeting were symbolic of the seedy underworld life he would later weave around her.

They had met in the underground of Flinders Street station. She was readying to submit her thesis. On her way back to her flat after her final meeting with her supervisor, she encountered him standing in the tunnel, busking. The incongruity could not have been more apparent. When Harriet had phoned Ginny that evening, curious to hear of her supervisor's comments and poised to enthuse and praise, Ginny had described the encounter, her voice all light and girlish. Harriet hadn't heard that tone since Ginny was fourteen with a crush on her peripatetic piano teacher. Garth had caught her eye as she passed him by and she had stopped and turned. He serenaded her, she said. With 'Hotel California'. She was transfixed, she said. Dropped a dollar in his guitar case, then another, and he kept on singing and playing, ignoring the others who had gathered to witness the moment, directing exclusively at her his gaze, his smile, his lust. Harriet knew then that Garth was no good. Her daughter love struck dumb. Whoever in any event calls their child *Garth*? And it mattered not one jot that he made good money busking, or that he had a prime pitch, and of course Ginny's insistence that he really had talent Harriet took to mean he had absolutely none at all.

Garth moved into Ginny's North Melbourne flat a few weeks into their relationship and that was when Ginny discovered his whisky habit. He was a stupid soppy drunk, argumentative when riled, in the hair trigger manner of the alcoholic.

Harriet only visited the once. There was an exhibition at the Sutton and it seemed to her appropriate enough that she should make use of her daughter's spare room. After all, it was only for one night. And a ghastly night it proved to be.

The flat was small and dim and plainly furnished, although nicely laid out with a narrow hall and separate kitchen. The living room was Spartan: two drab chairs, a television and a clutter of musical gear shoved into one corner. Ginny was at the Derwent and not due back until nine. Garth had returned early from a bad evening's busking, carrying a bottle of whisky and a parcel reeking of fish and chips. Harriet wished she had ignored the heavy footsteps lumbering to the door, the grunts then the turn of the key.

Entering the living room to the smell was bad enough—a sickly mix of fish supper, whisky and sweat—and the sight of Garth devouring his repast with all the manners of a hog made Harriet bilious. When he started slugging back the contents of his glass and reaching for a refill over and again, she succumbed to a mounting disgust.

She did nothing to mask her displeasure. He did nothing to hide his relish of her disapproval. Nothing was said. They both made pretence of watching television.

When Ginny at last arrived, Garth staggered to his feet and slobbered her with kisses. She pushed him away and Harriet caught a flash of annoyance in his face. Not wanting to add to the tension, she chose that moment to retire, and she was forced to listen through her bedroom wall to raised voices, one gruff, the other defensive.

Ginny stayed loyal to her beau and Harriet could not contain her chagrin. After that night she hardly saw her daughter. They were three difficult years. Harriet called it her Persephone period and she broke away from abstract art and produced a series of moody landscapes in pen and ink which, thanks to her friend Phoebe, she promptly sold to a cohort of mothers who met each Wednesday in Olinda for yoga and to bemoan their wayward daughters.

Harriet was not the only one to hold Garth in disregard. Ginny's peers at the university fell away one by one, presumably after suffering an encounter with the inebriated lover.

That he had devastated her career was little short of tragedy. Whenever Ginny telephoned, Harriet would inquire after this friend and that, or the progress of a band or collaboration. The truth was hard to elicit but between the lines of Ginny's evasive remarks she gleaned that Garth was at the root of the shedding.

Seated across the coffee table, Harriet watched her daughter take short sips of tea from the cup clasped in her hands, her lowered gaze, her worn and pale face. She would be sure to remain in withdrawal from the mayhem of her relationship for some time. Harriet felt concerned. Yet it was concern tinged with consternation. It was one thing having her daughter move back home. That was challenging enough, but to have her misery move in with her would be intolerable. Something would have to be done. Without that something, her daughter's mood would thwart her creativity. She wouldn't focus. She wouldn't paint. And seated there, sipping her tea, Harriet saw her immediate future cloud over.

For three weeks she put up with Ginny's glum mood. Then one night, she could endure it no longer. They were having dinner and for a good ten minutes Ginny shunted about her plate the salad Harriet had so painstakingly prepared, picking at the olives and little else. Harriet was ready to blast forth with frustration, incredulous that anyone, especially her own daughter, could wallow so wilfully.

She downed her black cohosh tea in several large gulps before its bitter taste took hold, then stood and leaned her hands against the table, commanding Ginny to the living room with, 'We need to talk.'

She held aside the beaded curtain, waiting for her daughter to pass through. She was determined to lift her up by her paisley socks if need be.

Rather than let her sit down on a sofa, she accosted her on the Kashan rug, blocking her movement with a sharp 'Stop.'

Ginny tried to walk away and Harriet put out her arm to block her. Defeated, Ginny stood limply and Harriet was about to tell her that she wanted her to pack her bags in the hope of shocking her out of her mood, when she saw her daughter in part profile together with the pianola and the artwork behind her, and she had an idea.

She envisaged a collaboration of music and art, an exhibition that was a concert, or a concert that was an exhibition. Either way, a marvellous ruse.

At first Ginny seemed nonplussed. Then resistant. Eventually, after much walking back and forth and Harriet trying every means of persuasion from the obvious, 'It will lift your spirits' to 'It will be a splash on the local arts scene,' the comment that secured her cooperation was 'It will give the gallery a lift,' as if Ginny had been waiting for the real reason to come along and that was it.

Ginny agreed, in principle, and went to her room, leaving Harriet in mild shock.

She pondered the artwork hanging above the pianola, her homage to Kandinsky, painted in the Eighties when she had been her daughter's age and her passion for abstraction had exploded on canvas upon canvas. And she wondered if this collaboration might afford her something of a renaissance, a chance to recapture her prolific pre-Ginny creativity.

Two years before Ginny was born, Harriet had been as free as any sandstone graduate could afford to be. She was the daughter of a corporate lawyer and a Bible-worshipping headmistress of a private school. They were British ex-patriots who had left South Africa with their wealth long before the collapse of Apartheid, and lived an erect and moral life in Mont Albert. In the face of her parents, Harriet felt an additional pressure to conform. Yet she forewent all their suggestions of careers that could be pursued with a degree and a Masters in Art History. 'The Heide Museum is looking for a curator,' her father would say, staring at her over the rim of his glasses. Or, 'Here's one for a conservator,' and her mother would look at her keenly, willing her to step in line. Harriet had no predilection whatsoever to become a curator or a conservator. She yearned to spend a few years exploring her creativity while she was still young enough to make an impression in the art scene. And she was naïve enough to believe she stood a chance.

Once, at her mother's birthday lunch at which Rosalind had been the only other guest, they were seated at the dining table, her parents at either end. Both were dressed formally, him in a grey suit, the collar of his shirt cutting into his plump neck, all shiny freckly pate and jowly cheeked and looking more judge than lawyer; her in a plain blue dress, grey hair permed curly, straight backed as she cut into her tuna terrine. Harriet, seated midway between, shot Rosalind an uncertain smile and scooped the last of her curried egg. Then, on an upwelling of courage, she announced she had spent the last five years attending art classes wherever she could find them.

Her parents exchanged glances, but she persisted, stressing the virtues of following her passion and insisting that they always said they only ever wanted her to be happy.

Her father looked stern, her mother equivocal. Then Rosalind spoke wistfully of her own youth and how she had longed to be a concert pianist but her parents thought her not worth the additional investment so she turned to philosophical pursuits instead.

At first Harriet thought Rosalind was siding with her parents, until she said, 'I often thought I'd have been equal to Eileen Joyce given the chance but of course we'll never know.'

Harriet bounded in with pleas and assurances. Her parents were swayed and, despite their disappointment, they gave her a small living allowance.

Ecstatic, she went home to her rented upstairs rooms in a two-storey house in Fitzroy—Number Seven Moor Street. The larger room she used as her studio: high ceilinged with a balcony that faced south. The room was bland. The rudiments of a kitchen lined the back wall. A box room at the back served as her bedroom. The bathroom, shared with the downstairs tenants, was down the hall. In the studio-room she had laid drop sheets on the carpet in the corner by the window and positioned her easel towards the natural light. She would spend many hours of each day standing by the window, pondering her latest work, and at last she could do it with a modicum of financial security.

She leaned back against the window frame, for once at ease with her surroundings, despite the incongruities of domestic and personal style. She had adopted a ladybird look, although she liked to think of it as colourist meets noir: curly hair, black as jet, held back from her face by a red silk scarf, her smock, black, protecting her turtleneck sweater of red cashmere, dog-tooth check mini-skirt and red tights. While many of her peers were pairing off or marrying, or moving away for promising careers and big mortgages, she clung fast to her bohemianism. Melbourne frustrated her. She yearned for Berlin, Paris, New York, cities where art thrived, where she felt sure she would find scores of her own kind. Yet here in downtown Fitzroy, thanks to her friend Phoebe, she was exhibiting, selling and receiving commissions and she had to be grateful for that.

Phoebe had a natural instinct for the niche market and a sharp eye for trends. Abstract, expressionist, symbolist—modernist art had been having a renaissance. All of their old student friends had a poster on their walls of a Matisse or a Munch or a Klimt. Being ostensibly naïve, Harriet priced her works accordingly and well below her competition. It was at once their subversion of the male-dominated neo-expressionist art scene and the all-pervasive Australian cultural cringe. Aussie art produced by a woman, selling like Rolexes from a suitcase in London's Petticoat Lane: Phoebe and Harriet were rapt.

So it was with much confidence that she applied a touch of raw umber to the work on her easel. She was working in gouache for the matte finish. The piece was to be her homage to Kandinsky, part of her homages series that had been keeping her busy for months. Upon selling her first 'Homage to Matisse' before the paint was dry and receiving a commission for a second, she had wondered if the title held the appeal, a title that framed and contextualised each painting, as if the buyer thought they were in some way taking home a real Matisse or Munch or Klimt.

Kandinsky was not so popular; buyers, it seemed, had a preference for the French, presumably inspired by the arty popularity of Edith Piaf, exemplifier of melancholia, passion, the suffering of the disenfranchised artist fallen on hard times, and chic. Or perhaps it was merely the presence of some sort of representational form: a chair, however distorted, still recognisably a chair. Pure abstraction was too difficult, nay meaningless for the plebeians of Melbourne, who therefore deemed it pretentious. Alas the work on her easel was her indulgence, for it was really quite good and when finished would hang on her wall.

She stood back from the work, moving aside to let what light there was of a dull day shine directly on the canvas. The work depicted her faithful application of Kandinsky's rules of colour and form, a series of interconnecting geometric shapes splayed along two intersecting planes that vanished at separate points. Shapes in muted tones, negative space earthy, and the three contrasting yellow circles tense before a blue rhombus. Then there was the dominating black moon that took up the top left corner. It was possible to see in the work representations of buildings, roads, pyramids and references to time, another viewing and a building became a city, the road a river and the pyramids pyres until there were no more mundane associations and the shapes became what they were, forms in themselves, and their interactions spoke then of something else, something ineffable, perhaps cosmological, even divine.

The piece had indeed achieved transcendence, and she knew she had fulfilled Kandinsky's spiritual aims for abstract art. With quiet triumph she jiggled her brush in a jar of water, removed it and wiped it dry, setting it down on the table where all her other brushes were lined up in order of size; flat with flat, round with round, sable with sable, hog bristle with hog bristle.

She removed her smock, folded it in half and draped it on the back of a chair. Then she leaned against the window and looked up and down the street. To the east, the terraced houses with their lacework verandas receded in two straight lines into the grey of the day. Directly opposite, three bikes were chained to the railings. She was about to pull away when, cornering Nicholson Street, a figure approached in a steel-grey trench coat and matching fedora, and she recognised as well Phoebe's purposeful stride.

She turned back to the room. On the draining board, sauce-pans and crockery were stacked about ten high. The bin stuffed full. On the floor before a low cabinet her records, in and out of their sleeves, arced like a fan. The lid of the record player was open, with Nick Cave and the Bad Seeds on the turntable. She took it all in with the domestic indifference she had contrived to suit her persona and walked from the scene and out to the landing, ready to call down to Phoebe that the front door was on the latch.

'Great,' Phoebe said as she entered the hall without an upward glance. She climbed the stairs in twos, wheezing at the last tread. Harriet looked on, thinking ones would have better suited her condition.

Phoebe followed her into the studio-room, tossed her fedora on the sofa and ran both hands through her slick-backed hair. Phoebe was petite, flat chested, and plain of face. Yet there was a slight hood to the eyes, a firm set to the mouth and a definite uprightness of gait. Altogether her presence was formidable, as if she had spent her whole life fighting for the spotlight, forever passed over by the tall and the beautiful. Condemned to the wings, she had learned to make the most of the obscurity, adopted the part of the hustler and, with ruthless resolve and an astounding efficiency, made her-self indispensable in the local arts scene, undoubtedly in a similar fashion to her cor blimey forebears. Phoebe hailed from rough and ready parentage from London's East End and had been adopted for health reasons by an aunt on her mother's side, growing up in Melbourne. The aunt managed to divest her of the accent but not the asthma or the attitude. Harriet, herself no mouse, might have cowered inwardly in her presence had she not been her closest friend.

Phoebe was in Harriet's class at high school. They studied the same subjects, and became school-based best friends, neither Harriet's parents nor Phoebe's aunt enamoured with the bond. The only time Harriet did invite Phoebe home, Claudia Brassington-Smythe called Harriet aside and asked her why she was associating with a commoner. Harriet overheard Phoebe's aunt say much the same when she visited her house, only in reverse. 'She's up herself, that one. You'd do better mixing with your own kind.' Instead, their bond grew stronger. Flying in the face of their respective family's wishes, each secured a place in art history at the University of Melbourne and their lives had intertwined ever since.

Phoebe stood in the centre of the room, one foot only an inch from *The Firstborn is Dead*. Harriet was about to rescue the record from her friend's absent-minded foot when Phoebe said without preface, 'Have you finished the Klee?'

'Tea?' Harriet said, wishing Phoebe would sit down.

'The Klee, sweetheart.'

Realising she was not in a sociable mood, Harriet reached behind the sofa and pulled out a canvas.

'Ah superb,' Phoebe said, giving the work a brief but appraising glance before adding, 'Can you knock out a Matisse by Thursday week?'

'Sure, but…'

'No buts. The buyer is a nonce. Couldn't tell a Cezanne from a Mondrian.'

She went to the painting on the easel then took a step back, tilting her head to the side. 'You've surpassed yourself with this one,' she said and stared a while longer. 'Have you thought more about the Klimt?'

'Too fussy.'

'Thought so. I'll negotiate a Hirschfeld-Mack. Something gold though.' She looked back at the easel. 'That one won't sell. Needs a human face, lovey.'

Harriet paused then laughed. 'Or a chair.'

And so it went. Phoebe took thirty per cent of sales. They did good business and neither felt compromised. Naïve her work may have been yet Harriet was no dilettante. Not only had she attended art classes throughout her university years, during her Masters she had secured private tuition from a cash-strapped doctoral student in fine art. She would whip round to his flat in Carlton after her Wednesday tutorial, and spend an hour or two, sometimes more, acquiring the methods of the craft. His name was Fritz.

The night they had met was fated, of that she was sure. For it had been with much trepidation that she took the number ninety-six tram to St Kilda. Bauhaus were playing at the Crystal Ballroom; not her sort of venue but she was curious to hear the band live, having found their music conducive to the production of Kandinsky and Klee-inspired works. It was a muggy October evening and she was feeling peeved that Phoebe had chosen a night in. Hadn't wanted to brave the air, she said, in case it set off her asthma. But Harriet suspected otherwise, a suspicion confirmed when she alighted the tram in Fitzroy Street and stepped into St Kilda in the rain and had to skirt two semi-conscious drunks propped against the façade of the Seaview Hotel before confronting a melee of Goths under the portico. Phoebe's bugbears; the former would have brought to mind her father, the latter her derision. Goths, for Phoebe, were a pretentious perversion of good taste.

Harriet sympathised with Phoebe's prejudices. The Siouxsie Sioux hair, the leather, the black, the theatricality of the garb, altogether the look might have carried vaudeville appeal if only the wearers wouldn't take themselves so seriously. She filed in behind and headed upstairs, acutely aware of her own apparel: an oversized vee-neck sweater of black, a red satin mini skirt, un-laddered black stockings, and fur-trimmed pixie boots. The kohl about her eyes, the pale make-up, the vermillion lipstick, the silky black locks of her hair, and the uninitiated might suppose her a conservative version of those hustling ahead of her. But she knew, and the Goths knew as well, that they didn't belong at the same gig.

The fug of the Crystal Ballroom hit her as she walked in. Despite its size and high ceiling, the stench of sweat, dirty damp coats and cigarette smoke seemed to have nowhere to go. The huge chandelier that gave the venue its name was lost in the haze, its crystal indistinct and bereft of glimmer.

While the support act was playing she queued in the crush at the bar. Then she found a spot far from the Goths and downed her can of beer in long steady draughts. She preferred to drink wine but didn't trust the labels behind the bar. The beer was bitter and gassy but left her feeling more courageous. She put the can on a window ledge and, even though it meant mingling with the diehards, she squeezed into the crowd until she was some way toward the front and equidistant from the speaker stacks. She wasn't a diehard, here for the worship like the Goths. She could never lose herself to a pack. Yet Bauhaus were compelling. At twenty-one she was all attuned senses to the uncomplicated music, the insistent pulse, the melancholia. She shared with the crowd an impatient expectancy. When Bauhaus took the stage, and Pete Murphy the microphone, she felt deep inside her the jagged guitars and the rich baritone vocals.

Yet it wasn't his bonhomie, his frenetic dancing, the way he dominated the stage or the sophistication of his voice that mesmerised her. Neither was it the aliveness of the brooding music coursing through her every cell.

At first she thought it was the lighting, but the colours were too elaborate and too precisely bound to the music. Besides, Bauhaus would never be lit in pink. Ten bars in and she realised she wasn't only hearing 'Bela Lugosi's Dead', she was seeing the song, seeing every note, the whole forming an intense kaleidoscopic light show. She stood, transfixed, the audience rocking and swaying all around her receding into an amorphous blob of insignificance.

As the song ended someone jogged her arm and the moment was gone. The band launched into 'Kick in the Eye' over the applause and Murphy was soon leaping from the speaker stacks. Yet for her, nudged back to the reality of the ordinary, heightened as it was, the song and the antics seemed trite. Suddenly, she wanted to leave.

She tried to slip through the crowd behind her, but her path was blocked by a plainly dressed man whose gaze could not be diverted from the stage. Not keen to force her way through the pack of Goths who seemed to have taken over the gig, she made to squeeze by him. He didn't move an iota. At the end of the song she made a second attempt but he was oblivious to her, or so it seemed. She waited. Then, as if the piercing feedback at the end of 'In the Flat Field' jolted him into an awareness of her standing before him, he looked at her, smiled and inched aside.

She went to the bar, empty save for one inebriated punk who lingered at the end, and bought another beer. She took a large gulp, grimaced, then went to stand in the darkest corner furthest from the stage.

For Kandinsky it had been Wagner, for her Bauhaus. When she had read about Kandinsky's synaesthesia in her undergraduate years she was convinced it wasn't true. That he had been hallucinating, probably on something, or he was a fraud, for he could no more have seen in colour Wagner's music than people see auras. She relied on this assumption to inform her final third-year essay, a controversial piece that raised an eyebrow or two, in which she argued that he had based a life's work on a fabricated event and upon this false foundation erected a contrived, almost delusional set of correspondences between painting and music.

Standing in the corner of the ballroom, beer in hand, those assumptions collapsed and she cringed inwardly. She knew with the conviction of the born again that she, too, had seen into a secret realm, sharing with Kandinsky an inner knowing. He had been right all along, and her essay, which had earned her a high distinction, was crap.

After the gig, she beat the crowd downstairs and stood beneath the portico, sheltering from the drizzle. Her ears were ringing. She scanned from the corner of her eye the Goths filing by—raucous and drunk—and the contempt she felt in the ballroom was replaced by unease. In the melee she noticed the plainly dressed man who had stood behind her in the audience and blocked her path. He was heading for the tram stop. She threaded past the others until she was beside him and together they crossed to the centre of the road.

At the other end of the tram stop an altercation was breaking out between a spikey-haired punk and a thickset thug, some of the others jeering them on. Harriet faced her chosen ally, looking up to catch his gaze.

'Hi,' she said. 'I'm Harriet.'

'Fritz.'

He was fair-haired with angular features, intelligent blue eyes beneath a high forehead lending him a serious yet not unattractive appearance. She assumed from the way he said his name that he was German.

'Are you on holiday?' she said.

'I'm a student.'

'Summer school?'

'I'm a doctoral student.'

'An international student? You must be talented.'

'My mother is Australian.'

'Father German?'

He frowned. 'Bavarian.'

'German then.'

'Does it matter?'

She thought he sounded irritated and she placed her hand on his arm. 'I don't mean to be rude,' she said.

He made no reply and they stood together in silence.

When the tram pulled up and the doors opened she made sure she stayed by his side. He sat behind the driver and she took up the empty seat set at right angles to his. She stole a glance at the others on the tram and didn't relish the long ride back to Moor Street.

As the tram clunked and jolted and swayed she made another attempt to strike up a conversation, explaining without preface that she was studying art history at her parent's behest, but she really wanted to pursue fine art. Up until the Bauhaus concert she had more or less acquiesced to their wishes.

'What's changed?' he said with interest.

'I'm not sure. I was seeing the music in there. I mean, really seeing it.'

'Might I suggest you drop the acid,' he said, looking away.

'I didn't.'

'What?'

'Drop acid. This was real as day.'

She went on to explain and by the time they had reached her Moor Street tram stop, he had offered her private art classes. She wasn't to know it then, that those classes would culminate each time in his bed.

She stood on the pavement and watched the tram trundle on, thankful that Fritz's stop came after hers, then she dashed down her street to her house. Climbing the stairs she was pleased that Phoebe had chosen a night in.

Later, she was pleased for an altogether different reason, for she surmised that had Phoebe been with her at the Crystal Ballroom, she would have been required to stand at the back where there was more air, and there was every chance her synaesthesia would not have occurred without the immersion in the throng.

On the strength of her Kandinsky essay her tutor, Dawn Vector, had suggested she consider a Masters the following year. When she explained in a tutorial in the week following the concert that she wanted to explore the impact synaesthesia had on the pure abstract art of that great Russian painter, Miss Vector was astonished by the reversal. Harriet didn't offer an explanation, other than that she had changed her mind. Secretly, she thought of it as atonement. And she knew she would be able to approach the matter with much authenticity.

Upon completing her masters, in between knocking out commissions for Phoebe, she transmuted her synaesthetic epiphany into her Kandinsky painting. She had always thought of it as her masterpiece. About a decade later, when she moved to Sassafras, she had hung the work above the pianola and there it had remained.

Standing on the Kashan rug, Harriet pictured the composition she had glimpsed moments earlier, a composition that had triggered her idea of a collaboration, a composition of her daughter, the pianola, and the painting. The three objects formed a triangle, scalene and obtuse, its longer side descending along an almost vertical plane from the painting to the pianola; Ginny, the third object, at the obtuse angle. The two planes formed by the pianola and the painting were partially contained in the third, Ginny, who consisted of an irregular point that included pairs of lesser points, the eyes, the ears, the breasts.

Imposing a concave effect upon the whole, she distorted the uniformity, stretching the perimeter and creating a convergence at the centre. A convex imposition and the centre was spread, the edges compressed. Harriet wasn't sure which she preferred.

Together, Ginny, the pianola and the painting represented the whole of her life, three significances in a state of tension, of dissonance, and there was no mistaking that Ginny was the dominant force, taking up the whole left half of the composition, foregrounded with her extremities beyond the frame, as if challenging her, as if they were rivals, subject and artist, vying for power. And Ginny dominated the pianola, which stood in submission, cowering beneath her imperious pose, head raised, mouth set, eyes staring off into the distance.

Harriet felt drained. She crossed the Kashan rug, a little heavy of foot, and sat down on the sofa facing her artbook collection, casting an eye along the spines. She realised she couldn't expect Ginny to be as pleased as she with the idea of a collaborative exhibition and it seemed to have taken much to persuade her of its virtues. Although Harriet couldn't tell if Ginny's stubborn resistance was directed at her, the project or both. That her daughter was still capable of behaving like a teenager she found disappointing and she was burdened with a recollection of the scorn Ginny used to cast over her taste. As if on cue, the heat rose up from her chest and she found herself clammy and fidgety.

Ginny must have been fifteen the day she flounced through the house to greet her best friend, Veronica Hunnacot, at the front door. After an exchange of giggles and raised voices, they had gone straight up to Ginny's room.

Harriet had turned to Rosalind and smiled. They were taking tea after Ginny's piano lesson. Rosalind had been teaching Ginny piano for years, just as she had Harriet. Back then Harriet knew her as Miss Spears. 'Rosalind' came later. She observed the woman seated before her, all square and upright, her formal posture accentuated by her green tweed skirt suit and brogues, and her silver hair pulled back in a comb, hair that framed a face round as an apple. She was a Cox's Orange Pippin, both traditional and comely, with a rosy flush to her cheeks, her nature a subtle blend of delicate qualities that combined into something robust. She was mild in her manners yet neither meek nor complacent. She had had the whole world figured out long before and knew her place in it. Nothing surprised her. She took a sip from the bone china cup Harriet always gave her, and placed it back in the saucer on her lap.

'It occurs to me the child has an aptitude for jazz,' she said reflectively.

'Ginny? What makes you say that?'

'Pure intuition my dear. And her manner of approaching Bach.' She raised her gaze to the ceiling, to the muffled thuds, as Ginny and Veronica cavorted about upstairs.

'I must be going, Harriet,' she said, handing Harriet her cup and saucer.

After seeing Rosalind to the door, Harriet thought about making falafel wraps because Veronica Hunnacot was vegetarian. Falafel from a packet. Harriet was not a packet-instruction cook. Neither was she a recipe-following cook, preferring to chuck whatever was to hand into a pot to stew for several hours. She would put on Count Basie to drown out the noise upstairs. Or perhaps Scott Joplin. Music to chop to and there was much chopping to be done.

By the time Ginny and Veronica came downstairs, Harriet had moved on to Duke Ellington.

They bounded through the beaded curtain, one of the strands catching on Veronica's hair clip. She disentangled herself with a penitent smile. She was a well-developed girl, typical of the female Hunnacots, the too-short top she wore revealing a narrow yet fleshy waist that bulged upon meeting her too-low cut, too-tight jeans. It was a look thankfully Ginny had not taken to. Although, already tall for her age, the teenage fashion of the day rarely met around her middle. Veronica had the opposite problem, her middle parting clothes that might otherwise have hung with modesty.

Harriet had never taken to the Hunnacots. They resided in Gwenneth Crescent and Veronica attended Ginny's school. Veronica's parents were both teachers of a liberal persuasion: the sort that sponsored a child from some forsaken land; the sort who attended fundraisers and joined societies. Between them they had taken office on every committee in the village. It was the Hunnacots who had set up a fundraising stall outside the gallery one Saturday morning when Phoebe had arranged for some buyers to view her new collection. The request to move on was met with much resistance and it was only the knowledge that their daughter was her daughter's best friend that held back Harriet's fury.

The girls had regressed to sly giggles. Veronica was nudging Ginny's arm and reaching to whisper in her ear. Upon which Ginny said, 'Can we listen to something else?'

'I thought I'd play jazz,' Harriet said airily.

'You only like *old school* jazz.'

It was true in a fashion; Duke Ellington, Count Basie and Scott Joplin were in keeping with the Twenties, but more's the point, their music didn't stimulate her synaesthesia, a spiritual state she found distracting and tiresome in the kitchen.

'This isn't old school,' she said, maintaining a blithe tone. 'It's timeless.'

'Only for you.' Ginny turned to her friend and, using a turn of phrase beyond her years, she said, 'At least one of us here has moved with the times.'

More giggles.

Harriet managed to contain herself, but when Ginny bent towards her friend and said in a loud whisper, 'She makes me play the pianola,' Harriet struggled not to reach out and swipe her.

The pianola had been Harriet's grandmother Emma's greatest joy, a Steinway of polished mahogany, gifted for Emma's eighth birthday. The family story had it that little Emma would peddle through Ragtime and jazz rolls till her legs ached from the effort. Harriet's mother had learned to play on it, as had her mother's older brother and fine pianist, the adorable Uncle Phillip. That it was Harriet's eighth birthday when Uncle Phillip lost his life to cerebral malaria during a spell in Kenya, and the pianola had been gifted to her that very day, caused the instrument to take on a greater significance in her heart. Soon after, she left with her parents for Cape Town and she never saw her grandmother Emma again.

She had had little ability but she treasured the instrument just as she had treasured her uncle. And in the cool dark dining room on Cape Town's hot summer's days she would peddle the old piano rolls, just as her grandmother had done, until her legs were sore.

The winter sun dipped below the mountain and the room darkened. Dusk was hours away but a match would soon have to be taken to the fire she had laid in the grate earlier in the day. Harriet didn't stir. The atmosphere remained tense; Ginny, seated at the pianola, idly pressing a key here and there. Plinketty plonketty, Rosalind called it. That she remained seated and thoughtful, however, did seem promising. It was a sure sign that she was beginning to take the proposition seriously.

Harriet discovered she was pinching the soft flesh of her forearm and desisted. She had not envisaged they would labour over the selection of a number. At least on twelve they were agreed. That left eleven numbers, eleven possibilities, eleven opportunities for disagreement. With Ginny in a fractious mood, for a fleeting moment Harriet considered postponing the decision making until another day, a moment soon eclipsed by a suspicion that an impasse now would see the entire collaboration falter. She would persist; that minutes before, Ginny had prowled back and forth across the Kashan rug, evidence that she gripped the project in her jaws.

Ginny closed the pianola lid and swivelled round to face her mother. She looked careworn beyond her years and Harriet felt a sudden sympathy for her.

'Seven,' Harriet suggested, hoping to bring some life back into the discussion.

'Why seven?'

'I've always liked seven.'

'We can't base a life's work on a number one of us happens to like. It's frivolous.'

Ginny was right of course, but Harriet did not care for her dismissive tone. 'It's a number of much significance,' she said defensively. 'Think of the seven colours of the rainbow. The seven chakras. The seven planes of emanation. Besides,' she added after stealing a quick glance at her watch, 'everything happens for a reason and seven came into my head at seven minutes past four.'

Ginny pressed together her lips. 'Perhaps we should forget about the number altogether.'

At that Harriet felt a strong urge to throw a cushion. The heat rose and sweat beaded on her brow. 'But the number is crucial,' she said. 'It sets up the initial conditions. Besides, we have to agree on *something*. If we can't manage a sodding number, then we might as well give up.'

Ginny stood and made to leave the room before changing her mind and pausing by the fireplace at the very spot Harriet's imaginary projectile had landed. She turned back to her mother and said, 'Then three.'

'Three,' Harriet repeated flatly.

'What's wrong with three?'

'I hate three.'

'You can't hate a number. It's silly.'

'What's silly about it?'

'It's just a *number*.'

'It's too religious and too obvious. Makes me think of trinities and triptychs.'

Ginny was silent.

'And three has never worked for me.'

'How can you say that?'

'Three Gore Street was a disaster.'

Ginny looked ready to explode. 'That had nothing to do with the street number,' she said between her teeth.

'It might have,' Harriet said indignantly. 'Seven, on the other hand, has always brought me luck. Seven Moor Street, for example: I was happy there.'

'You're doing it again. Ascribing your experience to a number. It's self-centred.'

Harriet felt sure she was about to go on to say something like, typical of you. 'Then how do we arrive at the number?' she snapped. 'Pull one out of a hat?'

'Might as well.'

'Pure chance?'

'Better than a contrived correspondence.'

They were still for a while, both lost in their own thoughts.

Harriet pulled a handkerchief from a pocket of her dress and dabbed at her brow. 'What about Pythagoras?' she said.

'You mean the Pythagorean progression.'

'One becomes three becomes seven. At least seven has a sound metaphysical dimension.'

'If you say so.'

'It's true.'

'No, it isn't. It's just a pattern.' She paused, and a reflective look appeared in her face. 'Your choice of seven is interesting though. Three and seven define the quality of a diatonic chord.' She went back to the pianola and without sitting down opened the lid and played a chord. 'Hear that?' She played the chord again, and then again.

'What am I meant to hear?'

'A major seventh.'

'Seems a bit off.'

'That's because it's a semitone from the tonic, and also because the seventh note is the most out of tune with the natural temperament. In a sense the musical seventh is a contrivance. And trust me, it will end up being one you will despise.' She played the chord again then closed the lid and said, 'This would be so much easier if we picked four.'

'I would never, ever pick four.'

'This is ludicrous,' Ginny said to the ceiling.

'Four is a square,' Harriet said defensively, 'and a square too easily becomes a cross. I'd feel crucified.'

'Oh for Christ's sake!'

'Then what's your suggestion?'

'Nine.'

'Ambitious.'

They fell silent. Nine paintings would be easy enough if she applied herself but nine pieces of music seemed an onerous task in light of Ginny's maudlin state of mind. Then again, it might be just what she needed.

'I think nine is the most beautiful interval,' Ginny said with sudden enthusiasm. 'You can flatten or sharpen a nine and it will still be a nine. The same occurs with the fifth but it doesn't have the same sense of mystery.' She sat down, opened the lid and played a chord, accentuating a note, no doubt the ninth note, and Harriet had to admit it did sound rather nice.

There would be no point voicing the thought that her daughter's preference for nine was tinged with the same egotism for which she had criticised her mother. How else does anyone choose anything? We are all, even the best of us, in some measure selfish.

'Nine?'

'Very well. Nine.'

'Then it's settled.'

Ginny walked across the room and when she reached the hallway door she looked down at Harriet and said with a slow smile, 'It's three sets of three.'

Harriet succumbed to a rising unease. She would never have considered had Ginny not drawn it to her attention that nine was three sets of three, magnifying the very number she had rejected three-fold. Perhaps she should have stipulated a prime number from the first and eliminated nine from the odd numbers altogether. Yet Ginny thought nine a beautiful interval and Harriet felt she had no choice but to bury her misgivings.

Tuesday, 4 April 2017

Fernley Cottage

Judith tinkered with a wobbly paintbrush stem and pondered a reply. She found she was lost for words. She scrolled through the comments; the initiator of the thread, Franken Form, alleging a conspiracy behind Daesh. Celestial Petal chiming in with an accusatory barb at the Illuminati. And then there was poor Fred Spice, who had protested the claim, being told by a motley crew of bizarrely named participators that they could help him recover from the brainwashing. Hadn't he seen Lawrence Pike? Lawrence Pike! That conspiracy evangelist, better known as compere on 'What a Blast!' She hit the keys for the shit-pile emoticon then thought better of it. Franken Form followed on with a list of Youtube links to hour-long documentaries claiming to reveal the truth about Agenda 21, involving a zany plan to exterminate twenty-five per cent of humanity before the next financial meltdown. A couple of smiley faces from supporters and a string of fat pink love hearts from an obsequious Franken Form fan eager to demonstrate allegiance.

Thankfully, Fagbutt Oilcan had started another thread on the twin towers conspiracy. Equally absurd and she might have scrolled on but the significance of the date drew her in: Nine eleven, the anniversary of Pinochet's coup in Chile, the day of the celebration of Mohammed's birth, America's emergency number, and so it went and she was transfixed by an extensive list of nine elevens, including numerological calculations of the flight numbers, and one surprisingly coincidental observation that there were nine hundred and eleven days between the fall of the twin towers and the Madrid bombings. She wondered what sort of person would calculate that. Other observations were so farfetched they were ridiculous. Yet taken together, the prominence of the numbers was striking. Conspiracy theorists had noticed, surmised and contrived all those nine elevens, as if the preponderance alone were significant. Pure chance, or perhaps someone planned it. Planned it with conspiracy theorists in mind. An elaborate web of associations designed to attract every conspiracy nut on the planet. Well, it had worked.

She whittled time seeing if she could collate the speculations by fact or contrivance until she reached an addendum on fives, Fagbutt Oilcan pointing to the significance of the Pentagon's five-pointed star design, a design he claimed was based on an occult symbol.

The same occult symbol that Madeleine had clumsily sewn on her black canvas shoulder bag. For her, it had been an emblem, superficial yet meaningful, fashion defining her dark cultural interests. Certainly not anything deeper. Madeleine was never that deep.

She shut down her laptop and left it on the hearthrug, annoyed at her own susceptibility, rueing the moment she let temptation sway her and follow Bethany's link to the Forum.

A distraction for bleak days, Bethany had said in her email. She glanced at the time. It was four o'clock. Four o'clock on the fourth of the fourth month. Four threes are twelve. Which had to mean nothing. She poked at the logs in the grate, watching as fiery red sparks shot forth and died as they fell. Then she took herself to her studio.

The room, large and imperfectly square, had a low ceiling, exposed beams at three-foot spacings running the length of the fractionally longer wall. The window, set in the northern wall, overlooked her garden and the undulating hills beyond, all ploughed fields of red earth, stone walls and hedgerows, and tall trees casting long shadows, their leaves fresh with spring. Tranquil and picturesque, a perfect juxtaposition to the chaos beneath the sill, her workbench strewn with a comforting jumble of notebooks, sketches, paints, and tubs of pencils and brushes. Two stacks of paintings at various stages of completion wainscoted the opposite wall. Above, the wall was covered in prints, photographs and grubby scraps of paper scrawled with ideas. It was her favourite room in the house. In here, only in here, would serenity dawn in her.

Madeleine had rarely entered the studio. Not since one cataclysmic morning when she was three and she had slipped in unnoticed and gone on a paint splodging rampage and ruined several artworks. It was the one time Judith lost control of her temper and slapped her.

She felt a pang of regret over that slap.

She contemplated the landscape on her easel, her most painstaking work to date, depicting the remains of an old-growth ironbark. Rough, fissured shades of grey and thin tracks of sanguine sap, the trunk stump and felled logs desolate in a paddock of stubble and straw bales rotting to black.

She dipped the tip of her brush in the splodge of sepia on her palate and dabbed the canvas at the sawn end of a log. She was a slender woman, dressed as she often was in a pair of paint spattered dungarees over an old battleship-grey T-shirt. She was sure she gave the local farmers the impression she had become a bra-burning feminist trapped in the Seventies. Born and raised in Fernley cottage and still they eyed her as an interloper. Yet the outfit was born of pragmatism, not politics. Beyond the confines of these fields she would never be mistaken for a rabble-rousing troublemaker or a placard-wielding activist. Women of the warrior class terrified her. Judith was of a type. She lacked that temerity of spirit so admired by the liberated woman, so scorned by the chivalrous man. She had an open, youthful face, and at forty, few signs of ageing had altered its soft features, although lately few smiles parted her winsome lips and her once lively brown eyes were dull.

She was named upon her mother's parturient affection for *Jude the Obscure*. Boy or girl it had mattered not. What mattered to her mother was that no offspring of hers should suffer as Jude had suffered. Unlike her namesake, she had been provided opportunities of education, and Exeter society in the latter half of the twentieth century adhered to a moral framework largely free of hysterical religious censure. The foundations for a life without the anguish of banishment were set. Judith would never be ostracised. And, mercifully, for the most part her life had not resembled Jude's. Why give the child the name if it matters so much to you that your offspring leads an altogether different sort of life? Yet her mother, a dressmaker by trade, was entirely unsuperstitious, and Judith knew it had never occurred to her that she might invoke an echo. Oddly, it was the book's title that reflected Judith's existence. A recluse, determined to live out her life ensconced in a stone house on the edge of Dartmoor. And without Madeleine, she was living the life of her literary namesake to the full.

She stepped back from her easel and took a ponderous look, ignoring the rattle of the window, insistent in a whoosh of wind. All the windows in the old farmhouse were multi-paned casements and one or other if not all required repair and maintenance, something she would attend to before the following winter took hold. She had all summer ahead of her, all the time in the world, she told herself, and she choked down the wretched, broken feeling that lurked in her heart.

She was reaching for a tube of burnt sienna when she glimpsed the roof of a car approaching up the lane that carved its way between the hedgerows to the east. She listened. The engine noise drew closer. Perhaps it was her neighbour. She waited.

The engine noise faded and quiet returned. She squeezed a reddish brown blob on to her palette and looked past her easel at the tall trees in the distance, silhouetted against a gunmetal sky.

Correspondence

'Just imagine this room full of people,' Harriet enthused. 'Nine paintings on the walls and you, over there, perhaps even on a dais, performing nine musical pieces. One for each painting.'

'So the music corresponds to the paintings?' Ginny said dryly.

'And the paintings to the music.'

'Doesn't seem all that original.'

Harriet drew a breath. Ginny had been aspersing the project ever since Harriet conceived the idea. They had frittered an entire month, Ginny still mired in the aftermath of her sorry relationship. While the real Garth was no doubt boozing his life away, a psychic Garth had lodged in Ginny with the tenacity of a tapeworm, spiralling ever downward, and Harriet wondered if it would ever reach her bottom.

They were standing in the front room of the gallery, a short walk from the house and situated in the main street of Sassafras, sandwiched between an antiques shop and Agatha's Tea Rooms. Harriet sold a piece or two of her own, but the gallery served primarily as an outlet for Phoebe's auction finds. Viewing was by appointment, Harriet held a very occasional exhibition, and openings were never for the great unwashed.

The owner of Agatha's Tea Rooms and purveyor of dainty Devonshire teas was Mrs Pargiter, a woman of ample flesh and strident opinions, who would insist that should Harriet open her doors to passers-by her business would thrive. Mrs Pargiter really meant the tea rooms would benefit from having an open gallery right next door. Harriet pictured the interference, that irritating woman insisting on artworks with an Agatha Christie theme of one sort or another. Steam trains set in oriental landscapes perhaps.

Sassafras was already quaint enough.

The tea rooms were housed in a mock Tudor cottage replete with gables and ivy, an inauthentic visage that lured city-dwelling daytrippers covetous of something reminiscent of olde-worlde England. Despite having only the scantest recollection of her native land, Harriet knew with conviction that the Dandenong Ranges—where the tallest trees once grew, where tree ferns flourished in the cool moist air, where creeks carved their way down steep-sided valleys—upon the best efforts of scores of talented gardeners, about as much resembled England as the Amazon did the Nile. Yet other than the tea rooms, which oppressed her sensibilities, she wouldn't criticise the efforts of would-be British gentry, for the result was a charmingly eccentric mix of native and exotic, mountain ash and maple, fern and rhododendron, the garden centre opposite the gallery furnishing the locale's floral aspirations.

The gallery, unlike all the other businesses in the village, was plain-fronted, flat-roofed, and in every respect unremarkable. The window displays to either side of the entrance door, consisting of two drab landscapes propped against white Masonite screens, gave passers-by no indication of the vibrant works within, and invited no inquiry.

The space above the screens afforded a pleasing view of the street. Maples were budding to life in a flush of green. Heavy clouds threatened rain. A young man in a short-sleeved shirt and shorts shot past an elderly couple rugged up in hats and scarves who were strolling towards the tea rooms, and a party of women milled about in front of the bric-a-brac shop opposite.

Harriet turned from the window. 'Tea?' she said to Ginny, who was standing in the doorway to the back room, staring blankly at nothing.

'I need to get on.'

'What on earth for?' After all, Ginny had done nothing but mooch since she entered the gallery, as she was wont to do every day since her return.

Harriet looked around, hoping for a painting to straighten.

The main room was a good size for a small collection; rectangular with polished floorboards and matte white walls. The room had dimmed and Harriet was about to flick on the lights when the sun shone through the trees across the street, shafting in and glistening on the floorboards. She almost said, 'There you are,' as if the weather itself augured a positive resolution, but held back, knowing Ginny would dismiss the remark as poppycock.

Opposite the front door was an open fireplace, the chimney blocked off, the grate containing a decorative arrangement unchanged since Harriet purchased the shop with her inheritance years before, and deposited in the grate all the pine-cones Ginny had daubed with gold paint as part of her school's Christmas activities.

Harriet used the back wall, including the chimney breast, to hang her work. Hers were the first pieces spectators saw when they entered the gallery, yet they were overshadowed by Phoebe's finds adorning the screens and the two side walls.

Currently, Harriet had five pieces on the back wall, all of greater complexity than her Homage to Kandinsky that hung above the pianola at home. This was her Wessex series, the works in essence depicting beneath acres of sky an undulating green and yellow-ochre landscape, replete with hedgerows and cottages, coves and cliffs, rendered in a style reminiscent of Matisse, and scumbled. And if she had left well alone they might have sold, yet her obsession with abstraction had bent and twisted and refined until there was little sense of a traditional landscape. She found the works inspired when she had painted them last year, but the moment Phoebe saw them she said, 'They'll be hard to shift.' And she had been right. No one had taken even a skerrick of interest and Harriet was in half a mind to paint over the canvases.

Phoebe's finds appeared coherent: a collection of modernist works from the early twentieth century, lesser works of known but not famous artists, and one or two obscure pieces that had caught Phoebe's eye at auction. They wouldn't be left hanging for long.

'We'll have tea,' Harriet said firmly, and made for the rear door, flicking on the lights on her way, the room again dim.

She had reached the kitchenette and was about to put on the kettle when there was a rap on the front door. She rushed back to answer it, noticing Ginny idle in a corner of the room.

Rosalind was sheltering beneath the door's narrow awning, shaking her umbrella free of rain and drawing it shut. Harriet, her mind flitting to the washing she had left out to dry on what had been a fine spring day, stepped aside as Rosalind entered the room.

'What a pleasant surprise.'

'Saw the light was on, Harriet, and thought I'd call in. Good afternoon, Ginny.'

'Hello, Miss Spears.'

Ginny raised a smile but her churlish look didn't lift with it. She shifted as if to view a painting.

Rosalind, who never missed such moments, was quick to respond with, 'I hope I'm not interrupting.' Then, addressing Harriet, she swept over the situation with, 'I was intrigued to see your Wessex series. This is them I take it.' She went over and studied the painting nearest the back room door. Ginny edged around the room towards the screens. Harriet waited, not keen to disturb Rosalind's contemplation as she made her way along the wall, although she doubted the dear old thing would make a purchase. But one could never tell with such matters and she found her breathing was shallow in anticipation.

When she reached the last of the series, Rosalind said, 'Harriet, had you considered that these works might do well in Britain?'

'I really can't imagine that they would.'

'Why ever not?'

'I don't think the British would care for Dorset depicted this way.'

'Nonsense.'

Harriet felt uneasy. It wasn't like Rosalind to take an interest in her art.

'I don't see them as Dorset at all,' Ginny said. 'They are an interpretation of an interpretation, an impression of an impression. That's how they should be viewed. Not as representations of Hardy's Wessex.'

Harriet looked at her with surprise. She was moved to hear her daughter talk in an appreciative and perceptive manner. Then again, Ginny had always been astute. She had been privy to Harriet's conversations with her two friends her whole life, read *Sophie's World* when she was ten, and, in her first year of high school, wrote a remarkable essay on aesthetics, having engaged with a little Schopenhauer and Kierkegaard. Her interest culminated years later in a unique perception that rejected metaphysical explanations of the universe in favour of a sort of philosophical mysticism. To that end, mother and daughter rarely agreed.

Rosalind seemed dissatisfied with Ginny's remark, but she didn't pursue it. 'I'm particularly taken by this one,' she said, pointing to the Eustacia piece, her most obscure work of all. It was a rendition of the Dorset Downs like no other. Even Harriet found excessive her application of the principles of abstraction and her emphasis on colour and form, trees becoming elongated triangles with hair, the Downs rendered a modular series of square blocks, the resulting piece, rich in lime green and deep blue, featuring a trapezoid in startling black with two rhomboid shapes of translucent aquamarine veering off to a vanishing point in the top right corner of the canvas.

'What are you asking, Harriet?'

She concealed her amazement. Rosalind was conveying all the decidedness of a special purpose.

'Rosalind, I…'

'The full price please. No favours.'

'But I'm…'

'Child, this work is symbolic of a moment of supreme importance, an occasion I wish to mark and I can think of no better manner in which to do it.' She gestured at the painting.

Harriet didn't speak.

'If you must know,' Rosalind said with certain triumph, although neither Harriet nor Ginny had inquired, 'I'll soon be off to that part of the world.'

Ginny, who had been leaning against the street door, suddenly stepped forward.

'When? What for?'

'In January. And there is much preparation to be done. I shall be attending the Theosophical Society's annual conference.'

'Fascinating,' Ginny murmured.

'More than that,' Rosalind said abruptly. 'We are understandably concerned for World Peace. There'll be a guest speaker from the United Nations. And Bournemouth is a fine old city, so I've heard.'

Ginny opened her mouth as if to speak then shut it again before slumping where she stood, deflated like a sorry little sausage balloon passed over at a six-year-old's birthday party.

'What is it dear?' Rosalind asked, addressing Harriet.

'Oh nothing.'

Apparently satisfied, or perhaps indifferent, Rosalind said, 'Price?'

'Five hundred. But I can sell it to you for…'

'Done.'

'Rosalind, really…'

'Harriet, I won't hear another word.'

'Ginny, will you…?'

She tried to catch Ginny's eye, but her gaze held fast to Rosalind's back. But she gave a small nod and went to fetch the painting.

Harriet led Rosalind to the back room where a pier table was positioned along the near wall. As Ginny approached with the painting, Harriet sucked in her breath. Stone-faced, Ginny leaned the painting against the table and returned to the main room. A silence hung as Harriet set about the wrapping and Rosalind wrote a cheque.

Transaction complete, Rosalind left the gallery wearing a look of tremendous satisfaction. The moment the door closed behind her, Ginny marched into the back room and said accusingly. 'Bournemouth?'

Harriet knew what would come. She had considered taking down the Wessex series upon Ginny's return, before she had a chance to see it. But that would have left an empty wall for she had nothing worth hanging in its stead. Which meant that days earlier, when Ginny had first seen the works, she'd stood in front of one then another, gazing at each for an inordinate length of time, and once she had viewed them all she swung round and said, 'What are you not telling me?'

'I have no idea what you mean.'

'Wessex!'

It was not like her to shriek.

'I felt inspired,' Harriet said, feigning casual indifference. The heat rose from her chest and she repressed an urge to remove her cardigan.

'Did you go there?'

'Don't be absurd.'

It was always the same suspicious antagonism. Ginny had been questioning Harriet over the whereabouts of her father since she was seven and they had fled to Sassafras. 'Where's Daddy?' grew into an openly hostile 'Why won't you tell me?' by the time Ginny was a teenager. Harriet had refused to offer an explanation. 'It's too painful to remember,' she would say and change the subject.

Harriet began to suspect that Ginny's homecoming had more to do with taunting her mother with the past than it did a chance to nurse her wounded heart. As if Ginny was using the break up with Garth as an excuse, part of a ruse to uncover matters better left buried, matters Harriet had vowed to herself never to resurrect. For who in her right mind would seek to pick up and consume a rotten peach long since tossed behind, a peach eaten away on the inside by the grub at its core?

She put away in the pier-table drawer the paper, Sellotape and scissors she had used to wrap Rosalind's painting, her mind trying to make sense of the situation. Rosalind was off to Bournemouth and the synchronicity could not have been more unfortunate. What might it augur? She reassured herself that most likely the intersection of her Wessex paintings and Rosalind's trip foretold of matters artistic and she imagined selling the whole series, perhaps even receive a commission on the strength of their merit. Yes, the implications probably had nothing to do with Ginny at all, who had simply jumped to conclusions. She rummaged through the drawer without a clue what she was hoping to find.

Ginny's latest interrogation began the day after they chose the number nine for their collaboration. Harriet knew it was the mention of Three Gore Street that had triggered Ginny's probing. They had gone to the gallery, entering via the rear courtyard to deposit some groceries in the kitchenette on their way through to the back room, where the matte white walls displayed a range of the lesser of Phoebe's finds. The room was windowless, the only natural light filtering through a transom above the door to the main room, which Harriet kept locked. Ginny had taken up the petite hard-backed sofa positioned in the centre of the room, and was pushing back her cuticles. Harriet hovered by the pier table trying not to look.

Ginny had scarcely uttered a word during the grocery shop in Olinda that had left Harriet hoping she wouldn't encounter a Pargiter or a Hunnacot, for her charge wore her angst like a badge and it was not something Harriet wished seen, sensing the whispered suppositions that would follow. Still, seated there in a frenzy of cuticle mutilation, she seemed reluctant to give voice to her concerns.

Harriet was wondering why she didn't return to the house when Ginny said, 'You never speak of him.'

'Who?'

'You know full well.'

'What do you want to know?'

'Everything. Anything. I don't know the first thing about him.'

'You do. You know what he looks like.'

'That's hardly enough.'

'You'll make your fingers bleed.'

'Is it any wonder? I feel as if I don't know half of myself.'

Harriet glanced at her watch. Phoebe was due at ten to collect a triptych of silver birches hanging on the far wall. Painted by an unknown artist in gouache, black against a white background with minimal grey shading, the pieces were skilfully crafted. The artist obviously had talent, but the works were not to Harriet's taste. Ideal, Phoebe had said, for an entrance hall or small study and she had found just such a room at the Fitzsimmons's. Harriet took one of the pieces to the pier table to wrap, pleased to have the works gone, at once pleased that in less than an hour Phoebe would appear and break into the conversation, for she didn't wish to endure more than an hour dwelling on the events that had taken place when she had been about Ginny's age. Yet she knew that Ginny had reached an age when fobbing would no longer do.

'All right,' she said softly. 'I'll describe how we met.'

Business with Phoebe had been thriving; Harriet's 'Homage to Matisse' series of especial popularity amongst power suited yuppies with arty pretentions. It was the flamboyant mid-Eighties, the Hawke years, that age of conspicuous consumption, and Harriet's depiction of a Holden stationwagon in vibrant colours and textural brushwork, and rendered in neo-expressionist style, was also much favoured.

Phoebe unearthed her customers at garden parties, gallery openings, conferences, folk-club nights, birthday parties, weddings, and even the occasional funeral. She would home in with a diatribe on the scandalous prices of the known names, the known *European* names, kindling a swift reaction to all things un-Australian. She would quickly go on to explain, having then their full interest, that she herself was an art dealer; that she was in fact a champion of the underdog, the little known but incredibly talented, that indeed she was a feminist supporting women struggling artists. Or she would lure a punter with her well-rehearsed vignette on Séraphine Louis, a housekeeper painting by candlelight until discovered by a German art collector. Phoebe omitted her apparent psychosis and her demise in an asylum, insisting instead that she had made a similar discovery and they really ought to consider the works of Harriet Brassington, wisely dropping the Smythe. At which point she would reach into the breast pocket of her trench coat and extract several photos of sold works. Being little known, of course Ms Brassington's works were affordable and she never let the punter go until she had their number and not the other way around.

One cool evening in October, Harriet watched Phoebe in action at a private function at Maryvale's. Harriet was seated at the bar, sipping the daiquiri her friend had proffered and observing her gestures in a long mirror that extended the full length of the back bar. Moments later her gaze was diverted to a strange young man who had appeared as if from nowhere, and was staring at her reflection. He was of average build, his face large-featured and forthright beneath a shell of thick black hair. The corners of his mouth were upturned. He exuded a magnificent charm in his black suit, white shirt and tie, clothes that set off his remarkably salacious eyes.

By then her liaisons with Fritz had become dull, their affair little more than casual, although perhaps to him it meant more, but he never spoke of how he felt. She gazed at the mysterious man at the bar and smiled. McCoy Tyner's 'Passion Dance' was playing and desire curled its way from her belly to her throat like a snake.

Phoebe had broken the moment, nudging her arm with a grin. She leaned to Harriet and whispered, 'A Munch by Sunday week,' and Harriet watched her leave the room. When she looked back, the man had gone. She might have been disappointed had she not seen his business card on the counter.

'McCoy Tyner?' Ginny said. 'That's amazing. He's one of my favourite jazz pianists.'

Ginny's attentive fascination was disconcerting and Harriet strained to think of ways to edit the past and leave Ginny with a semblance of truth, even as a voice in her insisted there could be no harm in telling a story that must be told, begged to be told. Isn't it a child's right to know their parentage? Besides, it might help Ginny out of her morass.

Harriet secured the first artwork in bubble wrap before easing it into a sleeve of cardboard. She leaned the package against the wall beside her then she went for the second artwork and placed it face up on the table. The stark black of the silver birch leaped up at her.

'So obviously you called him.'

Harriet hesitated. Yes, she had, and they had met at the Evelyn on Brunswick Street. In fact, she had taken him back to her flat and straight to her box of a bedroom, and in the soft light of a gibbous moon filtering through red chiffon curtains she had devoured him. From then on those early weeks were a hedonistic frenzy of lovemaking. She felt debauched in the recollection and duly censured the narrative.

She told her daughter that initially she learned nothing much about him. Her attention, and his, was exclusively on her. Her body, she thought. Her art, she said. He was German like her art tutor, Fritz. He had a brooding manner as if a thought of significance had just occurred to him that demanded contemplation, which she thought evidence of his cultural inheritance since Fritz was apt to brood as well. Careful, exacting, measured, he spoke to her in a heavy accent of Munich, the Bauhaus and the village Kandinsky had lived, and it was as if Kandinsky himself were with her in her room.

It wasn't until Phoebe came round a few weeks later that she emerged from her love-nest bubble. Wilhelm was in the shower when her friend knocked on the door.

'I've come for the Munch,' she said, her eyes narrowing at the sight of the half-finished painting on the easel.

'Phoebe,' Harriet said apologetically.

'And to warn you. Seems I'm too late.'

Phoebe shoved aside Wilhelm's jacket and sat down on the sofa.

Harriet hovered for a moment, thrown off balance by Phoebe's barely contained annoyance, then offered her tea in a gesture of placation.

'Tea? I don't have time for tea! Can you finish the Munch by Wednesday? That's the longest I can make the client wait.' Her tone was uncharacteristically curt, almost threatening, as if she had transformed in the face of the sudden knowledge that Harriet was letting her down into her common-as-muck forebears. Harriet's mind flitted to Wilhelm in the shower and she hoped that was where he would remain.

'Sure,' was all she could think of to say.

'Sure?'

'I will.'

'He's a leech, by the way.'

'You don't know that,' Harriet said, instantly defensive.

'I know he's not for you.'

'How can you say that? Besides, you're wrong. I think we are compatible. We share an interest in the Bauhaus and Kandinsky.'

'He has a reputation.'

'Everyone has a reputation.'

'Wilhelm Schmid's is not the sort of reputation to brush aside,' Phoebe said emphatically. 'You know he knows Fritz?'

'Yes,' she lied.

'They come from the same town. You should talk to Fritz.'

As if she would do that! 'I think you should mind your own business,' she said. 'He seems lovely and that'll do for me.'

'Your call.'

Upon which Phoebe had stood up and left.

Harriet stopped, unsure where next to take the conversation.

'Did you talk to Fritz?' Ginny asked. She had shifted to the edge of the sofa and sat with each hand on a thigh. There was a measure of impatience about her and a dogged attentiveness that made Harriet feel guarded.

'Fritz? No. Well yes,' she said, which was scarcely a coherent answer.

Determined not to appear flustered and discomforted by a glow about her neck, her cheeks and her brow, she told Ginny how she had met Fritz for lunch at Mario's, newly opened on Brunswick Street and just around the corner from her house. He had finished his doctorate in fine art and was now lecturing, and he had wanted to meet her near his campus on the Yarra River's south bank but she wouldn't hear of it. Instead she insisted he catch the tram to Fitzroy to soak up the setting: tiles, chrome, shiny glass, and walls covered in band posters, and two moustached, pot-bellied men in black serving the best espresso in the southern hemisphere.

He would never have come across to her like a jilted lover, but she could tell he was disappointed when she pledged loyalty to Wilhelm. She reached for his hand across the small square table and he pulled away and leaned back in his seat, but was immediately forced to cram closer in when a corpulent woman took up the seat behind him. Irritation appeared in his face but his natural reserve and their friendship held sway.

Yet she couldn't believe him when he told her he didn't care for her new beau. When he warned her that Wilhelm had quite a reputation back in Munich she assumed it was his hurt feelings talking. What reputation? For what? But her insistence was met with reticence and he had said no more.

'It was gossip, I thought. Just gossip and not a skerrick of truth in it.'

'So you didn't take much notice.'

'Of course not. Not of him and not of Phoebe.' Harriet looked at her daughter. Already, she was on tricky ground. 'Phoebe isn't a suspicious sort,' she said, steering the story a little aft. 'She saw that my passion was interfering with business. As far as I could tell, business was her primary concern and not my welfare.'

She set the second painting beside the first, then went and placed the third on the table. Her thoughts drifted back to Gore Street. It was a dismal house of reddish-brown brick and, unlike the rest of the houses at that end of the dead-straight street, lacked the rounded arches of a porch and the balcony above, a balcony shaded beneath its own awning and trimmed with a fancy lacework railing. Instead, an out-of-true iron veranda shaded the front door and just the one double-hung window, misaligned in the façade. The upstairs windows were exposed to the elements. The house faced west and for a time in the afternoon, sunlight would kiln dry the upstairs room, eventually finding its way through the small downstairs window to heat the front room as well, revealing the stained wallpaper where a previous tenant had perhaps hurled a beer. The skirting boards had dry rot and the kitchen out the back was small, dark and damp.

Ginny had heard the Gore Street vignette many times, and each time she had taken not the least interest. Harriet would meander in her mind from room to room, detailing the faults in minutiae. Often Ginny would stand up and leave her to it before Harriet came back to herself, realising with mild contrition she had given the impression that her sole reason for leaving Gore Street was the house itself and not the demise of the relationship of the inhabitants. This time, in deference to Ginny's obvious need, and with about half an hour before Phoebe was due to arrive at the gallery, she applied herself to the task at hand and dredged up a long-buried memory.

Three months had passed since Harriet met the gaze of the enigmatic man at the bar. Three months of snuggling in the womb-like confines of her bedroom. Wilhelm's presence occupied her, leaving scarcely any time for painting, or Phoebe's mounting consternation. In those three months she had never been to his Gore Street house. Sometimes she would mention an interest and his reply was always, 'But here is perfect. So intimate, so private.'

Then one day Wilhelm telephoned her to say his housemate had moved out and would she like to have his room, his manner so perfunctory she had no idea how to answer. There was her independence to consider, her life in Moor Street. Then again, she had to share the bathroom with shifty Frank Como, who had taken the downstairs back room last month, and in the downstairs front room, Bella Lotta, a dancer who slept all morning and occupied the bathroom for half the afternoon. Whenever she encountered Harriet in the hall, she only ever said, 'How's it going?' before flouncing off in a cloud of chiffon and scent. Then Wilhelm offered Harriet the use of the front room of his Gore Street house as her studio and she said yes without hesitation.

She moved two weeks later, having had no trouble finding a replacement tenant for her Moor Street rooms. They were cheap and large with plenty of natural light, in the heart of the trendy end of Fitzroy.

She could have had no idea that the passion broiling for those few months would cool at the Gore Street threshold.

Wilhelm was too busy with his doctoral studies to provide assistance on the day she moved in. As arranged, he had left the key under an empty lonely terracotta pot positioned beneath the window on the narrow strip of concrete that served as a front garden.

Phoebe was furious at his absence. She complained as she climbed the stairs, grappling with a suitcase, that house moving was too much for her asthma. As if to reinforce the point, on the landing she blustered and wheezed and scrambled for her puffer. Her Cortina, parked outside, was loaded to its roof. Harriet unloaded the rest while Phoebe sat recovering on a chair in the middle of the downstairs front room. Back and forth Harriet trudged, laden with bags and boxes, dumping her things in an arc around Phoebe's feet. Then they went back to Moor Street.

Two more trips and Harriet, too, had cursed Wilhelm for not taking a day off his studies.

'I should have realised there and then,' she said reflectively.

'Realised what, exactly?' Ginny was examining a cuticle. She bit away at the quick. Harriet winced.

'Don't.'

'Don't what?'

'Do that.'

Ginny folded her hands in her lap in mock obedience. 'You were saying?'

'I should have realised that your father was a harsh man.'

'To you, maybe.'

'Yes, to me.' The smile she gave her daughter was pinched.

A draught of cold air wrapped around her calves as Phoebe entered through the back door. 'Is the kettle on?' she called out before seeing Harriet in the doorway.

She deposited a painting at her feet and went to close the door. Ginny stood and made her way past Harriet and then Phoebe, muttering something about piano practice.

Harriet sensed she had done little to sate her need.

The light was dim except where she stood, rendering black as pitch the realm beyond its reach. She sensed she was in a cave. She could feel the cold dirt beneath her feet, scrunch her toes in the powdery dry of it. The air smelled earthy and damp. The silence was close; in the distance the sound of water splashing on rock. A cool down draught stroked her back. An impulse urged her onwards, into the cave's depths. Yet she had been told to stand where she was. By whom? She stared into the gloom, made out the low roof and the boulder-strewn floor. Another smell, sweeter, flowery, wafted on the air. Deep inside the cave, somewhere to her left, she caught sight of a flickering light moving her way. Her heart thrummed in her chest. A voice whispered, 'Run. Run. You can still get away.' But her legs held themselves fast. She couldn't even raise an arm. A quick movement behind her, ahead of her, circling her, and she saw pairs of eyes, glinting red shards. The smell grew stronger and became familiar: incense. A shadow passed across the dim circle of light. She was aware of her nakedness, her back, her buttocks, her waist, the fall of her breasts and the vee of her womanhood. She felt his touch before he touched her. The urge to run grew strong, the urge to struggle and scream. Yet there was another feeling. A feeling sapping her impulses. A feeling that grew in the presence of the shadow: defeat.

Ginny woke in a slick of fear. She had had dreams before in which she found herself unable to move despite being free to do so. It was a bizarre feeling, unique to dreams, a loss of will or control of your faculties as if your body had been taken over by a hidden power. But this dream was different. In this dream she wasn't free. There had been someone in the dream with her but she had no idea who. Someone menacing? A stranger? Someone she knew? Someone capable of draining her of her will, leaving her resigned to whatever was about to happen.

Most likely it was Garth. The dream was a symbolic impression of her relationship and the gloom that had descended on her since she left her North Melbourne flat—a warning not to go back to him? She hadn't even considered it. She had already put her things in storage. The lease had expired and she had paid the rent in advance to the very last day with the funds of a windfall gig—the wedding of the daughter of a Derwent regular. She paid the rent to ensure that Garth wouldn't squander her earnings, nagging her in his pleading, obsequious way to borrow that for this and this for that until there was nothing left. He had pumped her as dry as a beer keg on a stag night and had she not met him she might have had a tidy sum put away. Not enough for a deposit on a house unless she wanted to live back of Hall's Creek, but still.

She was depleted in more ways than one, her finances a surface symbol of a deeper inner loss, an emotional numbing in the face of his perpetual emotional spilling, his feelings a feedback whine of wants and imagined hurts. She knew, even if her mother didn't, that it would take a long time, months not weeks, to overcome the turmoil he had left in his wake.

She lay on her back, clasped her hands together across her chest and stared at the ceiling. It wasn't just Garth souring her spirits. She had somehow allowed herself to be railroaded into collaborating on an exhibition with her mother. It was a ghastly prospect and probably had as much to do with why she couldn't move her feet in that dream as anything else.

Last night, Harriet had suggested she join her at the gallery. She suspected Harriet thought it would stimulate discussion of the collaboration, but she had little inclination for her mother's company. She felt less disposed to do anything with her mother with every day that passed.

She was penned by Harriet's insinuated stance that she awaken each morning in better cheer than the previous day, that her mood should miraculously lighten under her mother's arrogate watch, as if being back in the folds of her skirts were enough to restore her to her former good spirits. Yet her mother's form of nurture was questionable. It wasn't intimate chats by the fireside she offered, or shared talk of misdeeds of flawed lovers: how men were all the same; that it was the women who were strong, who carried the man like a beast on their backs; that men today had lost the provider spirit and their sense of obligation and were led instead by primal impulses and therefore were a gender in evolutionary retrograde. Instead, after she had accosted her in the living room, her mother conjured an exhibition, and Ginny knew it would put a greater distance between them even as it bound them together.

She got out of bed and threw on her paisley jacket. Winter, and her mother was being uncommonly frugal with the heating. Let the sun do its job, she would say. What sun? Even if it did show itself it wouldn't reach her bedroom window until the afternoon.

Without turning on the light she took her laptop from the small desk near the window and sat back on the bed. Harriet insisted she keep 'the damn thing' in her room, her abhorrence of all things technological verging on the hysterical. She didn't even own a blender. Mobiles, computers, in fact all things electronic, let alone digital, were anathema to her preferred mode of living, which Ginny placed somewhere in the dark ages. She had had to secretly buy a pre-paid dongle when she moved back.

It was a good connection. She opened her search engine and typed 'Wilhelm Schmid'.

Nothing.

Schmid Wilhelm. Nothing.

Wilhelm Schmid academic.

Wilhelm Schmid lecturer.

Books Wilhelm Schmid.

First on the search list was a link to the list she had come across before on similar searches, of chapter contributions in tomes all dated from the time he was at the University of Melbourne, with nothing after 1995.

She closed her laptop. She had no choice but to quiz her mother, which was not a happy prospect.

Harriet's reticence when it came to talking of her father had been maddening her for years. Her suspicion that Harriet was holding back vital clues as to his whereabouts aroused again last night at the mention of Three Gore Street. Three: a number she had managed to amplify into nine. Perhaps she would have a better chance extracting the details of that distressing time in her child-hood at the gallery.

Vitalised by a new sense of purpose, she showered and changed.

'Dorset is bigger than you think, Ginny.'

'Fritz is living there.'

'So?'

'So he might know where my father is.'

'Ginny, drop it. Your father disappeared. That's all anyone knows. We'd do better to think about the exhibition.'

Ginny couldn't understand why her mother always changed the subject with one of her ridiculous smiles, lips pressed together and stretched out, slightly downturned at the corners. She wondered at what Harriet was aiming to achieve with an expression that made her look like a goanna in pain.

She recoiled inwardly every time her mother put on that face, and each time her reaction grew stronger. One day, the wind will change, she thought. But it was more than that. The smile was a form of closure, a zipper on whatever had gone before. Those lips would fasten shut, as if her smile were a clear sign that some imaginary more behoved her to move on to another topic and that she was, in spite of it all, older, wiser, and well within her rights to do so.

Ginny shifted back on the small hard sofa, resisting an urge to push back her cuticles that had started to smart. Upon Phoebe's arrival, she had left the studio and wandered up the street, browsing at shop window displays and puzzling over the number of day-trippers in the cafés on that dreary Saturday. Then the sky darkened and she had taken shelter beneath the veranda of Bertie's Antiques. She had stood for a while, realising were she to head home she would be drenched. Reluctantly, she made a dash back to the gallery.

Thankfully Phoebe had left. She had always found Phoebe intimidating, her no nonsense manner cold and uninviting, her alliance with her mother, a firm unity of two, serving to push Ginny even further from the scarcely evident intimacy of their mother-daughter bond. Yet Phoebe's loyalty was impressive and she had to acknowledge a touch of envy, for she hadn't such a bond of friendship of her own. Her two friends in the Dandenongs, Poppy and Veronica, were also a unit of two, and for a long time she had regarded herself superfluous.

Harriet returned from the storeroom carrying three pieces to replace the triptych.

'What do you think of this one?' she said, gesturing at a Modigliani-inspired portrait, the acrylic applied in a painterly fashion that even Ginny could see undermined the artist's intent.

'I like it,' she said blandly.

'Really? I think it's a clash of style and technique. Phoebe's slipping.'

'If you say so.'

'At least we are rid of the triptych.'

'You didn't like it?'

'You did?'

'I thought it was quite nice.'

Harriet leaned the other two paintings against the wall and hung the portrait. Ginny could tell from her evasive demeanour that she would divulge no more for the day. The rain pattered on the roof and Ginny wished it would stop and she could go home.

A month later and Ginny was standing in the gallery beside the stretch of blank wall where Harriet's 'Eustacia' had hung before Rosalind had bought it to commemorate her trip to Bournemouth. Bournemouth, where her mother's friend Fritz was teaching at the university. Not that Ginny thought for a moment that her mother had sneaked off overseas on the pretext of artistic research for a secret liaison. It was just that whenever Ginny inquired about Wilhelm, her mother was too evasive and too obscure. She had to be hiding something. The shock she felt learning of Rosalind's imminent trip had subsided and she slowly realised that for the time being she would do better to let the matter go. In its place, she let grow a feeling of quiet achievement that her efforts to avoid engaging in conversations about the collaboration had proven successful, indeed her avoidance of her mother in general was a small feat.

Harriet appeared holding a canvas she had fished out of the storeroom: one of her early works, a Brassington on Boyd land-scape that she presumably decided complemented the Wessex works. With her back to Ginny she said without preface, 'Why don't you compose the music and I'll depict the musical phrases in colour and form.'

'Unoriginal,' Ginny said. If she persisted in blocking, maybe her mother would cease her pursuit and they could drop the whole thing.

'We could use slides. Have moving shapes and colours too.'

'Again, unoriginal.'

'We would be doing it our way. That will make it unique.'

It was hopeless. Her mother as tenacious as ever. Ginny thought she knew what lurked behind her suggestions. Hadn't her beloved Kandinsky attempted something similar? And a few years before, the Tasmanian Symphony Orchestra had collaborated on a synaesthetic extravaganza at the Museum of Modern Art in Hobart. If they followed that path they would be seen as bandwagonists. Besides, she couldn't see the point in recreating for non-synaesthetic types phenomena they could never hope to experience for themselves.

'It's too literal,' she said. 'This equals that. And there's little left for the audience to interpret. It's all been done for them.'

'Kandinsky believes such abstractions stimulate the mind of the viewer,' Harriet said with hauteur. 'It isn't about their interpretations. It's their responses and reactions that matter. He knew art contains the power to stimulate a spiritual experience. That was what he set out to achieve in his own work and how he taught painting to others.'

Her mother's tone was infuriating, as if only she were privy to some supposed superior knowledge and Ginny, a non-believer in all matters theosophical, an ignoramus.

'He sounds like an egomaniac,' Ginny said, a remark calculated to ire. 'He's assuming that his abstraction is the only way.'

'He was attempting to convey the spiritual essence. I don't think you can get less egotistical than that.'

Harriet took a stray flier from the mantelpiece and fanned her face. Watching her go through the discomforts of a flush afforded Ginny a private pleasure. As if now that her provocations made Harriet hot, she was provided the opportunity for vengeance. It was a new phenomenon, one as much fascinating as it was incomprehensible.

She went on, warming to her newfound power. 'In trying to

invoke an imaginative response Kandinsky leaves nothing to the imagination. He's effectively telling the viewer what to look at and how to look at it. To me, that's inflexible.' She was careful to confine her argument to Kandinsky but the subtext was there and she knew that Harriet knew this was an attack on her. She knew too that Harriet would rise up in defence.

She was still fanning her face.

'You are being unfair. There are so many ways to view a triangle or a circle. And the relationships between the shapes and colours stimulate the imagination and speak to the soul. The ego doesn't enter into it.'

'One can just as well have a soulful response viewing a Stubbs.'

'A ruddy horse! How ridiculous! Next you'll cite the Mona Lisa. Just to be contrary.'

'Contrariness has nothing to do with it. Abstract art invites a limited response amounting to "Oh how clever, how inspired", totally undermining its intention which is, as you say, to inspire the spectator. Abstract art is nothing more than a great chain of literal correspondences masquerading as a great chain of inspiration, a baton passed between an elite group of no doubt exclusively male artists. It's what happens when the intellect hijacks creativity.'

Harriet didn't reply. She stood back and eyed her Boyd, then went forward and nudged the canvas straight.

'Then what do you suggest?' she said softly, in one of her sudden changes of manner, designed, Ginny thought, to dismiss the truth of her words as much as diffuse the tension between them.

'I have absolutely no idea.' She gave Harriet one last look, raised her shoulders in acknowledgement of the impasse and left the gallery.

Monday, 16 January 2017

Fernley Cottage

It was a quarter past one in the afternoon when, after days of mild weather, a cell of bitter air released its wrath on Devon. The local news reported uprooted trees, power outages and traffic chaos as blizzards swept down from the moors. The view from Judith's studio, moments earlier a patchwork of green and brown beneath a milky wintry sky, transformed as whorls of agitated snowflakes, ensconced in a thick haze of grey, shrunk the depth of field.

She switched off the radio and returned to the work on her easel, losing herself in a riverbank scene set against a backdrop of vast undulating plains beneath a blue vault of sky. The trees in the foreground were giving her trouble. They were nothing like the trees outside. Mottled trunks and splayed branches that ended in clusters of grey-green leaves, the complexity of subtle hues of red and purple a struggle to capture from a photograph. They were the river red gums of Australia and she wished she could smell the air there, feel the heat.

Time passed without notice and when she pulled away from her easel and cleaned her brush, the blizzard was easing, revealing a landscape of white. The wind persisted, the snow still fell, the clouds heavy and low in the fading light. She was thinking of cooking up a pot of soup when her creative poise shimmied to the sound of a hurried rap on the front door. She jiggled her paintbrush in a jar of murky turps and dried it on one of Madeleine's old T-shirts then looked at her watch. It was eighteen minutes past three.

The rapping stopped, then started again. The wind gathered pace and screamed through the valley, rattling the studio window. She strove to quash the apprehension stirring in her belly, reassuring herself on her way to the front door that it was probably a neighbour.

Instead, Madeleine cowered in the porch, shivering and grim in a shabby black coat. With a bulging bag slung over her shoulder she had the visage of an itinerant hag.

'Hi, Mum,' she said in a desultory voice, striding past and on through the house, leaving a trail of drips and wet footprints in her wake. Judith closed the door and followed, keeping her pace slow, her insides listing back and forth like unsecured cargo on the deck of a pitching ship.

'Madeleine,' she said cautiously. 'What are you doing here?'

'Visiting you.' She stopped in the doorway of the kitchen and swung round, her bag banging the doorjamb, the straps sliding down her arm. She let the bag drop to the floor with a thump. She was a short girl, big boned, her hair a cropped bush of black, setting off her rows of ear piercings and the tattoo on her neck, just below the left ear: a pale black outline of a skull. There was a lack of balance to her face. Her lips were wide and full, her eyes small and narrow, elongated further by a line of kohl. Too often those eyes smouldered black fire.

'Will you be staying long?'

'I'm moving back.'

'Here?' She did her best to disguise the horror she felt. 'But what about your degree?'

'Stuff college.'

'Oh no, Madeleine. Don't say that.'

Madeleine grabbed her bag, slung it on the dining table and went to pour herself a glass of water, scanning the room as she gulped it down. Judith stayed by the table. Separating her and her daughter, a chunky pine bench partitioned the dining area from the kitchen. It was a room filled with culinary potential. Over by the stove, assorted utensils hung from hooks. There were chopping boards and utensils galore. Grubby jars of spices, herbs, nuts and dried fruit jumbled the shelves that framed the window, shelves that ran all the way round to the studio door situated disproportionately close to the dining area side of the bench. At the end of the bench a bowl of fruit accompanied a chipped mug of pens. It was the same room, but Madeleine made everything in it seem strange.

Judith glanced at the bulging bag as if it were a culprit—old and battered, on one panel the logo of a five-pointed star, grubby and frayed.

Her gaze slid to her daughter. 'Madeleine?'

'Me and Zol are finished,' she said to the floor.

'Would you like some tea?'

'I'm leaving him.'

'Madeleine, I...'

'What?'

Judith hesitated before desperation made her speak. 'Just because you're leaving him doesn't mean you have to leave university. You've only one semester left.'

'It does.'

'Cocoa maybe?'

'You should be pleased I'm back.'

She marched past Judith, heaved her bag to her shoulder and left the room, disappearing down the hall.

Succumbing to an overwhelming need for air, Judith put on the coat, woollen hat and scarf hanging on the back door and went outside. She stood in the courtyard—sunken, paved and hemmed with trellises, a wrought iron table setting in its centre—and braced herself. The wind was unrelenting. The herb terraces that flanked the courtyard were in the lee of the wind but beyond, the small orchard and vegetable patch on the north-eastern rise were receiving a pummelling. Another gust whipped and whirled.

She pulled on her gardening boots—muddy, scuffed and perfectly moulded by her feet—and grabbed her gloves off the stoop. A week old and they had holes in the thumbs, the leather too thin for the tasks they were made for. She took the shovel leaning by the kitchen window and cleared the steps free of snow. A rusty wheelbarrow was lying on its side on the grass. She gripped the handles, feeling the cold through her gloves, and wheeled it up the path to the woodshed. From there, looking back to the house and the fall of the valley, she could see the thatched roof of Mr Fletcher's, now snow-capped, and the church spire that remained free of snow, a beacon of normalcy in an otherwise violent white setting.

In the foreground, her house nestled in its blanket of white. Fernley cottage had belonged to the Fernleys for three generations, her grandfather, Stanley, purchasing the house in the Fifties when granny Fernley was carrying Judith's mother. The Fernleys were originally from Exeter; Stanley, a tailor as his father was before him. They were the haberdashers of Sidwell Street. Fearing the worst during the Exeter Blitz, Stanley evacuated the family to Dartmoor. When they returned their shop was gone. Stanley never recovered from the loss and wanted nothing more than to spend the rest of his days far from the memories of that terrible raid.

Grandfather Stanley made much of Devon's fertile soil, giving over half the garden to vegetables and a small orchard. A tradition was set; Judith's mother, Florence, instilling in her daughter the same affection for gardening that she shared with Stanley. The garden was much the same as it had been in Stanley's day, orderly and well maintained. Judith's favourite features were the elegantly shaped garden beds with their scalloped borders of bulbs and perennials, and the herb terraces, three tiers in all, each containing plantings in a herringbone pattern of foliage. The herb terraces were a collaboration of Stanley and Florence. He built the retaining walls and backfilled with soil and she chose the design.

Soon after, Florence married Bernard, a teacher at the village school. Bowing to the family's wishes, he moved into Fernley

Cottage and a few years later Judith was born in one of the upstairs bedrooms. Fernley Cottage was the only home she had known and would ever know.

She loaded the barrow, taking her time, splitting two large logs and chopping others for kindling. The descent back to the house, wheeling the laden barrow on the slippery white ground, and she was tense again. She needed to persuade Madeleine that if not Bournemouth, then Exeter was where she belonged, amidst the hubbub commensurate with her age and interests, where she could express her passion. Here, here there was nothing to amuse her. Perhaps that had been the problem all along, Judith thought: boredom.

Before she reached the courtyard she paused, struck by the sun, low in the sky to the south, shining its thin light through a copse of trees. The fields were white. Hedgerows and stone walls a grid of black.

She parked the barrow outside the kitchen door, lifted a wicker basket off the cast-iron hatstand beside it, and went back up the path to the vegetable patch that was sheltered from the north and west by a low stone wall. A quick gust of wind and her hair lashed her cheeks. She picked a bunch of kale and pulled up nine turnips and crunched her way back, leaving behind her footsteps in the snow. She stopped beside the herbs for rosemary and thyme. The wind lulled. She cherished the moment as if it were her last fragment of calm before she ventured inside.

She entered an empty kitchen. She put the herbs and vegetables on the bench and ferried in a bundle of kindling and two armfuls of logs. She stoked the fire in the living room, stood for a minute warming her back, then returned to the kitchen to prepare dinner. She rinsed, peeled, sliced, fried and stirred all with an ear turned, listening for movement in the house. She heard nothing.

At five past six she called Madeleine to the table. After half a minute of silence, she heard footsteps on the stairs and thuds down the hall.

Madeleine entered the room and flopped onto a chair. 'What's this?' she said.

'Turnip bake.'

Madeleine lifted the lid off the other dish. 'And kale,' she said indifferently.

'Yes, kale.'

She levered a square of the turnip bake onto Madeleine's plate and passed her a spoon for the kale.

'Zol only eats pizza.'

'I imagine he does.'

Judith pictured him, a lumbering troll, and grimaced inwardly.

Madeleine poked at her food. Judith hoped those years with Zol hadn't changed her tastes. The one, and possibly the only sentiment she shared with her daughter was a commitment to healthy food.

'And what about you?' she said. 'What do you like to eat these days?'

'Not pizza.' At last she loaded her fork.

'He wasn't your type.'

'I know.' She looked at Judith coolly and said, 'But don't judge me.'

'I'm not judging you.'

They fell into silence, a silence that wrapped itself around the word 'judge'. Her gaze drawn back, Judith was sharply aware of her daughter, the dismay she felt at this invasion of one.

When they had finished their meal, Judith set about clearing the table. Madeleine took her by surprise when she said, 'I'll be able to help around the house,' and she left her seat and followed Judith to the sink. She put in the plug and turned on the taps, rolling up the sleeves of her sweater. Yet this new obsequiousness in her manner only made Judith suspicious.

The wind gathered pace and another blizzard rolled in. Judith went around the house, drawing the curtains on the inclemency, her mind a flurry of uncertainty and self-blame. Maybe she should never have allowed Madeleine that first tattoo. Her permission seemed to mark a point of descent. Yet opposition had seemed futile at the time.

Five years before, Madeleine had sat crossed-legged on the sofa, a textbook open in her lap, the plugs of her MP3 player in her ears, her thumbs on her mobile. She didn't look up when she asked in that desultory tone she would put on. 'Mum. Can I have a tattoo?'

Judith had already allowed her to dye her hair, bought her band T-shirts, posters of death-metal heroes and tickets to concerts. She had even relented when Madeleine nagged her for a septum piercing. All in spite of a visceral dislike for the youth culture she followed. But a tattoo?

She had reasoned with her, the standard arguments: a permanent marking, and what if she changed her mind when she grew up? And of course Madeleine was her usual adamant self. She would never change her mind.

Madeleine held up a calligraphy sketch, all angles and lines. Judith squinted at the page, managing to discern the words 'Dying Fetus'. It was downright macabre.

'They're a band,' Madeleine said. Which didn't change a thing. Uppermost in Judith's mind was the nagging thought that if she didn't attempt to fetter her daughter she would find no inner limit. Yet if she did refuse, Madeleine would no doubt pursue her self-mutilating interests with even greater vigour.

How old had she been then? Judith cast her mind back. Sixteen and one, two, three months? She couldn't recall the date. Her twenty-first birthday now just days away, six days, and here she was, the same Madeleine. How would she ever cope?

She went to the living room and put another log on the fire. Madeleine wandered in from the kitchen and sat down on the hearthrug. The room still contained the old family furniture, some of it from Stanley's day: the wingback chairs, a teak veneer sideboard, a single tall bookcase.

'I thought you were enjoying History.'

She caught Madeleine's gaze as she sat down in the chair closest to the fire, her daughter's eyes sharp, evasive.

'I was.'

'Then why drop out?'

Madeleine hugged her shins, resting her head on her knees. She was an incongruous black lump on the lively pattern of the rug, a dance of flowers and leaves in Persian style.

'You were getting good grades.'

Madeleine made no comment.

'Is it a problem with your lecturers?'

'Don't interrogate me.'

Judith desisted. There was in her daughter's manner a puzzling and uncharacteristic defeat. They were silent for a while. She listened to the wind roaring through the trees outside. Somewhere in the house, a window trembled.

'Mum.'

'Yes?' Judith said cautiously.

'Will you help me move my stuff?'

'To where?'

'I told you, I'm moving back here.'

She might have framed it as a request. 'You never liked it here,' Judith knew it was futile to attempt to dissuade. And she had no idea where else Madeleine might go. Certainly not her father's.

'You couldn't wait to get away.'

'That was before.'

'Before what?'

'Nothing.'

Madeleine stood. She said she was tired and took herself to her room.

Overnight the snowfall continued and by the following morning an icy north wind blew, adding to the freeze, and sending forth eddies of fallen snow. Snow that had drifted, burying stone walls. As far as she knew, Madeleine was still asleep, an impressive feat, her room bearing the force of the wind.

When she was small, Madeleine would climb into Judith's bed on windy nights and hold her forearm tightly. Concerned for her now, Judith left the studio and knocked on her door. There was no answer so she went to the kitchen and switched on the kettle.

With a mug of rooibos tea clutched in one hand she stood in the studio doorway and took in the painting on the easel. Shortly before dropping out to have Madeleine, she had borrowed a book from Exeter university library on the Australian landscape of the Modernist era, and she had found an immense affection for both subject and style. Drysdale, Nolan and Boyd conveyed not only the harsh and sparse plains typical of Australia's interior, those artists mythologised the landscape; reality became mystique, death never far. It was Boyd she favoured. She had no clear idea the location of Wimmera, but for two decades she had lived in her mind on that dry brittle land beneath the largest sky there ever was.

She was at peace with her own work too, the pale ochre of the dry wild grasses, the burnt-sienna earth, the hues of cream and smoky lavender of the tree trunks, the viridian green of the river's shady bank.

The trees still needed work, and the river.

She put her tea on the bench and squeezed onto her palette raw umber and a skerrick of white, and dipped in a fine brush, gently blending.

Before long she heard footsteps and Madeleine appeared in the doorway dressed in what she had on yesterday.

'Morning, love. Sleep well?'

She gave a small nod. 'What are you working on?'

'A commission.'

'For…?'

'A friend of Bethany's.'

She came into the room and looked around before flipping through the canvasses stacked against the wall, affecting interest. Judith made to return to her painting then pulled back, brush poised. Madeleine had paused, eyeing a scene of a derelict shack and a stand of dead trees, their few remaining limbs raised like contorted metacarpals.

'I like this one,' she said.

'Thank you.'

'Is it a commission?'

'No.'

'It reminds me of those tree pictures you did for Bethany.'

'The triptych?'

It wasn't possible. The only similarity between the two works was the emphasis on the form of the trees. Perhaps Hannah was on her mind. Madeleine had seen a lot of Bethany's daughter around that time. And they were at Bournemouth university together too. Judith wondered how much Madeleine saw of her friend and if she was missing her.

Madeleine stood in the doorway, gazing out the studio window as if transfixed. Judith turned to see what held her interest. The low morning light glistened on isolated patches of snow amid swathes of pale grey.

'You've never liked Zol,' Madeleine said without preface.

Judging her tone she was angling and Judith found she had tensed in anticipation. 'I won't deny it,' she said slowly, picturing the oaf.

'He won't be at the flat.'

'Oh.'

'He'll be at a tattoo convention.'

'I thought he was a piercist.'

'He is.'

Judith was silent, foreboding growing in her mind beside a fatalistic maternal resignation.

'So it would be a good time to move my stuff,' Madeleine said. 'You won't have to see him.'

'There's no persuading you to stay in Bournemouth?'

'No.' She sounded resolute. It was another of those moments when Judith thought the temporal order of mother and daughter might as well be reversed; Madeleine held the authority of a parent.

'Today is Tuesday.'

'I know.'

'You're asking me to take you tomorrow?'

Madeleine held her gaze.

'Why didn't you just phone me?'

'You wouldn't have done it.'

Which was true. She didn't want her back. Life with Madeleine had always been stressful, her daughter on an unstoppable decline, her mid-teens beset with episodes of binge drinking, drug-taking and stealing from her mother's purse. When she was home she was an irascible wreck. Judith could do little to steer her from self-destruction, and when Zol came on the scene, her influence deteriorated exponentially. Judith had no idea at first that her daughter was seeing him. She had been too busy toiling on Bethany's triptych. As far as she knew Madeleine was spending alternate weekends at Caitlin's and her father's. It took a love bite to disabuse her of both.

Model

Two weeks past the spring equinox and the last rays of sunshine slinked through the trees and the kitchen window, glinting on the knife she held. She was poised to chop a bunch of parsley for a leek and potato soup. Cooking was not Harriet's strength yet she liked to spend time in her kitchen, donning an apron, pretending to herself she was back in her grandmother Emma Smythe's house in Dorset. Picturing herself not as the grey-haired Emma she knew before she was uprooted to South Africa, but as a joyful youngster in a flapper dress and headband, hightailing down country lanes in an Aston Martin. A woman who knew who she was because she was where she was, among all her family and their friends.

The room lent itself to such imaginings. It was almost square with a geometric Dutch tiled floor. Green painted, glass-fronted cupboards hung above a black Formica bench top that lined the back wall. A retro-style fridge sat uneasily beside an authentic free-standing white porcelain sink. A vintage gas Kooka on cabriole legs was set into the inglenook fireplace that took up much of one end of the room, an antique oak dresser the other. A matching oak table occupied the room's centre. The dresser and the table had belonged to her grandmother Emma, who passed them on to her mother and formed part of the much-travelled furniture she had inherited years before, furniture once comfortably at home in the old manor house in Dorset's verdant pastures and now equally at home here in this clinker-brick cottage that sheltered in the cool moist air beneath the canopy of the mountain ash.

Replacing the rows of painted plates her mother had displayed on the dresser shelves, Harriet had arranged candles, trinket boxes, incense holders, a pair of carved elephants, a bamboo canister of I Ching sticks with accompanying book, a pack of tarot cards, a velvet pouch of runes, and, in frames less ornate than those on the living room mantelpiece, a single pair of photographs, one of Kandinsky, the other Klee.

Both men had prominent foreheads and a serious defiance in their manner. Klee stared with an almost violent intensity and Kandinsky, who barely raised a smile, imposed his wisdom on the room with fixed determination. They were the *avant garde* of their day, and Harriet was rather attached to the *avant garde*. She was aware that her affection for the Bauhaus movement might seem to others at odds with the hedonistic trends of Twenties' fashion she also admired, yet Harriet did not for one moment consider her aesthetic position contradictory. She was adamant there existed a logic to the incongruity of her tastes. In culture, fashion and design the Twenties was an era for the bold, the flamboyant, the beaded. In domestic style she revered the era itself. In her art she might emulate the modernist styles of abstract expressionism, but in interior design she did not, for she abhorred the austere when it came to the realm of the home. Abstraction in art was one thing, stripping a building to its barest elements of form quite another. After all, a home had a mundane purpose whereas paintings, and art in general, served to lift the spectator out of the ordinary and the everyday. It seemed to her that those elements applied in art, when applied in architecture, served not to spiritualise the population, but to oppress it.

She set aside the parsley and stood at the sink, washing grit from inside the long leafy shafts of a leek. When she turned off the tap and shook dry the leek, she observed the trail of fine dirt that settled on the white porcelain on its way to the plughole.

The window above the sink looked over the back garden. The long and cold winter had merged seamlessly into spring and only now, as the days lengthened, were the warmer nights hastening growth and bringing to an end the winter harvest in the small but productive vegetable patch. In the half light, Ginny was gathering salad greens spaced out along the edge of a raised bed that was retained by a low stone wall. It was the painstaking way she went about it that captivated her mother, pondering over each plant, bending, hesitating, gently picking then straightening and moving on with bowed head.

A full moon rose in the east, backlighting a stand of trees in the neighbour's garden. Harriet thought of its cycles, the way it waxed and waned. And an idea glided its way through her mind like an owl and she wondered if the moon might hold the key that would unlock the creative impasse, an impasse that had thwarted her collaboration with Ginny from its inception. She moved away from the sink, unsure what to make of the idea, baffled as to how the Moon, indeed anything cosmological, would assist in the creation of art and music when one of the collaborators was, despite her mystical bent, a stalwart rationalist.

She dried her hands, went to the dresser and pulled open the bottom drawer. It was still there, rolled up beside a ball of string, last year's Christmas cards and some packing tape. The Moon planting guide of 2000 that Ginny's school friend, Poppy, had gifted her to mark the millennium. When the podgy little Pargiter, daughter of that meddlesome Mrs Pargiter of Agatha's Tea Rooms, had appeared at the gallery bearing on upturned palms her scroll, all wrapped up in shiny silver paper, Harriet had thought it the strangest moment of her life and could do nothing but smile. A curious happenstance, Poppy must have been under instructions, which made the gift and the ceremonial manner of gifting all the more strange. The only reason she hadn't tossed it out was it had become a memento of a remarkable celebration, the village alive with bonhomie, restaurants and hostelries in neighbouring Olinda apparently bursting with clientele. Not that she had participated in the merrymaking, preferring to stay at home and slosh Pol Roger with Phoebe.

Ginny had spent the night at the Hunnacots and the planting guide was still on the kitchen table where Harriet had left it since bringing it home, partly wrapped in its glittering paper. Halfway through their second bottle, Phoebe had launched into a mocking diatribe on the notion of planting by the phases of the moon. 'Let the elementals take care of it, I say. Or the pixies. Let them plant the little sprouts. No, no, let the moonbeams do it.' Harriet had laughed, but it wasn't the lunar premises that confounded her. It was the distasteful way the information was portrayed, calendar style, on a poster.

She unrolled the chart and laid it on the table, securing the ends with the cruet set and a stout candle that formed part of the table's centrepiece. She followed the Moon on its anti-clockwise journey around Earth, waxing from new through crescent and gibbous to full then waning again, thirteen times to complete the circle. She wondered how to broach the subject with Ginny, who held a remarkably severe view of the esoteric. Other than tides, which were indisputably related to the moon's pull, she regarded all lunar correspondences, including the growth of plants and the menstrual cycle, with disdain.

Harriet only had herself to blame. Few were predisposed to theosophical teachings, and a light touch was called for when it came to non-seers and sceptics, or a door that might one day have thrust open would be sealed shut for the entire incarnation.

Several years earlier, after an afternoon of theosophical musings with her dear friend Rosalind in which they had discussed at length the root races and the Moon chain, she had imprudently raised the topic with Ginny and was met with merciless derision. Ever since, she'd refrained from using the word 'Moon' in Ginny's presence, and she wished she'd managed the same last night regarding the root races, but her tongue had got the better of her.

A tongue riled was a tongue loose, especially when the rest of her heated up like a radiator.

She traced a finger along the Moon's trajectory. She didn't want to alienate Ginny further from their collaboration. Ginny's reticence was already a considerable irritation and she worried about her state of mind and the depression that shadowed her, at once wishing she would snap out of it. She had become hypersensitive and Harriet felt she was forever handling fragile glass. That a woman of rarefied intelligence could become locked inside such gloom Harriet found not only disturbing, but a maddening waste. She left the planting guide where it was and returned to preparing the soup.

Ginny set the bowl of salad greens on the grass at her feet, squatted down and reached over the English spinach for a few leaves of red mizuna. She was in no rush to go back inside. Knowing her mother was watching from the kitchen window, she avoided looking in that direction.

Ginny was cross with her mother and she knew it. After their altercation last night she had half a mind to pack a suitcase. She would get a job, put her qualifications to some use. After all, she had attained the highest education possible, commencing her doctorate at the tender age of twenty-one upon her spectacular undergraduate success. That ought to count for something.

Academics had been falling over themselves to supervise. Although she had to admit that the enthusiasm waned when she devised her research topic: Musical Expression as a Transformative Experience: A Phenomenological Inquiry.

It wasn't the phenomenology that put them off. After all, once the turgid, obscure and convoluted is stripped away, or left for sycophantic study groups to ponder, the philosophy could be whittled down, and often was, to mean nothing more than the study of the essence of something. Not an objective study, for that would be heading in the opposite direction. Phenomenology demanded a subjective mode of investigation. Her own inquiry involved unpacking in minute detail what 'musical expression' was for the person expressing it.

'Transformative experience', on the other hand, was a touch mystical in connotation and not to many of her academics' tastes. Only one of her supervisors came forward with empathy and understanding. The others adopted doubtful stances and quizzed her ruthlessly as though determined to remain unable to see the merit in her work.

Exploring transformative experience led her on a fascinating journey. She visited Jamesian depictions of religious experience, explored the nature of mysticism in Evelyn Underhill, and went on a brief but intense foray into the works of Stanislav Grof, before she arrived at the thickets of metaphysics and concerns of scope and tangent reigned her in. But not before she entertained Neoplatonism and found herself back with Pythagoras and the music of the spheres, upon which she spent a whole week pondering those connections in *Gödel Escher Bach*. Shortly after, she changed the title of her doctoral inquiry to 'Musical Composition as a Transformative Experience', which seemed to her more focused.

She would compose music and record the experience in a journal. She would divest herself of theory and secondhand knowledge using Husserlian brackets. What in essence is transformative in composition? She would enter the epoché and find out.

It was a thrill to have secured a scholarship to finance her immersion in her passion and she didn't notice the shrinking of her life. Her peers fell away, some taking up juicy contracts in television and film, others gigging with the purist jazz musos at Dizzy's, Paris Cat and Bennetts Lane. There were those who had caved in to security and enrolled in a diploma of education, and the diehards, admirably scratching a living while throwing their all into their various bands, hoping to make a name for themselves and tour overseas before age dashed their chances. One way or another her peers were part of the social fabric while she was set apart, a lone thread weaving its own cloth in a North Melbourne flat.

The flat was in a converted warehouse tucked down a lane off Errol Street, and consisted of two small bedrooms and bathroom accessed on the right hand side of a narrow hallway that led to the living room, and on through to the kitchen. The layout was compact, with high ceilings and polished floorboards, and all the rooms were oddly shaped. The second bedroom a rhombus, the end wall narrowing to the width of the two-door built-in wardrobe. Its window looked out on a high brick wall about six metres away. The other bedroom, the bathroom and the living room also looked out at the same brick wall. She knew just about every brick: the various cracks, chips, the places where the mortar needed pointing, the old paint stains.

The kitchen was the flat's redemption, although it was long and thin, its narrowness accentuated by a faux granite bench that stretched below the window, and an island bench that mimicked the elongation. Both benches ended abruptly to allow space for a dining table. There was enough room on the near side of the island bench for bar stools and little else. Ginny didn't mind. The window that took up much of the north-facing wall overlooked a courtyard with small trees and plants in tubs and handkerchiefs of lawn. She had shoved a Formica dining table against the windowed wall and put her Roland at the end, cramming into the spare corner a small cane armchair. She ate, composed, wrote, contemplated, lived her every waking moment in the flat in that corner of the kitchen.

For respite, every weekday she would walk to Victoria markets, then zigzag the grid of streets down to Flinders Street station, cross the Yarra river and on past Hamer Hall and Victoria's National Gallery to the Victorian College of the Arts. There she divided her time between the library, a practice room and the café where she would sit in a corner watching first years cavort about, smiles stretching to their ears.

The walk home was the worst part of her daily routine, every footstep bringing her closer to isolation.

She tempered her loneliness with lofty thoughts, knowing she was one of a few privy to specialist knowledge. While the heaving mass of society vilified those who pursued academic heights, a society that sought to keep a well-clipped lawn in which nothing tall-stemmed stood a chance, her own stem grew tall and straight, a single bloom in a garden of mediocrity, or so she thought at the time. The truth was, she felt exclusive and excluded all at once.

She would have relished discussing with her mother all that was running helter skelter through her mind. Perhaps Harriet might have provided some structure, or been some sort of anchor, but the one time she mentioned her work there had been a full moon and Rosalind had just left the house, and all her mother could talk about were the evolutionary descendants of the moon chain.

Ginny felt sucked into madness as her mother swiftly circled over the subject of root races, landing at the feet of her favourite fact, that skulking about on the planet were too many Lemurian types, knuckle draggers with passions of the lowest order. It wasn't hard to conjure examples. Ginny had only to recall the Ice-crazed jittering wreck who attacked the driver of the eighty-six tram the other week. Or the sleazy old man that hung around the entrance to Victoria markets, leering at short-skirted young women passing by.

Harriet insisted those low Lemurian humans were little more than animals that couldn't tell instinct from desire. They were obsessed with sadism and sex, being capable of feeling only raw pain or orgasmic joy. They were impulse driven and insatiable. They therefore had no moral compass. 'And we all know what happened to that root race,' she said with pomposity. 'Their very form was deemed inadequate for the purposes of spiritual evolution, and incinerated.'

Ginny had dared not inquire who had done the deeming. Neither did she ask whose spiritual evolution stood most to benefit, the Lemurians or some other higher form. It would have triggered an avalanche of metaphysical mumbo jumbo.

She stood up and stretched her legs. She had been crouching beside the garden bed for too long and the colander was overflowing.

She should return to the kitchen but she couldn't yet take herself back into Harriet's psychic sphere.

She knew her mother's view of root races was immutable. She used it to distance herself from the 'great unwashed'. Root races justified her very existence, and her isolation, as if she were highly evolved, and contact with those of a lesser root race would taint her soul. Which was why, when Veronica and Poppy were round last night, and Harriet had called her father the Lemurian, Ginny had all but choked on her food.

They were seated round the oak table sharing a bottle of Chablis, Harriet with her back to the cooker, comfortable in the large-armed ladderback chair at the end, and Poppy and Veronica side by side opposite Ginny, whose chair afforded her an absorbing view of the garden, and of the dresser, should she wish to turn from her mother's overbearing presence.

Poppy wriggled in her seat, adjusting the fall of her dress beneath the vivid green mohair poncho she had found in Savers. Her fork clattered to the floor. With an 'Oops silly me' chuckle, she leaned down to retrieve it. She sat still after that, all wide-eyed innocence. With her dyed white bob framing her round and pale face, she had the appearance of a China doll.

Veronica caught Ginny's eye and they exchanged a knowing look. Veronica was her marmalade friend, at once sweet and tart, with a pithy undertow. Her lips were a lush orange-red, and her hair glossy, black and straight with baby bangs. She had taken to wearing jeans rolled up above the ankles, layering up her torso with ill-fitting Savers' tops, their cuffs reaching well beyond her wrists. Beneath her sleeves she wore a number of bangles. Having little chance of using her hands for anything without shaking back her cuffs, the moment she moved she jangled.

Ginny sipped her wine and privately surveyed her friends, wondering how they had both grown into adults committed to pop culture pastiche. Then again, she was in no position to judge. She saw without looking the paisley jacket she had rarely taken off since her return, having found it in her wardrobe, puzzled and pleased that her mother had not tossed it out. She knew Harriet despised paisley. There was a time she wore paisley trousers, paisley shirts, and paisley skirts and dresses. Her affection for the design kindled the day they went shopping in Chapel Street and she had stood outside the Salvos admiring a paisley dress and Harriet had gasped in distaste at the sight of it.

The paisley jacket had been hanging in her wardrobe from the moment she moved out and when she had opened the door to see it hanging there, she felt an unanticipated rush of comfort. As if in the wearing she reclaimed a pre-Garth self. More, that it took her back to her high school years. It was a uniform, and dressed in it she felt surface her remnants of that former self.

As a teenager, what had then been a belligerent grudge against Harriet for refusing to divulge anything of her father found expression in paisley. At twenty-eight perhaps she no longer needed to state her defiance in cloth. Yet, absurd as it might have seemed to her friends, she wasn't quite ready to take the jacket off.

A smell of burning cheese wafted across the room. 'I'll check on the food,' Harriet said and left the table.

Ginny didn't move. The oven door opened and closed with a thump. A chink of plates. She focused on Poppy and Veronica as they discussed the merits of eyelash extensions.

That afternoon they had gone for a walk down by the creek, enjoying the dappled shade beneath the mountain ash, the verdant undergrowth, the tree ferns. They had strolled along, edging off the lane for the occasional car. They were paying scant attention to their surroundings, not heeding the screech of cockatoos in the canopy above, concentrating instead on each other: first Poppy's account of her turbulent love life, then Veronica hers. She was meant to take the cue but Ginny avoided talking of Garth, keen to avoid the humiliations: the broken career, the broken heart. Instead, she maintained interest in her friends' conversation, their various losses and successes.

Veronica was a beauty editor for *Ra-On*, an online Melbourne-based hipster magazine that followed the latest fads and frivolities of urban trendies, concerning itself with everything from kale to lattes to the art of looking careless. Yet there was nothing frivolous about Veronica. For her, the colour of lipstick was a matter of life and death. She would wax about the launches, the freebies and the lovers she accumulated, who all sounded as seriously superficial as she.

Poppy was a copy editor for Dark Moon, a small but thriving publisher of teenage fantasy novels, her bouncy ebullience spilling over into all manner of enchanted realities and fruitful if arduous quests. Her perception and interpretation of the mundane imbued with magic finds, treasures, trials and tests, that it could be hard to be in her company without feeling half-crazy from the effort of sifting the reality out of her conversation.

She wondered if they reflected on her in a similar fashion. Sometimes she viewed her friends as schoolyard vestiges. Yet they were quirky and fun, and she was glad they were up the mountain for the weekend visiting their parents, glad she had invited them over.

They reached a T-intersection and came to an abrupt stop. Nobles Lane wended its way up to the crest of the mountain. On the left, a smattering of houses clung to the slope, obscured by dense foliage, save for a touch of roof here and glint of window there. On the right, barely visible beyond the overgrown nature strip, was Alfred Nicholas Memorial Gardens, an elegantly landscaped and intensively planted rectangle of land, the main feature a lake at the bottom, accessed via a steep zigzag of paths. It was a tourist attraction, but in winter, when there were fewer visitors, Ginny used to like to walk down to the lake and sit on a bench and watch the water tremble in the breeze.

Poppy took one look at the ascent and said, 'Let's go back,' so they did, neither Veronica nor Ginny hesitating. Conversation during the walk in reverse was much the same, Veronica relating a detailed and rambling account of her and Poppy's recent day trip to Bendigo on the train. How they hadn't anticipated the weather and found themselves huddled in a hotel listening to some old dude sing the Blues. Ginny couldn't see the point of the tale except to convey a sense of fun, Veronica egged on by Poppy's embellishments. Poppy had been convinced the old Blues singer was the reincarnation of Robert Johnson in white skin, and that an old photo of the Campaspe River hanging above his head, and the stocky wire-haired bitzer asleep at his feet were certain proof, for the devil hangs close by rivers and it was the devil's dog that shocked the blues out of Robert Johnson's strings.

Veronica didn't question the veracity of her friend's claim, leaving Ginny struck by the allowances she made. By the time they reached The Crescent, Ginny had to fend off her envy. Her friends had careers that suited and satisfied them, and they had each other, sharing a small but well-lit flat in Brunswick. They might skimp on food, eat at Lentils and claim the occasional suspended coffee, but their lives were whole, and hers was in splinters.

Her gaze drifted from her friends, seated across the kitchen table, to the window, to the black of the night, to the room reflected in the glass, her mother by the stove. And suddenly she viewed her friends as allies.

Harriet placed in the table's centre a large casserole and two serving dishes and when she removed the lids they were all staring at the Boston baked beans topped with overcooked cheese, the mashed turnips and the braised savoy cabbage they were required to eat. It must have been intentional, all that stodge and flatulent potential in one meal.

Earlier in the day she had offered to cook, but Harriet wouldn't hear of it, yet with Poppy vegan and gluten free, and Veronica vegetarian and lactose intolerant, she knew her mother would struggle to invent dinner and knew too how much she would resent the inconvenience. So this, it seemed, was to be their punishment.

They helped themselves.

Conversation proved as laboured as consuming the repast.

Several mouthfuls in, Poppy smiled politely at Harriet with an 'It's yummy, thank you.'

'You're welcome,' Harriet said. She had taken a portion that would barely feed a baby.

Veronica was swift on Poppy's heels with, 'Tell me, Ginny, which one of those is your father?' pointing at the photos on the dresser.

Ginny was taken by surprise. Veronica had visited the house many times, sat in that very chair, and had never shown an interest in those photos. Perhaps Mr Hunnacot's recent appearance on the front page of the parish newsletter for his service to the community had prompted her question.

'Neither of them,' she said flatly, aware that her father was as much a mystery to her friends as he was to her. She returned to her food, forking a few threads of cabbage.

'Who are they?' Veronica asked.

'Kandinsky and Klee,' said Harriet.

'Sounds like a folk duo,' Poppy said.

Ginny kept quiet, sensing her mother's mounting irritation.

Veronica studied the photos. 'They look dorky enough,' she said.

'They are the great artists of modernism,' Harriet said, putting on one of her outlandish smiles.

Ginny closed her mouth on a forkful of beans.

Poppy looked from Ginny to Harriet and emitted a sheepish giggle. 'I thought they might have been...'

'...former lovers. No. I wouldn't countenance such a display of sentimentality,' Harriet said, her tone suddenly pompous. 'And neither would I under any circumstances have on full view an image of the Lemurian.'

Ginny swallowed quickly, reaching for her glass to swill her mouth.

'The Lemurian?' Veronica looked puzzled.

'Yes. The Lemurian.'

'She means my father,' Ginny said in a low voice, shooting her mother an icy stare.

Harriet stretched out her hands and thrust forward her face, eyebrows raised.

Upon which Ginny shoved aside her plate and pushed back her chair. She went to the dresser and opened one of the doors below the hutch and lifted out a shoebox coated in a decoupage of pictures of paintings cut from magazines. She placed the box heavily on the table before her. 'I shall show you, Veronica, since you asked. And you too, Poppy.' Her mother hated poring over the past. So she would ruin her evening with it.

'Oh goody,' Poppy said awkwardly, although she would have meant it. Poppy had a thing for the pre-digital age. Ginny suspected, too, that she was relieved not to be compelled to eat more of what had proven to be just as it had looked.

Veronica removed their plates to the sink and drew up her chair.

Harriet said nothing. Leaving her plate where it was, she stood, hovering. When Poppy said, 'Who's that?' she removed herself from the room, passing through the curtain with a louder than normal clatter of beads.

The photo box remained on the kitchen table the following morning. Harriet had left it there when she had returned after the others vacated the room, to remind herself that some penance was required.

'Coffee?' she asked as Ginny appeared, and she poured a second cup from the cafetière.

Ginny let the beaded curtain fall behind her, pulled up a chair, and began sorting through the photos at the top. She seemed less angry than last night, much to Harriet's relief.

'How old was I in this one?' she said, holding up a baby photo.

'Doesn't it say on the back?'

She turned the photo over and shook her head.

Harriet held out her hand.

Ginny was wrapped in a shawl, its tasselled fringes draped over Harriet's cradling arm. She was endearing with her tiny face, eyes gazing up, an almost smile on her lips. 'You must have been about ten days old.'

'Is my father taking the photo?'

'Yes. He took many photos.' She looked again, this time at a younger self in a light summer dress standing in front of a high brick wall. Then up at her daughter, now so grown and not resembling her or her father at all. A cuckoo in the nest, yet her parentage was not in question; she was a Brassington-Smythe, and a Schmid. Seated beside her she seemed vulnerable, awkward, part of her still a child, and Harriet felt a sudden tightening in her chest.

It was a windy day in July when Wilhelm, camera in hand, insisted she take the baby outside for a photo in the natural light. A wonder Ginny hadn't caught a chill. She recalled he had bought the Canon just before the birth.

'The day you were born I was finishing a painting for Phoebe,' she said reflectively. 'It was to be my last Matisse, but I didn't know that then. You were patient, waiting until I cleaned my brushes before choosing to make your way into the world.'

'Where was Wilhelm?'

'Leading a seminar on the Thule Society. We didn't have mobiles in those days so I phoned the college and left a message. Minutes before you made your appearance he arrived at the hospital, camera to the ready apparently. I'd had so much gas I didn't know he was there. The nurse told me later that she couldn't help noticing he was only interested in capturing the moment, so to speak, and not in providing me with any comfort. Fortunately you were an easy enough birth, or I think I might never have gone home to Gore Street.'

'You weren't happy with him, even then.'

'No, but a child changes things. One can't abandon an unsatisfactory union on an impulse, not when you share a child.'

'I suppose not.'

That was exactly what she had done, seven years later, but neither mother or daughter said a word.

'And he worked hard and I admired his passion, his intensity, his intellect. And he wasn't cruel. Well, not to you.'

Ginny passed over her remark. Yet she looked curious and doubtful all at once.

Feeling a measure of contrition, Harriet went on. 'I should take that back. I'm not sure he was cruel or had ever been cruel to anyone. Yet neither was he kind and he displayed little compassion. What bothered me was the harshness of his ideas and the harsh way he extolled them. It was as if he had the answer for everything, the final or ultimate solution.'

'You make him sound like Hitler.'

'Well, there was little humanity in his solution. He was all for de-populating the planet. He was scathing of what he called the lumpen masses. It was the intellect that mattered to him, a particular sort of intellect. I suspect he thought himself the incarnation of Übermensch.'

'Lots of people hold harsh views. Does that make them bad people?'

Harriet had no answer. She had already said too much. Knowing Ginny's attitude to Theosophy, which was a complete rejection, any judgement she might make of Wilhelm's esoteric predilections would be taken as ideological—little more than disagreement on the basis of competing metaphysical beliefs. It was not worth pursuing. Besides, she had criticised him enough.

She drained her cup then delved in the box, extracting a pile of photos tied with green ribbon. Before she pulled on the bow she said, 'It was with you that he displayed tenderness. He doted on you. He prized you.'

'He did?'

'It was as if he thought you held some sort of promise for the future. He'd been like that ever since I told him I was pregnant.'

'That's nice.'

Ginny's smile lit her face. It was the first time Harriet had seen Ginny smile like that in a long time. It made her doubt the veracity of her recollections, if only for a moment. 'I found it surprising at the time,' she said. 'I'd been hesitant to tell him. I was twenty-seven and not yet ready for motherhood. He was thirty-two and had made no indication of a desire for a family. We'd been together little more than a year and I had never thought it would be a forever sort of relationship.'

'I was a mistake?'

'Not a mistake. An accident. And yes, I had misgivings. But I was not prepared to have an abortion. So I kept you a secret from him for three months.'

'Three months!' Ginny looked at her with serious expectancy, as though anticipating her mother would reveal something of grave import previously withheld.

'Oddly, I thought at the time that he was overjoyed. He'd arrived home from a meeting with his supervisor who'd been nagging him not to veer too far into speculations on the origins of Freemasonry in his literature review. I was in the studio. I'd gone to greet him but he'd already dumped his overcoat and rushed upstairs to the bathroom. He was telling me all about his run in with his supervisor through the closed door when I interrupted him with the news. He exclaimed with delight instantly. A little Schmid he kept saying and chuckling, and I kept thinking no, a little Brassington-Smythe.' Harriet refrained from drawing attention to the fact that she had told him while he was releasing the contents of his bowels.

'I'm Ginny Smith, in fact.'

'I wish you wouldn't.'

'I said Smith, not Schmid.'

'All the same.'

'But Brassington-Smythe is so pretentious.'

'It is your name, Ginny.'

'At least you didn't insist on Virginia.'

Harriet made no reply. She untied the green bow and sifted through the photos.

'Why the ribbon?'

'I think these were before you were born.' She held a photo and gazed at it for a moment. 'This one was taken in the Evelyn. We used to go there often, for the music.'

Wilhelm, Harriet and Fritz, seated in the bar. Harriet with a slight lean towards Fritz. They were an incongruous crew. Wilhelm in his vintage Fifties' suit, head tilted back, jaw forward, wide smile unconvincing. He was visibly drunk. His presence leapt from the photo, a look of smarmy triumph on his face. Fritz looked more intellectual than ever in his round, thin-framed glasses. He seemed gaunt too, his cheeks a little hollow, then she remembered that was the year he had caught the flu. And she was all camaraderie with her closed-mouth smile, eyes staring straight at the lens. She had on her scooped-neck red dress with matching bow in her ruffled black hair, and with those vermillion lips she was all glamour-puss.

'I must have been about six months pregnant. Still drinking dark beer of course.' She emitted a short and solitary laugh. 'For the iron.' She passed Ginny the photo.

'Who took it?' Ginny asked.

'That must have been the night Fritz brought his friend from Munich along. A nice young man. Quite shy. Gunther Fuchs with the single black-painted fingernail. He didn't say much, but Wilhelm had taken an aversion to him from the first. Gunther took the photo before the men went outside for a cigarette. Fritz told me later that Wilhelm had lectured the poor man on the perils of adopting a symbol of which he knew nothing.'

'What symbol?'

'The black fingernail. Apparently Wilhelm accused Gunther of trivialising something of symbolic significance, undermining by appropriating what amounted to iconography.'

'People do that all the time. Veronica wears an all-seeing eye necklace.'

'An eye within a triangle within an uroboros, I know.' Harriet paused. And she wears it upside-down, she thought, but now was not the time to digress. 'Wilhelm told Gunther that in all likelihood he'd invoked a taboo and for all he knew brought upon himself his own downfall at the stroke of the varnish brush. He went on and on, Fritz said, and his manner so strident that matters occult must remain occult, that Fritz felt compelled to tell me.'

'Why?'

Harriet glanced out the window. 'He wanted to protect me. Fritz despised dogmatism and in this instance he would have found Wilhelm's doctrinaire attitude alarming. As do I. He said Wilhelm went on to insist that the symbol was the preserve of an Elect, and not for the general populace. Fritz said that as the music got louder, so did Wilhelm, and he thought they might get barred.'

'From the Evelyn?' Ginny said doubtfully.

'The point is that when Fritz later related the story, I first thought of Wilhelm as the Lemurian. I was so annoyed.'

Ginny didn't respond. Harriet could feel her prickles. That night was also the first time she had seen black flickers of light about Wilhelm. The Letters were playing and at the time she attributed the flashes to the music, not the man. Or rather, she tried. But there was a darkness in him, of that she felt sure, making the flickering black lights she was seeing less synaesthetic and more, what? The light was triggered by the sound of the music, it had to have been, yet she saw beyond sound, something she had no wish to see at all.

She wouldn't mention this to Ginny. Besides, she wanted to clarify her Lemurian comment. Despite Ginny's prejudices, she deserved a fuller explanation.

'You see by then I'd developed an interest in Theosophy. Rosalind had given me a copy of *The Secret Doctrine* for my twenty-fifth birthday. A curious gift, I'd thought at the time, and I'd started dipping into it. Ludicrously difficult to read but I'd gleaned enough to gain a vague understanding of the root races. I suppose I was predisposed after my Masters on Kandinsky. So I was intrigued by the notion of the evolution of consciousness.'

Ginny shifted in her seat. She was hunched over the photo and showed no sign of lifting her gaze.

'And the Lemurians are lower on the evolutionary scheme,' Harriet added.

'But Wilhelm was an intellectual,' Ginny said. 'You always describe Lemurians as animal-men.'

'Initially I was insulting his appearance.'

Ginny was quick to censure with her cool blue-grey eyes.

'I'm sorry. That wasn't fair of me. It wasn't until years later that I saw the significance of the appellation.'

Ginny placed the photo on the table and leaned back in her seat, folding her arms across her chest. Harriet gave her an awkward smile. She knew Ginny would never accept what she had to say next. So she stood and went to make black cohosh tea.

'You can't stop there!' Ginny said, her voice uncommonly shrill.

She could and she would. Damn that Veronica Hunnacot for stirring this up. Although she couldn't blame her. Ginny was on a quest to find out what she could and it was hardly surprising. She was twenty-eight, about the age Harriet had been when she met Wilhelm. Only natural therefore that she should now demand the truth. As if a gong had sounded out upon the repetition of the number, a resolution of one sort or another was required. It was the way the universe worked and there was nothing to be done but flow with it. Yet for now there was another matter to address.

'You mustn't dwell in the past,' she said. 'It isn't healthy. Besides, I've had an idea.'

'Oh, god.'

'You've been here six weeks, Ginny. You need a new direction.'

'The exhibition,' she said glumly.

'Something else. Paid employment in fact. Phoebe is forever arranging weddings, functions and garden parties.'

'I thought her thing was flogging art.'

'The functions are her mainstay and her source of art clients. And she phoned last night complaining that the pianist for one of her events had cancelled. I mentioned your name of course.'

'No, Mum.'

'She'd already thought of you. It's why she phoned.'

'When's the gig?'

'Friday week.'

The kettle boiled. She prepared her tea, adding a little honey and grated ginger to mask the taste, and when she turned back to the table the photos were back in the box and Ginny had managed to slip through the beaded curtain without a tinkle.

Later the same day, Harriet watched Ginny through the kitchen window, hoping her explanation and her divulgences had appeased her. Ginny was far up the garden, near the studio, and making her way back to the house, colander of greens in hand. Recalling her ambivalence, Harriet went to roll up the Moon planting guide, then she changed her mind, leaving the chart pinned to the table by candlestick and cruet set.

She had long been fascinated by the planets and had often wondered what had compelled those ancient philosophers who looked to the heavens and watched the moon's strange and wondrous course through the night sky. How bizarre and inexplicable the moon must have appeared to them, changing its shape, sometimes shining milky-white full, sometimes not there at all.

Pythagoras had made much of the heavenly spheres. No doubt Plato or Aristotle felt their influence when they conceptualised the cosmos under an Athenian sky. Perhaps Alexander the Great timed his conquests by the movements of the planets. Copernicus and Galileo had gazed at the heavenly stars, but had they gazed at the stars in their horoscopes? Newton may have drawn inspiration from the heavenly spheres as he developed his theories of motion. It would have been planetary motion with all its earthly significances that caused Leibniz to write his esoteric philosophy, a body of work he kept secret his whole life. And what about Goethe or Dante? Or Byron, Shelley and Dryden, all of them interested in the heavenly spheres? These men were still celebrated geniuses. She wondered what was it about the movements of the planets that had attracted such minds. The allure of hidden knowledge, decipherable by only a select few, or perhaps it merely satisfied the need for mental stimulation, like chess.

The back door opened and Ginny came inside with the colander brimming with produce. She set it down beside the sink then looked askance at the table.

'I refuse to compose music to a moon planting guide,' she said shortly.

My, how that girl could rankle! Why couldn't she be placid or pliable? Amenable would do. 'I wasn't thinking that you would,' she said. Not anymore.

'Then what's that there for?'

'The moon has cycles and phases. I thought we could make use of that.'

'How?'

Harriet hesitated then, thinking on the run, she went on. 'I have an ephemeris. We could track the Moon over a period of time, say nine months from the day we agreed on that number, noting down all the aspects or connections the Moon makes with the other planets.'

'You mean, *the* planets. The moon is a moon.'

'Don't be pedantic.' She felt the heat rise and went to the sink to splash her face.

'Anyway, I don't follow,' Ginny said. 'You were talking about aspects.'

Harriet quickly dried her face with a hand towel then stood with her back against the sink.

'Think of the zodiac as a circle,' she said, eyeing Ginny cautiously. 'When the Moon sits on top of another, I mean, a planet, they are said to be conjunct. When the Moon is on the opposite side of the circle, that's an opposition.'

'Figures.'

'There are a few more.'

'Go on.'

'A sixty-degree sextile, a ninety-degree square and a hundred and twenty-degree trine.'

Ginny was silent for a few moments, then she said, 'So this is harmonics then.'

'Exactly.'

Ginny frowned. 'And how fast does the Moon travel?'

'It moves through one sign of the zodiac every two and a half days. Does a whole circuit round the zodiac in twenty-eight.'

'So we would be talking lunar months, not solar months?'

'All thirteen.'

'Over a period of nine months that's a lot of movement.'

'You think so?'

Ginny was quiet for a few moments. Then she said, 'Yes. I think it'll be too much information. If the Moon takes only twenty-eight days to do a circuit then it will have made every sort of aspect with every planet in each lunar month. And you are suggesting nine times that. And some of these planets would hardly have moved at all. I mean, Pluto for example, would be just sitting there in almost the same spot. So the whole dynamic would be repetitive.' Her gaze was wide, distant, turned inwards.

Harriet was astonished at how quickly Ginny conceptualised planetary motion. She wouldn't mention it, but that sort of immediate knowing is the hallmark of the esotericist. Must run in the family.

'Then what do you suggest?' she said, not caring how Ginny answered.

Friday, 10 August 2012

The Harmony Centre

Bethany's rooms were at the southern end of Fore Street, opposite Nicholas Priory—a Benedictine Abbey built about a thousand years before and thankfully not bombed in the Blitz as it afforded Bethany a charming outlook of rustic stonemasonry, which she said atoned for the fact that she was sandwiched between a tattoo parlour and a vintage record store. It was the August school holidays and Judith had been lucky to find a parking space despite the dreary weather, pulling up between two sedans further down the street.

'Got everything?'

No answer.

Madeleine had her shoulder bag, stuffed full, on her lap. She got out of the car without a word. Judith doubted she had even heard her speak, the tinny pulse from her headphones audible above the engine of her Volvo estate for the whole ride into town.

They headed back up to Bethany's, stopping a couple of doors down to cross the road. Directly opposite, a venturesome restaurateur had opened an Australian-themed bistro that advertised its hamburger and meat pie fare on a billboard outside. Judith felt sure there was more to Australian cuisine that that. With its ritzy façade the bistro altogether lacked the Wimmera of her imaginings.

Her gaze travelled past Vintage Vinyls and lingered on Bethany's new signage: The Harmony Centre, written in purple in sloping copperplate against a pale pink background.

Before crossing the road, she caught a glimpse in the window of the tattoo parlour of a black-haired hulk she would later know as Zol. He was working the counter and when his customer left, he glanced in their direction and she quickly looked away.

They made a dash across the road and passed by the record store to the sound of Jethro Tull spilling onto the pavement. Recalling her pre-Madeleine youth when she would play her father's records—everything from Camel to Cream—Judith thought she wouldn't mind making a detour to flick through the stock, but Bethany would be waiting.

At Bethany's, Judith stepped through the old wooden doorway set at an angle in the porch. Madeleine slumped in behind. Drop sheets covered the floor and in the far corner, scattered around the legs of a sawhorse, were lengths of timber and open tins of paint.

Madeleine made a show of casting about for somewhere to sit and seeing that there was nowhere, stood off to one side, hunched with her left hip thrust forward, a pose in vogue with all her friends.

Judith looked around at the bare walls before gazing out the shop-front window, her hands deep in the pockets of her cardigan. The tension she had felt earlier that morning returned with force. She always felt tense when someone commissioned a painting. She had clipped back her hair, something she only did for weddings, funerals and business meetings. She recalled Madeleine trying to gain her attention at breakfast, how she had stared blankly, half listening as Madeleine complained about Mr Tweedie's inability to explain trigonometry, until, exasperated at Judith's lack of response, Madeleine had stomped to her room, slamming the door behind her.

There was a short trill and Madeleine reached into the pocket of her jeans. Judith watched her read her text message. She looked like a street urchin, her canvas shoulder bag so often over-stuffed, two of its zips were broken from the strain. Judith refused to buy a replacement until it had completely fallen apart, something it seemed Madeleine was committed to bringing about, as if the bag were a humiliation she suffered grudgingly. Not its colour, black, but the Green Day logo on its front flap. Convinced all discerning passers-by would notice and scoff, she would drape her jacket over it whenever she went out. She stuffed her phone back in her pocket. She was immediately lost, consumed by the dark fantasy of the music she listened to.

Judith went over to her and nudged her arm. 'What is that?' she said, close to her ear.

'"Submerged in Boiling Flesh".'

'Might be an idea to turn it down.'

Bethany had entered the shop through a door in the back wall, rounding the sawhorse and narrowly avoiding brushing the hem of her skirt against the rim of an open tin of paint. 'There you are,' she said, putting on a smile. She seemed flustered; her cheeks, beneath a thin smear of makeup, flushed. She took in the empty paper coffee cups and takeaway cartons left by the workmen, sighed, left the room and returned with a plastic bag and a pair of rubber gloves. With the air of a punctilious housewife, she picked up the cups and cartons between her thumb and forefinger and dropped them into the bag, exiting the room to dispose of the detritus before returning to greet her visitors.

She was an excessively well-groomed woman, dressed that day in a beige skirt suit, tights and low-heeled shoes, her hair, dark-brown and usually straight, arranged in elegant waves about her face. Judith had never seen her dress casually and fully expected to one day find her weeding her garden, bent on her knees in a silk shift and court shoes. Despite their friendship, formed when they had sat together in Maths in Grade Three, Judith had always been wary of Bethany. That a quibbling woman called herself a therapist seemed to Judith at best self-delusory, at worst destructive for her clients. She always felt unsettled after an encounter with her friend.

Bethany removed her rubber gloves and placed them together on the sawhorse. 'Judith,' she said, extending her arms in welcome. They exchanged a cordial hug. 'So pleased to see you.'

'Making good progress?'

'I'll be glad when it's over.'

Bethany glanced at Madeleine as if suddenly aware of her presence and put on a forced smile. 'How's school?'

Madeleine pulled the plugs from her ears. 'Good,' she said and, in what Judith thought was an admirable effort to sound sincere, added, 'Thanks.'

Bethany's eyes scanned her from her face to her feet. 'You'll be planning your revision timetable no doubt,' she said. 'Hannah's made wall charts for each of her subjects. Such a studious girl.'

Madeleine was silent.

'Now, Judith,' Bethany said, returning her gaze to her face, 'I've had a terrific idea for the paintings.'

Judith stiffened. This was the moment she abhorred. The loss of artistic control. The knowledge that her creativity would be constrained to fulfil the wishes of someone with limited or no sensibility for art. She was in her best spirits when she worked on her own exhibitions, in her worst when required by loyalty to labour on a work for which she had no enthusiasm.

'I want you to paint three panels,' said Bethany. 'Each one a silver birch on a white background.'

'A triptych.'

'Indeed.'

'Of birches.'

'Yes. I wasn't sure for a long time what I wanted, but the other night it came to me in a dream.' Bethany paused, a glazed look appearing in her eyes. 'One of those vivid dreams,' she said. 'I was standing right here, facing that bare wall, staring at three panels. On each one, a silver birch in a wintry setting.'

Judith looked at the wall. 'Stark,' was all she said.

'Painted exclusively in black and white of course.'

Judith pictured the idea, the two-dimensionality.

'And grey?' she said tentatively.

'Perhaps a little grey. If you must. But absolutely no colour.'

She made an effort not to appear stone-faced as she clenched her hands behind her back. Her paintings were deep, complex, subtle, arresting, demanding attention, drawing in the viewer. To be told she had to paint in monochrome was as good as suggesting she cooked curry without spice.

'I'll make it worth your while.'

'Bethany…'

'A thousand pounds.'

'Framed or unframed?'

'Just the canvasses.'

'Then that's too much.'

'I insist. I'm planning an opening in mid-November. Will that give you enough time?'

That gave her ample time, too much time, a whole two and a half months of tedium, but the cash would help pay the rates.

Madeleine's phone again burst into life and this time she slipped outside. Judith thanked Bethany for the commission and reassured her that the time frame was adequate. They shook hands on it and she left the shop. Madeleine was standing on the pavement, holding her phone. Judith was about to offer her a lift to Caitlin's house when Madeleine told her she was meeting Caitlin up the street. Judith thought nothing of it. She kissed her daughter goodbye and went back to her car, passing Vintage Vinyls, now playing The Sex Pistols, thinking at least without her daughter the weekend would be quiet.

On the eve of Bethany's opening, Judith rested on the easel the last of the triptych canvasses. The trunk and main branches were painted against their white background. She leaned back against the bench, sucking on her bottom lip. White and black were not her colours. Mixing them to grey, she found she liked them even less. She studied her sketch of a single silver birch then dipped a fine-tipped brush into the blob of grey-black on her palette and traced filigree lines of leafless branches over what she considered to be a patina of snow.

She hunched in front of the canvas, eyes focused, hand locked steady and two hours later her right shoulder was cramping and her head ached. The air in the studio had chilled. She turned up the thermostat on the column heater tucked under the bench. She would have liked to take a break, walk briskly round the garden, bake bread, anything to circulate the blood but she couldn't afford the time. She had put off making a start on the work until early October, leaving her rushing and as eager to finish as Bethany was to receive it.

She was beginning to detest silver birches. 'They're highly symbolic,' Bethany had said airily on the phone the other day. Despite Bethany's dream, Judith had assumed Bethany commissioned the paintings simply to complement the space, but Bethany had said in a conspiratorial voice that another word for birch is Beth. Which took Judith by surprise. For six weeks she had been unwittingly painting some sort of symbolic portrait, satisfying the vanity of her friend in a veiled manner, and she had all but thrown down her paintbrush in disgust, until she slowly realised that the stark, bleak, shallow images did in fact capture the essence of Bethany, a woman bent on living a life of gloss and superficial manners.

Judith looked from the painting on the easel to its companions leaning on the bench. The overall effect was austere. The crisp lines, the naked trees, the harsh sterility of winter, evoking not just aspects of Bethany's personality but desolation, deprivation, even death. It was hard to connect this impression with the fertility and birth symbolism of the birch. There were no new buds auguring spring. No sense of something about to burst into life. Miró's single skinny black line, the meandering trail of an idea, uncertain of its destination across three vast white backgrounds, had vitality, a sort of vigour about it. In her commission there were too many lines, none of them ponderous. All fixed in place by the form of the birch. She wondered if she had failed in her execution. She should have deviated from Bethany's directive, taken artistic control instead of slavishly giving in to her desire. Now the work enslaved her and she didn't feel good about it.

Another two hours passed, and it was three minutes to four. The rumble of a bus coming down the hill resonated gently through the house. Madeleine would be home in minutes. She jiggled her brush in a jar of grey water, making a promise to herself never to work in monochrome again, no matter how much she was offered.

When the front door thudded shut Judith called out but Madeleine offered no reply.

She took another look at the triptych then went through to the kitchen. The pantry doors were open wide. Madeleine was standing on a chair, rummaging through the jars on the top shelf. The further in she reached, the more Judith saw of her midriff, her blouse riding up her back. Judith privately admired the soft curve of her waist, the innocent flesh.

'If you're hungry, I'll make you a sandwich.'

'No thanks.'

Having found what she was looking for, Madeleine pulled back and Judith caught a glimpse of a red-purple love bite the size of a fifty pence piece on her neck.

'I forgot to ask,' she said casually. 'How was your weekend?'

'Meh,' she said, stepping off the chair with a lone packet of two-minute noodles left over from a school camp.

'What did you do?'

'Not a lot,' she said, avoiding Judith's gaze. 'Caitlin was tired.'

'Madeleine,' Judith said softly, 'was there a party?'

'At Caitlin's? As if.'

'Somewhere else?'

'What are you on about?'

'A party. That's the place boys give girls love bites.'

'The hickey.' Madeleine laughed, but she looked awkward.

'Tell me where you were.'

She was silent.

'I'll phone Caitlin's mother then.'

'I was at Zol's.'

'Zol?'

'My boyfriend.'

'Boyfriend?'

'Are you a parrot?'

'Madeleine,' she censured.

'Okay,' Madeleine said churlishly.

'Who is this Zol?'

'He works at the tattoo parlour next to Bethany's.'

Judith thought back to the day they had stood at the kerb waiting to cross Fore Street and she had spied a troll-like figure at the parlour counter. Was that him? She couldn't decide which was more disturbing, the deception or the man. There was little to be gained pursing the matter with her daughter. Besides, she needed to hold on to what was left of her equanimity. There was a pressing decision to be made.

She left Madeleine to cook her noodles and went back to the studio. She wanted to call Bethany's commission finished. She looked at the painting on the easel for a long time, taking in the negative space, zooming in to the form of the birch, tracking the fine lines of the branches, before deciding the works would have to do. She couldn't bring herself to paint another stroke.

She went through the kitchen and on outside. The day was still and cool, the sun dimming to dusk. A few crinkled brown leaves clung to the otherwise bare branches of the apple trees. She pulled on her boots and wandered around the garden, pulling out a weed here and there.

Her life had a rhythm—painting, gardening, keeping house—and with Madeleine almost fully grown she would soon have the solitude she had craved all her daughter's life. Sometimes she thought this yearning evidence that she was an awful mother and Madeleine deserved better, but she refused to feel guilty about it. Not a day went by when a small part of her didn't wish that Madeleine's father would beg for more contact, custody even—things she would happily have given.

She pulled two bay leaves off a small tree growing in a large earthenware tub in the corner of the courtyard and kicked off her boots.

An hour later, she was folding grated cheese into a white sauce. The phone rang. She turned down the gas and went out to the hall. It was Bethany.

'Just checking on progress.'

Judith knew her too well to be convinced by her casual tone. She would be pacing the floor, ticking through a to-do list on a clipboard.

'They're done,' she said. 'I'll drop them by tomorrow afternoon.'

'Thank goodness. Can you be at the office at twelve?'

Not ideal. Lunchtime cleaved the day in two, neither half long enough to gather her thoughts and focus on her next project. But there was no point trying to negotiate with Bethany.

When the phone rang for the second time, it was Peter. She said she would call Madeleine and he told her not to bother. 'It's you I wish to talk to,' he said in a hurried, irritable voice.

'Go on,' she answered slowly.

'You know she's cancelled our day.'

'I had no idea.'

Which was true, but Peter didn't seem to believe her.

'I suppose now you're going to tell me you had no idea she's got herself involved with some lad,' he said. 'Some lout in fact, who works at the tattoo parlour in Fore Street.'

She pictured Peter, lips drawn tight, frown lines deepened between the eyes.

'Opposite Nicholas Priory?' she said, trying to keep the exchange light, thinking back to that day when she had seen the troll in the tattoo-parlour window. She hadn't taken much notice, unaware that her daughter standing beside her knew full well who he was. She went on in a bland voice. 'I suppose she met him while she was waiting for you.'

'That's a maybe,' he said. 'What I do know is they spent last weekend together.'

'She was with Caitlin last weekend,' she lied, picturing the love bite.

'Is that right? Then why did I see her in town with that behemoth?'

'She's sixteen,' she said, as if age made a difference.

'She's in with a bad sort.'

'I'll talk to her.'

'She's ruining her life.'

'I'll talk to her.'

She hung up the phone. She had no idea how to approach Madeleine. She was above the age of consent and free to be with anyone she liked. It wasn't her fault the girl had no taste. Although she suspected that was what Peter thought. She felt defensive. She had surely done what any mother would have to raise the child with manners and values. She had been barely more than a child herself when she had had her. To be required by a normally indifferent father to challenge their daughter over her deceit: She stood by the phone for a long time before walking away knowing she wouldn't.

Bethany's opening started at six. Judith arrived with five minutes to spare, Madeleine slouching in behind dressed in runners, black jeans and a Necrophagist T-shirt; her hair, as usual not brushed, hanging limply about her face. She had paid attention to her makeup, her face chalky, the sockets of her narrow eyes woefully black. Judith didn't begrudge her appearance. In a burnt-orange two-piece and contrasting sage-green scarf she knew she would be just as out of place.

Bethany greeted her with a wave and beckoned her to a long trestle table laden with food and drinks. Neatly arranged on a white linen tablecloth were platters of canapés, dips, vol-au-vents and cocktail sausages. Bethany poured Judith a glass of white wine and looked inquiringly at Madeleine. 'Would you like a soft drink or juice?'

'Is there any Coke?'

Bethany ignored the request, her attention drawn to a smartly dressed couple walking through the door. Judith handed Madeleine a glass of lemonade, worried she would remain grumpy the whole evening.

Then Madeleine noticed Bethany's daughter Hannah slumped

on the settee and her face lit up. Hannah was a quiet, unassuming girl, not at all Madeleine's type, but once Hannah started listening to Slipknot, she had become one of Madeleine's girlfriends. When Madeleine had become a Slipknot fan her image changed from blue jeans and stripy t-shirts to everything black. The older she grew, the more entrenched her contempt for all things ordinary. It was a relief to see her huddling together with Hannah, both bent over their iPods, oblivious to the sharp looks they received from the grown-up guests coveting their seats.

The room was full of the middle-aged: women in formal dresses talking in groups of three and four; men in suits, men in pressed jeans and smart shirts. She recognised the mayor and his wife, both of them tall and rotund; the local conservative candidate talking to a beak-nosed and wiry woman with cropped blonde hair; three teachers from Madeleine's former primary school chatting with a local builder; and two farmers looking awkward, their wives over by the window, gossiping.

A young, eager-looking woman with a camera hovered beside the trestle table. Judith went over and dipped a carrot stick in a bowl of guacamole.

'Are you the artist?' the young woman said.

'Good guess.'

'Your work is terrific.'

'Thank you,' she said, not quite believing her.

'I'm Megan, from *The Exeter Star*. Can I take your photo? I'd like to do a feature on your work.'

Bethany must have overheard. Suddenly she was beside Judith, all smiles. 'So pleased you could come, Megan. Make sure you get a good shot of the signage as well as the room.'

She steered Megan away by her elbow, pausing and turning back. 'You might be interested in talking with that woman over there,' she said, indicating with a tilt of her head a petite woman, demure in a plain worsted skirt suit and cream blouse, sitting erect on one of the straight back chairs. 'Her name's Viv.'

The woman was gazing at the paintings, lost in a sort of trance-like repose, hands folded loosely in her lap, palms upturned. Judith approached and stared at the triptych, curious to know what was so captivating.

The triptych merged seamlessly with the wall, the birches diminished amid the larger expanse of white. They ought to have been displayed against a dark background.

'Viv?' she asked.

The woman looked at her blankly. Then she said, 'Are you Judith?'

'I am,' she said and proffered her hand.

After a weak handshake the woman's gaze slid back to the triptych.

'What do you see?' Judith said.

'In these paintings, an element is missing.'

'Colour is missing.'

'More than that. They are lifeless.'

'It was Bethany's choice, not mine,' she said.

The woman looked at her with the same fixed gaze she had given her paintings. Her eyes were a filmy blue and she was so self-contained Judith felt scattered in her presence.

'I can see that you are fond of colour,' she said with a swift look at Judith's attire. She returned once more to the artworks. 'That painting on the right is the one that troubles me most.'

'I like the perspective, looking down through the bare branches at the frozen ground.'

'You are the artist, yet you are not seeing death in the images you create.'

Judith's skin prickled. She made no response although she thought the same, not wishing to be drawn into further discussion.

'If you'll excuse me,' the woman said and rose from her seat, leaving Judith glad to be free of the scrutiny.

She was thinking she had had enough of the opening when Bethany rushed over and grabbed her arm.

'I'm glad you spoke with Viv,' she said. 'She's a clairvoyant. Did she tell you?'

'I had no idea,' Judith said, immediately dismissing the reaction of her own skin.

'Excellent ability. Spot on, every time.'

'I never knew you were into fortune-telling.'

'I wasn't until I met Viv. The accuracy of her predictions is astounding.'

'Really?'

'Never fails. I took Hannah to a consultation for her birthday last week. Viv said all Hannah's friendships this year would be positive and mutually beneficial.' She paused, her gaze drifting to the settee. 'You can imagine how relieved I was to hear that!'

'Madeleine told me Hannah's been a bit of a loner.'

'It's wonderful to see it coming true,' Bethany said, passing over Judith's remark.

Judith wasn't convinced she meant it. Besides, she would never have thought Bethany would be that fatalistic. Believing in your own mystical powers is one thing; having blind faith in another's seemed a ludicrous abdication of will. That a therapist should place her trust in a clairvoyant was stranger still. For all Bethany knew, Viv could be a charlatan.

Bethany beamed a smile at the conservative candidate and Judith joined her daughter and her friend and asked what they thought of the paintings. Hannah stared across the room. 'They're a bit spooky,' she said.

'I can see them on a CD cover,' Madeleine said without looking up.

'Yeah! Like your Opeth CD. All creepy in a graveyard.' Hannah's eyes opened wide.

'Can we go now?' Madeleine said with a whine in her voice.

Hannah appeared crestfallen. Judith smiled at her sympathetically and extracted her car keys from her purse. Madeleine stuffed her iPod in a pocket of her jeans. 'I'll see you at school,' she said as she stood.

On the way out Judith sensed the silver birches in their wintry settings, feeling an odd sense of loss. Odd, because she detested painting in black and white. Odd, since she didn't find the works compelling. Odd, because really, she would be happy never to see them again.

Part Two

Composition

Repetition

Despite the elegant design of the house with its clinker bricks and high-pitched roof, Harriet preferred the studio. Situated at the end of the back garden, the studio hunkered in a grotto of tree ferns and soft grasses in the dappled shade of two golden elms, the sturdy trunks of three mountain ash standing like stalwarts. Clad in flitches of ash, with a tiled roof, and casement windows in the south and west facing walls painted a glossy black, the building had an English farmyard charm. Formerly a wood-turner's workshop, inside the concrete floor was speckled with linseed oil and, since she had taken possession, paint. A long and high bench lined the back wall, and where once chisels and clamps and saws had lived, the accoutrements of the artist—tins and tubes, brushes and rags, scraps of paper, notebooks and palettes—were neatly arranged below a frieze of half-completed sketches tacked to the wall. Canvasses of works in progress leaned against the other walls. Taking up the centre of the floor were two easels, twins set apart and facing the natural light. Behind the easels was a wooden table, and against the far wall, beside a potbelly stove, a single club armchair covered in a violet and emerald throw. For there were times when Harriet chose to sit in comfort and warmth.

It was November and early spring rain followed by a run of warm sunny days had ushered a burst of new growth. She had called on her gardener, Malvin, to put in some additional hours. She went to the window and watched him prune the dogwoods and photinias along the western fence. Of Dutch descent, Malvin was a huge and hairy man sporting a full beard, and attired as usual in his army fatigues. He brought his own tools, even a wheelbarrow, reversing his old Pajero up the driveway and positioning the rear end for ease of access to wherever he was working. He had a surprisingly graceful charm that made him a pleasure to watch and if she had had the predilection, she would have rendered him in paint.

She looked back, her eyes adjusting to the dimmer light, and went to her club chair, skirting the easels without so much as a glance at the canvasses sitting there. Two large and perfectly square canvasses. She had applied a thin wash of grey-black gouache to obliterate the stark void of the white, for white she found deadened her soul. She couldn't see into white, couldn't conceive a single idea. Grey-black was proving little better.

She sat down, elbows on the armrests, fingers of both hands pressed together. What had begun as a simple idea, a collaborative project culminating in an exhibition of art and music, had grown into a cumbersome leviathan. She rued the moment she had noticed the moon and her mind leapt recklessly from that celestial sphere to the Moon-planting guide in her dresser's bottom drawer without any regard for the consequences.

Tracking nine months of Moon movement had been just as Ginny had said, onerous. She had spent much too much of October seated before the planting guide and her ephemeris, befuddled by astrological information. The Moon moved so fast that in any twelve-hour period it traversed a full six degrees of the zodiac, which meant she had to resort to mathematical calculations to ascertain the precise moment it passed over each planet from the Sun to Pluto. Ginny had suggested using a computer. The Internet was sure to offer a faster method, she had said. But Harriet had shooed her away. She wouldn't countenance such a thing. Although eventually she had no choice but to relent to the use of a scientific calculator, one that could multiply in degrees.

Other than that, Ginny was no help. She would sweep aside the beaded curtain, enter the kitchen with a pointedly averted gaze, inquire facetiously on the progress of dinner or, after sashaying about gathering the elements of a salad, leave the room, pausing at the curtain with a 'Still not finished then.'

No she hadn't finished, but since she had committed herself to tracking every major aspect the Moon made to all of the planets she would persist.

Ginny's dismissive attitude peaked the day they argued over the quincunx. She had swanned into the kitchen ostensibly to prepare herself some lunch, but Harriet knew to pour more scorn on her toil. Laid out on the table were nine long strips of Sellotaped–together paper, each portraying the lunar aspects dotted along a timeline. She had listed the planets on the vertical axis, and allowed a wide stretch of space for each day to allow for increments of six hours. The aspects she had colour-coded and listed in a key in the top right corner.

Ginny leaned over her shoulder and pointed at the key. 'Quincunx?' she said.

'That's right.'

'What's a quincunx?'

'One-hundred-and-fifty degrees.'

Ginny paused, hovering over her shoulder. 'I thought all the aspects were based on whole numbers.'

'Not this one.'

Ginny went to the fridge and rummaged about for a minute and Harriet returned to her labour.

Moments later Ginny stood, empty-handed and said, 'Then it's a contrivance.'

'What is?'

'The quincunx.'

Harriet threw down her pen. Apparently they were not allowed fractions.

Then she made to defend the poor quincunx. She had three in her own horoscope and had always felt their presence, the sense of being out of joint within herself. But Ginny remained emphatic. The quincunx, she argued, was based on the fanciful law of correspondence, and not the harmonics of a circle. Only angles divisible by whole numbers into whole numbers bore any significance, according to her.

Ginny grabbed a handful of biscuits from the tin on the bench and swept through the beaded curtain, leaving Harriet nonplussed. What then to make of her horoscope, her experience, her very self? She pulled out her horoscope from the dresser's bottom drawer and stared at her quincunxes. Picturing her aspect configurations in their absence, she felt bereft and she could scarcely fathom why she was entertaining Ginny's opinion. Yet if she followed Ginny's reasoning she might as well widen the orb of the fifth harmonic, which *was* based on a whole number, and she took comfort in the new fifth-harmonic aspects she found. Their creative and inspirational qualities duly ascribed, she rearranged her sense of self and no longer felt off kilter.

Yet she was uneasy. Ever since her synaesthetic experience she had followed the law of correspondence, there never being such a thing as coincidence in her universe. If Kandinsky had found truth in the matching of colour and form to the human condition, and since Theosophy relied on all manner of cosmic correspondences with the mundane, then who was she to quibble with the quincunx?

Ginny had proposed what amounted to a new law of harmonics and whole numbers, and a new harmony along with it, and she had no idea the implications. Besides, Ginny had no place contesting the wisdom of the ages. How dare she dispute the ancient astrologers! For them, each major aspect corresponded to a zodiacal sign. Aries being the first, aligned with the conjunction, Gemini and Aquarius with the sextile, Capricorn and Cancer the square, Leo and Sagittarius the trine, and Libra the opposition. The problem was that the method left four signs without a mate. The quincunx helped resolve the shortfall.

It seemed arbitrary and wrong, and dangerous, too, to undermine centuries of astrological reasoning accrued upon this fundamental metaphysic, supplanting it with another rule, one born out of Ginny's need for consistency.

Later that day, Ginny waltzed into the kitchen in her paisley dressing gown and went straight to the kettle to make tea. Harriet turned round in her seat and spoke in the aspect's defence.

'How come one aspect gets planted into an entire scheme of aspects,' Ginny said in response, a tea bag pinched between raised fingers, 'an odd ball, just to satisfy a whim for neatness? So somehow all the major harmonics must correspond to a zodiacal sign? Why? They are different concepts; aspects are harmonics and signs zodiacal. The signs pertain to the constellations and I guess have some basis in astronomical fact.' The kettle boiled. She plopped the tea bag in her cup and added, 'Although I'm not sure about their division into thirty-degree segments. That too seems arbitrary.'

'How else would you divide a circle by twelve?' Harriet said, feeling a sudden outflow of heat.

Ginny took a few paces towards the cooker, turned and made for the dresser, before changing her mind and pausing by the sink and making a show of gazing out the window. Then she swung round to Harriet with her thoughts.

'The confusion arises in the circle itself.'

'The wheel.'

'I mean the wheel, and the division of the wheel by the number twelve. There might just as well be thirteen constellations, or two hundred, any number in fact, considering the enormity of the universe. By what criteria were these twelve selected and deemed so important?'

Harriet was speechless.

'Anthropomorphism is at the root of it,' she said, folding her arms across her chest. 'For the ancients, the planets were animate beings, and they ruled the signs as if they were kingdoms. I think humanity has progressed from such naïveties. Surely?'

'You're being a purist,' Harriet said, at last thinking of a point of contention.

'How so?'

'Only the harmonic root is relevant to you. Why not divide a circle into intervals of twelve? And why not then ascribe to each twelfth a harmonic series? Why in fact can't there be a seventh or ninth or even eleventh harmonic?'

They both paused, realising simultaneously the error of Ginny's logic.

And the quincunx was back as five twelfths of a circle and the sense of being off kilter returned to Harriet with a resounding jolt.

She went back to her Moon tracking labour and Ginny left the room without another word. It took Harriet several more days to complete her nine scrolls of Moon travel and remove herself and her scrolls to the studio.

Seated in her armchair, gazing at the backs of her grey-black canvasses perched on their easels, she felt perturbed. Ginny had been wrong to dismiss the law of correspondence. There had to be rules, rules that created structure and structure meaning. Light and dark, the colour wheel, the way colours made the viewer feel, all were fundamental to her art. It was the job of the abstract artist to evoke in the viewer an experience that was transformative and correspondence was the way to do it. Yet she had no idea how to evoke such an experience while making use of the Moon model. To make matters worse, after all her resistance and outright opposition, Ginny had taken Harriet's painstakingly scribed Moon-model scrolls and written four compositions and was well on the way to completing her fifth. Harriet had no idea how she was managing to find the inspiration.

Ginny hadn't expected to compose. Lacking enthusiasm for the Moon model, she had anticipated a compositional struggle in the face of her mother's farcical scrolls, at best producing nine short and mediocre pieces, commensurate with the effort she had planned to put in. It was the day after her first function and she had woken in a grump. After throwing off the covers she put on her paisley dressing gown and went downstairs.

Finding the house empty, she went outside and on through the garden, entering the studio upon three sharp raps, and with a quick glance at her mother standing before her canvasses of grey-black, she said, 'So you're making a start,' and plonked herself down in the armchair.

'Not really.' Harriet paused, brush in hand. 'I'm ridding the white.'

'Fair enough.'

'And you?'

'Not a note.'

'I'm sure…' Harriet's words trailed away. A look of satisfaction appeared in her face as she returned her attention to her painting. In her A-line smock of paint-splattered maroon, her black hair gathered up in a green scarf and cascading every which way, she looked like a mop-headed hag and Ginny had to suppress a laugh.

'That function was awful,' she said, as if determined to appear ungracious.

'I'm sure…'

'Stop saying I'm sure.' She paused, shocked at her own snappiness, before altering her tone. 'A bunch of old fogies celebrating some dude's ninetieth and all they wanted from me was endless Gershwin and Fats Waller. I had to play "Ain't Misbehavin'" six times.' She paused again. 'I hadn't realised how drunk octogenarians can get or how flirtatious. It was creepy.'

'Still…'

'There is no still.'

The force of her remark surprised her. She sounded snappy and uptight, but her mother's platitudes were maddening as ever they were. Yes, she was grateful for the work, but she couldn't exorcise from her being the gnawing frustration that she had screwed her musical career; that Garth had wiped her presence clean off the billboard. Three years and her connections and her hopes were gone. There were times when she felt raw with the humiliation and she failed to grasp what had motivated her, moments earlier, to seek her mother's company. She would have done better to have dressed and gone for a walk. Yes, a long walk was what she needed. She would go to the gardens, down to the lake, leave her mother here with her ludicrous hair and her paint.

She was about to leave the studio when there was a light rap on the door and Phoebe entered, dressed as she always was in a double-breasted trench coat and fedora.

'Harriet, there you are! I'm taking delivery of a bunch of Suhair Sibai's from a gallery clearance.'

'Who?'

'You don't know her work? Syrian artist. Lives in the States of course. Marvellous finds too. Thought you might like a squiz. Hello, Ginny.' She put her satchel on the table and looked from the bench to the canvasses on the easels. 'So what's all this?'

'It's a joint project,' Harriet said. 'Ginny and I are putting together an exhibition. Nine paintings. Nine songs.'

Her mother sounded proud, but Ginny knew it was a front. She was surprised Phoebe didn't already know and she found this one omission of confidence in an otherwise frank and unified friendship telling.

Telling of what Ginny wasn't sure until Phoebe said in an instantly engaged voice, 'Fascinating.' She pondered for a moment as if running through a raft of possibilities before going on. 'A song for each painting or a painting for each song. Who gets to go first? You, Harriet, by the look of it. So, Ginny,' she said, her gaze held fast in the direction of the bench, 'you'll be composing something to suit?'

'We wondered that, but instead we are both drawing inspiration from an external source,' said Harriet.

'The moon,' Ginny said.

'Not all goddesses in flowing gowns, Harriet. You surprise me.' Ginny allowed herself a private smile, Phoebe an unexpected ally, and she waited for her mother to react.

'Not that at all,' Harriet said. 'This is conceptual.'

'Yeah. New, gibbous, full,' Ginny said dryly.

'More than that and you know it!' Harriet shot her a censorious look. 'The movement of the Moon in relation to the whole galaxy.' She handed Phoebe one of the scrolls rolled up on the bench.

Phoebe unfurled it and made a show of taking in the information. She wore the demeanour of a woman conditioned by efficiency, as if every moment were given over to business, leaving little space for frivolity. Although, Ginny suspected her manner belied a sensitive nature. Her hair was pulled back hard from her face, emphasising the feathering of lines about the mouth and eyes, eyes growing smaller as the years crept by, the hood of skin below the brow sagging on a slant, lending her an almost oriental appearance and Ginny wondered if one day the drooping fold would impede her vision. She rolled up the scroll with a flourish and handed it back. 'Ambitious.'

'Nine planets. Nine months,' Ginny said.

'Nine paintings,' said Harriet.

'And nine songs.'

'Now I'm interested. So you'll have the project finished when?'

'April.'

'Hmm. Just after the spring equinox.' She reached into a pocket for her phone.

Ginny watched her mother return the scroll to its place in the row on the bench.

'Okay,' Phoebe said after a long pause. 'I've just the thing. Party of devotees about to return from walking the Camino: priestess types, whole coven of them. They'll be gathering afterwards for some spiritual debriefing at Maryvale's. I'm function manager. I'll arrange for the ladies to attend the opening.'

'That's kind of you.'

'Don't mention it. Bit of a jaunt for them and I was looking for an outing to fill the itinerary.'

'Makes it a lot more real I suppose.' Harriet looked doubtful.

'Really?' Ginny knew it was her sardonic tone that caused Phoebe and Harriet to exchange glances.

Phoebe stepped forward and stood squarely before her. 'Ginny, your mother has a knack for these things. Except for the Wessex series,' she said as an aside, 'but we all have our flat times.' She looked resolute, eyes shining with the force of a hot-blooded will that was nothing short of intimidating, and Ginny shrank back in her seat. Phoebe went on. 'Tell you what. Nine songs sounds like an album. What do you think? I'll get in touch with Tommo the Tank. Record producer. You've heard of him? He owes me more than one.' Ginny caught a quick motion of her hand behind her back and her mother promptly fiddled about with things on her bench. 'And while I've got you here,' Phoebe said in a low voice, 'how's your diary? I've got a run of oldie birthday parties coming up and feedback has it you were a sensation.'

'All I did was play "Ain't Misbehavin'".'

'And the rest. You gave them what they wanted. Which is more than I can say for your predecessor.'

'Frank not coming back?'

'Nope.'

She knew she had to be polite, had to accept Phoebe's gigs. They were lucrative too. Phoebe paid her far more than her residency at the Derwent and that had been well paid. It was the sense of walking into a cul-de-sac. And there was little chance she would have the opportunity to play her own music. At least at the Derwent she could play Wynton Kelly and McCoy Tyner. Now it was all Count Basie and Duke Ellington and Fats bloody Waller. In spite of her misgivings, she smiled and thanked Phoebe and said yes she was free and would be delighted to perform at her functions.

Satisfied, Phoebe joined Harriet by the easels and they talked in low tones. Before long they told Ginny they were off to the gallery to view the new acquisitions, leaving Ginny seated in the club chair wrapped in her paisley dressing gown.

Alone in the space, surrounded by all the tools of her mother's artistry, inhaling the slightly acrid smell of paint, an unexpected curiosity swept over her. She stood and went over to the easels. The canvasses of grey black held no indication of what was in her mother's mind. Eight of the scrolls were rolled up in a neat line, the first month's rolled out and held down at each end by one of the large pebbles Ginny had found on a beach one year. Pebbles with bright pink love hearts she had painted on for a mother's day school project.

The creation of the scrolls had taken Harriet weeks. Every time Ginny went to the kitchen there she would be, pouring over the Ephemeris, noting down each aspect with the dedication of a medieval scholar. So much effort and by the look of those canvases Harriet hadn't a clue what to make of her depiction of the Moon's cyclic sojourn in the heavens.

Arranged on the scroll was a series of rows, one for each planet, and the bottom axis, marked out in increments, denoted the days from one New Moon to the next. The aspects were colour coded and marked on as dots. The result was a haphazard dot dance. There was no sense to be made of it, no sound to be heard. It was about as inspiring as a cardiogram.

She had no idea what possessed her to pick up *The Combination of Stella Influences* by Reinhold Ebertin, let alone open the book. Beyond matters mathematical she had barely a clue about Astrology and even less interest, her mind hazing up when her mother went on about eclipses or, as she called it, a gloomy old Saturn transit. Yet the Moon model seemed the only way forward if they were to persist with the exhibition and Phoebe's involvement made that more an imperative. At least the model was abstract and temporal, and it was all they had come up with that contained the number nine and circumvented the banal correspondence of painting and song.

She reached for one of her mother's numerous notepads stacked neatly at the end of the bench and settled into the club chair, laying the scroll for the first month on her lap and Ebertin on the armrest.

For each pairing of the Moon with a planet, Ebertin had listed a brief set of descriptors. She began with the first pairing after the New Moon, realising that were she to begin at the New Moon pairing itself, each song would have an identical starting point and there was enough repetition without that.

She was surprised to find the Moon's first pairing was with gloomy old Saturn. A cold, austere beginning, yet at least Ebertin also mentioned self-control. The following pairing was with fiery Mars, denoting volatility and passion, then came expansive Jupiter followed by mystical Neptune. Moving from one pair to another she found herself entering a flow, where the preceding pair coloured the next in her imagination. If the Moon/Saturn meant self-control, then the succeeding Moon/Mars impulsivity would be felt as release. A story unfolded as the Moon arced its way on, shining its full face back at the Sun, then waning until it was dark. And as she wrote, she became the Moon, responding to the influences of each heavenly sphere, writing not a verbatim list of descriptors but a story of her impressions, and the feelings they evoked.

Her creative sensibilities knew that above all it was the flow that mattered, the sequence and the intervals between the pairings, and that somewhere within it all she would find the music.

And she was pleased to find she was back in the sublime world of her thesis, exploring the very process of composition, a process too often taken for granted as simply happening, an event as mundane as shopping yet as ephemeral as ether. Most of her friends thought of musicianship as an aptitude, an ability you either had or lacked, and it was true that musical ability was not something that could be forced or contrived. Too many composers view composition as something that happens to the individual, not something the individual steps inside.

She thought otherwise.

For her, composing was an altered state, a zone but so much more than a zone, for the word trivialised the experience, reducing it to the level of maps, as if it were simply an area in the mind. A state of awareness cannot be conflated with a mere space. And here she was again, immersed in a timeless place where she was no longer who she was; Ginny with her foibles. She was more than who she was, less than who she was and absent to herself all at once. In a trance, yes, but a trance with a purpose. And she was free, unlike in her thesis years, in which she found herself constantly defending and justifying her approach to her dullard supervisors, whose enthusiasm had been quickly eclipsed by incomprehension.

She reached for the second scroll, then the third, and then the fourth. She paid attention to the emergence of pattern and change. Time slipped by, the sun soon high, the studio on that warm November day pleasantly cool. Five scrolls at her feet. Four narratives to go, and she could not stop until they were done; would not compose a single bar until she had a sense of the whole.

Hunger and smelly armpits caused her with much urgency to leave the scrolls and hurry to the shower. She came back dressed in jeans and an old T-shirt, taking large bites of the hunk of apple cake she had grabbed on her way through the kitchen.

Thankfully Harriet had not returned. She suspected Phoebe had persuaded her to have lunch in Carlton, as she often did. Phoebe always had to be on the move and thought Harriet spent too much time in the Dandenongs. Which was true, for without her friend, Ginny doubted Harriet would venture further than the foothills.

Ginny had just reached the end of the ninth scroll when she heard footsteps outside.

It was the sudden entry, the shock on Harriet's face at the sight of her presence in the space, the look as if she, the daughter, were an interloper, and Ginny's otherworldliness evaporated. She hadn't realised that for hours she had been captivated until she was back in the ordinary.

Harriet had changed into a garish shift, her hair swept back from her face and held in place with a large comb.

'I'll get out of your way,' Ginny said, gathering up the scrolls and replacing them, and Ebertin, where she had found them on the bench.

'Headway made?' Harriet said with one of her ridiculous smiles as Ginny made to leave with her notebook.

'I'm not sure yet,' she said.

She felt evasive, not ready to reveal how she'd engaged with the scrolls, and she succumbed to an upwelling of emotion, her equanimity so resoundingly lost. In its stead she felt trapped inside her mother's sphere of influence.

She couldn't remember ever feeling close to her mother. Harriet had always seemed alien, her mothering alternating between indifference and overbearing control. She was so colourful, Ginny felt insignificant in her presence. She was sure Harriet thought of her by turns a disappointment, an embarrassment, and an encumbrance.

She was here in her mother's house because she had nowhere else to go, here to reassess her life, here to make sense of her recent past, a past that catapulted her back on the search for answers, for revelations, for anything that would help her understand why she didn't have a father. For surely a lack of paternal guidance explained why she had fallen for Garth. And so grew in the place of her exalted creativity the resentment she too often carried in her heart towards the sideswiping axe-wielder, the woman who had snatched her away without explanation and offered her little explanation since. Her latest offerings were little more than embellishments on earlier vignettes and went no way towards explaining what Ginny knew to be the truth.

One time, when she was still a child, she had overheard her mother talking to Phoebe about that life-shattering day. Standing in the hall before the closed living-room door, her urge for a drink of water forestalled when she caught their conversation.

'Convenient for him,' her mother said. 'But I had to tram it to Mario's.'

'Bloody long, Gore Street.'

It was the street name that caused her to pause at the door. There followed a long exchange about music and someone's birthday party. She was losing interest and had her hand on the doorknob when her mother said she had been relieved to get out of the Gore Street house.

'If it hadn't been for the caveat you may never have done it,' Phoebe said in an even voice.

'True.'

'Blame it on the caveat.'

'Sounds like a band name.'

'Everything but the girl.'

'No, we took the girl, remember!'

Then an uproar of laughter and Ginny went back upstairs feeling confused. Her mother had left her father for a caveat. She had no idea what a caveat was, but knew that it must have been very serious: caveat.

She hurried back to the house with her notebook, her mind in the grip of flashes of memory, fragments like movie stills, no sense of before or after.

She was standing in the middle of her Gore Street bedroom, doll in hand, hearing a commotion of slamming doors downstairs. Her mother was upset. She could feel her mother's distress approaching with her footsteps up the stairs. The door flew open and there she was, black streaked cheeks, hair a tumble.

'Ginny,' was all she said. Ginny saw her mother all around her in flashes of red and gold. Watched her clothes fill a suitcase, her toys a box. 'Wait there.'

And she waited.

Her mother left the room. The next thing she was being bundled down the stairs and squashed into the back seat of a car, her feet on a box, the bags and boxes beside her crammed to the roof, and Harriet in the passenger seat in front. She could not see the driver but she knew it was Phoebe. It had to be Phoebe. It was always Phoebe.

They drove through the night and she never saw her father again. She had felt abducted ever since. Her mother her kidnapper. It was odd to be abducted by her mother. Impossible to make sense of. Especially when her mother had never offered elucidation.

Ginny had tried to extract the truth from her on numerous occasions but without success. She knew her grandparents had only recently died. That her mother was deranged by grief. There was the torn canvas when she'd hurled a heavy candlestick across the room. Her father restraining her, reasoning with her, calming her down. Without him Ginny had been perpetually on guard, her mother's temper unpredictable, her sudden outbursts terrifying.

She would hide in her room.

She learned to be obedient, learned to disappear, and she learned to listen behind closed doors.

November neared its end and an unseasonal wind had been blowing from the north since lunchtime. Harriet had spent much of the afternoon fretting over her garden as the hot dry blasts crisped tender leaves and shrivelled flower buds. Malvin was due tomorrow and she knew he would reassure her as he always did, dead heading here, lightly pruning there, and telling her the perennials would soon put out vigorous new shoots. He was right of course, and it was rare that any of her plants gave up on life after a ravaging. Her garden was robust, fed by moist fertile soil built up through decades of care, the previous owners as loving of the floral kingdom as she.

She moved away from the window and walked past her easels, both empty, and strode in slow steps along the length of the bench where the first of her nine scrolls was rolled out. She must have stared at those coloured dots a thousand times and still her mind was blank.

She turned her back on the scroll and sat down at the wooden table to peruse the selection of art books she had brought in from the house that morning. She had selected titles at random by running a finger along the spines and stopping when the impulse took her.

She might have spent her time differently. On other occasions when she had suffered artist's block, she had sat in the garden and read a Barbara Hanrahan, wandered round the Olinda shops, or called Phoebe to see what she was up to. She had even been known to invite Rosalind round for a Theosophical chat. Only this time she could do none of those things. A part of her wouldn't brook distraction. It might be counter-productive, and she thought that it probably was, but the grip of compulsion the likes of which she had rarely known wouldn't let her go. It was as if her very life depended on bringing the exhibition to fruition, as if it were fated and her own shortcomings were standing in the way. She was on a brink. Perhaps she was putting herself under unnecessary strain, but she knew of no way out. It was a test, a trial, an initiation she had to pass.

She was flicking through a series of colour plates of Mondrian's work when a streak of grey came down the garden path and Ginny's face appeared in the window. There seemed a hint of a smile.

'Come in,' she said and the door swung open.

'I didn't want to interrupt.'

Yes, you did, Harriet thought, but said, 'You're not interrupting a thing.'

'I thought you might be at work.'

It was an innocent remark belying a certain self-satisfaction, even jubilance. For her daughter was having no trouble at all with her side of the collaboration. No trouble at all.

Harriet had not anticipated finding herself in competition with her daughter, let alone losing the race. When the project first occurred to her she had wanted to help raise Ginny from her miserable torpor, but now that she was forging ahead in a burst of creativity and enthusiastic absorption, Harriet found herself displeased. She thought she should be happy and she would be happy if it were not for her own creative nihility.

'Are you using six?' Ginny said.

Harriet went to the bench, grabbed the sixth scroll and thrust it at Ginny, regretting as she did her display of irritation. They both looked at Harriet's canvases of grey and black lined up in the back corner.

'Shall I make tea?' Ginny said.

'Only if you tell me how you are composing from the scrolls,' Harriet said, finally summoning the resolve to ask.

'Simple,' Ginny said. 'I wrote a story for each month.'

'A story.'

'Well, an interpretation I suppose. I used that book.' She pointed at the bench where there was only one book, sitting on top of a small pile of scrap paper.

'Ebertin?' Harriet said, taken by surprise that her daughter would so much as touch a book of astrological correspondences.

Ginny didn't react, plainly keeping to herself how it was that she came to use Ebertin since the book hadn't fallen into her lap. It was remarkable that she knew how to use it, then again it was transparent enough even to the untrained eye. That Ginny would go to such lengths after her petulant display over the Moon model was unfathomable and Harriet wondered if she really knew her daughter at all.

'So I wrote the stories,' Ginny said, 'and now I'm drawing inspiration from the stories to compose.'

'An interpretation of an interpretation,' Harriet said slowly, wondering where she had heard that before.

'Why not? Otherwise all you've got is a series of coloured dots.'

Harriet shrugged. It seemed to her a method far removed from the model itself and she worried that there would be little if any correspondence between the musical and the artistic pieces, should she produce any. What she had thought of as thoroughly objective and abstract, Ginny had rendered subjective and personal. She had in mind something metaphysical, something cosmic that pointed at a higher truth. Ginny had reduced the model to the human and to the particular, her own self in particular. She supposed it inevitable, considering Ginny's introspective state of mind of late, that she would have chosen such a path, sucked into herself the model, rather than allowing her soul to expand outward to reach it on its own plane. Grabbed and encircled, rather than stretched forward. Perhaps there lay the solution. There would be a contrast, the music subjective, the art objective. The music would represent feeling, the art pure abstraction.

Harriet felt a soft tingle in her bones.

And in her mind she conceived the first painting. She would forego all meaning and rely on the coloured dots, their repetition, their formulation in clusters and spaces, and she conjured a shape, her first shape, a three-dimensional shape, and she arranged the coloured dots upon the shape and allowed the shape to curve and bend along several planes receding to a vanishing point.

And she glanced at her daughter busy making tea and, keen to make a start, she said, 'There's a Hob Nob in the tin in the kitchen. Your favourite.'

Tuesday, 17 January 2017

Fernley Cottage

It was eight-thirty. The wind had abated and the snow was falling snow-globe slow. In the studio, Judith felt the sadness that came with the completion of a good work. Earlier in the day she had foregone her commission for Bethany's friend—the riverbank scene with its complexity of red gums—in favour of her latest Wimmera landscape, a sparse depiction of an abandoned farm, and now the work required scarcely another brushstroke.

The painting was to hang in the Aussie bistro in Fore Street and she was pleased she had transcended her aversion to its burger and pie theme and gone in one day with a bunch of photos on her phone. The owner, a bubbly woman in her thirties, had been delighted and offered to exhibit and sell all of her Wimmera works for a ten per cent commission. 'They'll be decorating my walls,' she had said with a jolly chuckle, which up until then were all but bare.

She was putting the finishing touches on a post and rail fence when Madeleine appeared on the threshold and leaned with her back against the doorjamb. Judith felt her breathing become shallow and short, yet Madeleine seemed less fractious, almost amenable. Judith pretended to carry on with her work.

'You haven't told me what happened,' she said quietly.

'Zol you mean? He's a liar and a creep.'

She waited, keeping her focus on her work.

'If you must know,' Madeleine said with ruthless honesty, 'he's been hooking up with Hannah.'

'Hannah? Bethany's Hannah?' She pulled her brush away from the canvas.

'The very same.'

'I don't understand.' Madeleine and Hannah were attending the same university so it was entirely plausible that such a thing could occur. Beyond Judith's comprehension was the idea of Hannah with Zol.

'When I was at Dr Attenhofer's lectures in Romanticism and the pre-Raphaelites.'

'I thought you were studying History.'

'It's an elective.' She thrust her hands in the pockets of her jeans. 'And that's when they did it.'

'I'm sorry.'

'Why be sorry? She's done me a favour.'

Judith couldn't argue with that. She was about to turn back to her easel when Madeleine said, 'What's his number then?'

'Who?'

'My father.'

'Hang on.' She set down her brush and made to leave the room. Madeleine stepped aside.

She rifled through a kitchen drawer, privately delighted at the prospect of Madeleine and her father spending quality time together and she couldn't find the card fast enough.

'Here.' She handed Madeleine the business card.

'Doctor Peter Love,' Madeleine read aloud. 'Course lecturer in Rosicrucianism and Freemasonry. What is all that shit?'

'He'll be pleased to hear from you.'

'Yeah? Last time I saw him he told me I was ruining my life.'

'Things will be different this time.'

'Now I've left Zol, you mean.'

'Just see what he has to say.'

Madeleine disappeared and Judith returned to her studio. She listened out for Madeleine's voice but the house was silent. She picked up her brush and jiggled it in a jar of turps, watching the solvent turn grey. Then she reached for Madeleine's old T-shirt and wiped the brush dry, feeling the cool of the turps on her skin, inhaling the fresh pungent odour, thinking that Madeleine was handling Zol's betrayal with a certain pragmatism that was remarkable for her years.

She went to the living room and stoked the fire then sat on the hearthrug with her laptop. She scanned the news headlines in her browser with little interest, the stories of austerity, the Middle East, climate change, and the growing refugee crisis always the same. An item on an anti-globalisation demonstration caught her eye. They were protesting the secrecy of a G8 meeting. There were anti free-trade banners and several men in *V for Vendetta* masks and she wondered if Lawrence Pike would appear with his inane grin and his in-your-face commentary.

She typed 'Wimmera landscapes' in her search engine and scrolled through images of flat dry plains, dams and rugged hills, depictions almost mythical in style, captivating, and she wondered what it would be like to live in a place so desolate. She had her village, farmers, tourists, Exeter nearby. In the Wimmera there was nothing. Just insects, birds, animals. She pictured the absolute solitude, tried to put herself in the heat and the dry and the dirt and she knew she couldn't live in such an empty place. She needed a sense of others even as she shunned company. What she didn't need was Madeleine slumping about the house. Her nerves frazzled as she imagined the days ahead and the Wimmera looked more inviting.

She pushed away the thought that the following morning she would have to go to Bournemouth. It was too grim a prospect. Anticipating Madeleine had not made the call to her father, she reached for her mobile.

Inversion

Thankfully the day was cool, for Harriet was not. Why ever had she agreed to nine? She had thought at the moment of conception that nine paintings in nine months would be easily achievable. Perhaps she had overlooked the conceptual element, the time needed for its execution. Five months into the collaboration and she had finished just one piece and had the other eight in various stages of genesis. But today was Christmas Eve, and by necessity she had been forced from the studio for the festivities. Even so, she couldn't relinquish her preoccupation.

She was standing between the beaded curtain and the fireplace, hands on her hips, elbows thrust wide, grateful for the ventilation afforded by her smock. Her eyes were fixed on her Kandinsky piece hanging above the pianola, the interconnecting geometric shapes, the use of yellow and blue, the dominating black moon striking against a background of muted earthy tones. She saw in the work as she always did, something elevating, spiritual.

She thought for a moment. Ginny was at the local supermarket with a long list, no doubt fast approaching an even longer queue. Harriet made for the studio, sweeping through the beaded curtain on her way and returning a short while later with her one completed piece. She placed it on the pianola ledge, to one side of her Kandinsky, then stood in the centre of the Kashan rug, eyes flitting back and forth. Upon her immediate impression, she found it most strange that a cosmological model should have produced something so mundane, for in spite of all its symbolic significances, beside her Kandinsky the work appeared devoid of inner meaning. She had assumed the mapping of the Moon's monthly round would have produced something at least a little bit profound. Instead her kaleidoscope of coloured dots aligned on a series of three-dimensional planes evoked in her no lofty emotion. There was nothing uplifting, nothing venerating, nothing remarkable in the rendition. Beside her Kandinsky, the work looked not only lacklustre but contrived.

Never had she felt more demoralised. She averted her gaze as if dismissing the work altogether, as if it, and not her, were to blame. She thought with bitter irony that her eagerness to assuage her daughter's malaise had precipitated a crisis of her own. She imagined the opening of the exhibition, the looks of disbelief and incomprehension on the faces of guests as they viewed her paintings, and she succumbed to a sudden upsurge of energy that made her want to roar with frustration, and her skin blazed with sudden heat.

She flashed the work another look and with renewed determination she resolved to improve it. Although, on the heels of that resolve tramped the same frustrating block. Perhaps it was a crisis not of colour but of form. Yes, perhaps that was it, the form contained no inner meaning and no subtlety, and the composition lacked motion and harmony as a result.

She was comforted by the thought and permitted herself latitude. After all, she had never painted this way before, never made use of a conceptual map. A Moon map, for heaven's sake! It was no use persisting with the other eight works. She needed to find an alternative approach. Her eyes wandered, finally catching in the mirror the reflection of the other end of the room. The sanguine curtains and matching sofas became blocks of colour at right angles to each other, and in a moment of inspiration it occurred to her that she might align shapes with lunar aspects and then apply the colour. After all, scattering coloured dots about when she had allotted the lunar aspects no form could well be the source of her error. Or perhaps what was called for was neither a correspondence of aspect and colour, nor aspect and form, but that thought sent her mind in a spin. Of course there was a corresponding form to each aspect and if she couldn't see it then it was her failing, for the universe was never in error.

She took the painting from the pianola ledge and made for the studio, sweeping a fast hand through the beaded curtain, listening to the soft tinkling of glass, catching flickers of white light like tiny stars as the beads settled back to stillness.

Ginny struggled to the house with two bulging bags and her mother's shopping trolley, cursing its small wheels that dragged through the gravel. She would have pulled up outside the front door but Harriet would have none of it. She said she couldn't endure, not even for a moment, the shards of sunlight that reflected off the metal and glinted through the windows, blinding her on her way by. So Ginny had dutifully parked in the carport. It was a cool day, the weather fickle and as she crossed the threshold she felt a little chilled in her thin grey dress.

On her way to the kitchen she heard the back door close and when she battled her way through the beaded curtain, her mother wasn't there. She looked out the window in time to see Harriet slip inside the studio. It was a furtive move, uncharacteristic, disappearing like that when she knew Ginny would be laden with groceries.

In her mother's absence she set about emptying the trolley and bags, placing the contents on the table until it displayed from end to end all manner of yuletide fare festooned with holly and berry motifs: Brie and Roquefort, duck and port pate, smoked salmon and fresh prawns, ham, salami and prosciutto, cooked turkey breast, avocados and two bunches of asparagus, a loaf of crusty white bread, a Christmas cake and a Christmas pudding (both in tins), a tub of Jersey cream, shortbread (which Ginny had offered to make, insisting it was easy, with Harriet equally insistent that it be bought), mixed nuts and walnuts, figs, fresh dates, quince paste, prunes, a tin of chocolates, a bottle of Bailey's Irish Cream and a case of Sauvignon Blanc. Thinking of the guests it was ridiculous: Poppy was a gluten free vegan and Veronica a lactose intolerant vegetarian. Phoebe couldn't have sugar and Rosalind, who was sure to pop in, only ate unprocessed foods.

No one knew and no one asked why Harriet adhered to traditional English feasting when they may just as well have eaten a tofu laksa, which they all would have enjoyed, but the one time Ginny had made the suggestion it was met with an intractable scoff.

She went to the sink and poured herself a glass of water, returning to sit at the table, doing her best to adopt a positive attitude on this festive eve. She thought she might trawl through the photo box then dismissed the idea as unwise. She reached into her shoulder bag and extracted *The Prague Cemetery* and was soon lost in a world of plotting, spying and counterfeiting, amazed that she, that any reader could harbour sympathies for the protagonist: an unscrupulous, murderous psychopath. Ten pages on and she decided it was evidence of Umberto Eco's mastery that he could elicit such a response in his readers.

She put down the book and reflected on her compositions and what sort of effect they would have on the listener, whether her subtle interpretation of the ninth would evoke feelings of exquisite sadness or beatifying joy. She doubted she was capable. She had not the talent or the experience. Other people were geniuses. Not her.

There was a tinkle behind her and Harriet wafted in through the glossy black beads of the curtain, regaled in an ankle length tunic of fine twill, the weave the deepest green with a thread of violet crisscrossing on the diagonal. The tunic cut softly into the waist, the bodice ending in a scalloped neckline. Beneath the tunic she wore a figure hugging satin top of gold bespeckled with tiny soft balls of red and green, dangling on black threads.

'Ah, you're back,' she said, affecting surprise.

'Took ages,' Ginny said flatly, thinking that it was her mother who had taken ages since she saw her scurrying to her studio dressed in her smock, her furtive movements reinforced by the way she must have sneaked round the house, inside the front door and upstairs to her bedroom to change.

'Always does,' Harriet said, scanning the fare on the table. 'You've done a good job. Everything on the list?'

'Yes,' she said, screwing up the list in her pocket, hoping this time they would do without the Turkish Delight and its unbearably sickly smell.

There was a moment of silence. Then, 'No Turkish Delight?'

'They didn't have any,' Ginny said quickly.

'Run out I suppose. It's popular.' She rested her hands on the back of her chair. 'You could dash back. They might have some tucked away.'

'They were about to close.'

'So early?' But she didn't pursue it.

'Are we expecting anyone else?' Ginny said, eyeing the table thinking the amount even greater than usual.

'And who might that be?'

No one. She had no aunties, uncles, cousins. Her maternal grandparents were dead. It was just her and her mother. And of course Phoebe, who she supposed in a fashion had taken the place of an aunt, and Rosalind who was about as great-aunt like as it was possible to be. And Poppy and Veronica were fixtures at Christmas too. It was a habit formed when they were at primary school and Ginny had begged her mother to let her invite her new best friends. They were altogether a full complement, a family. A family without men. Which could never be an authentic family, could it? Although she certainly wasn't missing Garth. Christmases the three years they were together were a tawdry round of gigs and back then she had missed her Christmas at home.

Harriet set about attending to the fare, squeezing into the fridge the fish, cooked meats, pate and cream. Without turning she said, 'Put the Sauvignon Blanc outside, would you?'

'Of course.'

Harriet liked her white wine cool but not chilled and had discovered long before that the stone slab outside the kitchen that never caught a glimpse of sun was ideal, even on a summer's evening.

Ginny helped clear the table and after giving it a wipe with a damp cloth she laid it for Christmas with a white linen tablecloth and matching napkins, her grandmother's gleaming silverware, and a centrepiece of conifer prunings, replete with hand painted red fruits and gold baubles, all arranged around a tall and stout red candle that Harriet had made from beeswax when Ginny was a child, and had never lit.

Ginny found she was slipping into line with the ritual of Christmas Eve and her mood softened.

Harriet was a bustle of activity at the bench beside the sink and before long she was handing Ginny a platter of crudité and another of the fresh and dried fruits.

Ginny went over to a free space of bench and set about making guacamole before Harriet got to the avocados, thinking at least Poppy and Veronica could eat that. Why her mother never accommodated her friends' dietary needs at Christmas was a mystery.

'Music?' Ginny said, placing the guacamole on the table as she went and put on Count Basie in deference to her mother.

When she returned, letting the curtain fall gently behind her, Harriet poured them both a glass of champagne. She raised her glass with a 'Merry Christmas, Ginny,' and a pleasant smile, and Ginny smiled back. She saw for a fleeting moment a lonely old woman, a spinster, a crone, the wrong side of fifty with sagging flesh and wrinkles. Just a woman, a woman with foibles, with eccentricities. An unusual woman lost in a world a hundred years' past, a world she kept alive inside this house with its curtain of vintage glass beads.

Ginny took a sip of her champagne then went upstairs to change out of her thin grey dress, not exactly feeling festive—she was too tired for that—but willing to try. She had had a full week of performances playing Scott Joplin, old music hall numbers and sentimental wartime favourites. On two occasions Phoebe booked an accompanist, Peter, a violinist who, having played all the old numbers on his instrument for half a century, needed no rehearsal, only a set list and a discrete mouthing of the key at the inception of each piece. Peter was an accomplished soloist too, and his enthusiasm for the music spilled into her and they had played in a private world of their own, surrounded by a barely listening crowd.

Yesterday, after the last function of the season—a luncheon at a winery—Phoebe had taken her for coffee in Prahran. Ginny had protested it was a long way for coffee, but Phoebe insisted there was nowhere closer. They journeyed much of the hour in silence, Phoebe concentrating on the road and Ginny drifting through a stream of incidental thoughts.

When Phoebe crawled down Chapel Street looking for a place to park, Ginny realised they had spoken so little that she began to worry she had committed some inadvertent transgression at the winery and Phoebe was saving her remonstrations for a stationary moment, a worry she quickly dismissed as paranoid.

With a parking space found, Phoebe took Ginny to the first café they passed. And over coffee and cake Phoebe made small talk, filling her in on Peter the violinist's past, how hard it was to be a musician in Melbourne, especially if you don't sing, and how she felt for all artists, performing or not, who had to find ways to survive in a tough marketplace. Ginny relaxed and found in her mother's friend easy company.

They agreed to go their separate ways and browse the shops for an hour. Ginny made several purchases: a necklace crafted in Ethiopia for Veronica, a hand knitted beanie for Poppy and a vintage flapper headband for her mother. She was fast tiring of shopping when an outfit in a shop window caught her eye.

Seeing the outfit laid out on her bed she was pleased she had gone in and tried it on. She removed the hanger and yanked free the price tag. It was a light-weight calf-length dress of black and grey herringbone, slim cut with a square neckline. The matching jacket was tailored with peak lapels and ample give about the shoulders, and it hung flush to the midriff, ending somewhere between waist and hip. Sheer black tights and patent leather court shoes and she felt uniformed perfectly for her forthcoming performances, entirely in keeping with the music she would be required to play.

An outfit without fuss or pretension, and without ludicrous festive baubles.

In a pile on the floor beside her bed her other purchases, all wrapped up in festive paper, made a fine if small display. She was surprised to feel a childish thrill at the sight of them. It suddenly felt like Christmas and she noticed she had even begun to feel comfortable being back home.

Her room was bright and airy, the window in the north-facing wall framed in its own gable, and the last quarter of ceiling sloping. Other than a new double bed, the furniture had not changed since her childhood: a heavy walnut wardrobe and matching tall boy, a dressing table with winged mirror, and a small bookcase that still had Pooh and Alice and all her other favourites. Otherwise the room was bare. Her dolls and trinkets and precious objects she had boxed up long before and when she went to university she had taken down her band posters. Thankfully Harriet had replaced them with one of Phoebe's finds, a woodland scene she had found difficult to sell but Ginny quite liked. For one ghastly moment she hoped one of the Wessex series wouldn't go the same way.

She stood by the window and ran a comb through her hair, her gaze settling on the twin elms outside her mother's studio, their golden leaves and dark trunks, the tree ferns standing stout and proud, their fronds hanging loosely in a soft breeze, the low line of the studio roof, and then beyond, as the garden came to an end, the dark recesses where the sun never shone and only the ivy grew. She looked away, remembering in a sudden rush the dream she had had the night before and from which she had awoken startled to find herself, after switching on the bedside lamp, gazing into the fleur-de-lys motif on the curtains.

It was the same dream, one she had suffered several times now. Always the dark cave, her nakedness, the presence behind her, the sense of foreboding, the inability to move, the draft from above and the flickering light. Each time the dream recurred the gripping fear grew stronger. She felt exposed, vulnerable. She felt every flicker of light on her body as a caress of a hot tongue.

It must have been in the early morning when she awoke, and after taking in as much as she could bear of that awful fleur-de-lys pattern, she had switched off her lamp and, willing herself not to give the dream any quarter in her thoughts, slowly returned to sleep.

She had become certain that the dream represented the darkness in her heart, a darkness that had nothing to do with Garth. It was as though she were held captive by her mother's refusal to enlighten her about her father. As if she were about to be told something of significance and she awoke before she heard it. And each time she had the dream, her desire to find out more about him strengthened along with her frustration at the reticence and evasiveness of her mother.

It was a dream befitting her psyche. She had always thought that life had marked her out as one of those who must learn from experience and not from second-hand knowledge. Although she knew she had been saved the worst excesses of suffering life could offer. It was just that she had always sought to know a thing from the inside, in a manner that was direct and sensory. She had to feel something to know something and the dream was heavy with possibilities of knowing. And standing in her fine grey dress, comb in hand, she knew she would never be satisfied unless she tracked down her father and paid him a visit.

There was a knock on the front door. She left her bedroom and went downstairs to answer it.

Phoebe gave her a warm grin. 'Hello maestro,' she said, struggling inside with a holdall and a large canvas bag, the strap of her leather satchel sliding off her shoulder on her way by. 'Here,' she said and handed Ginny the bag.

They made their way through to the kitchen, Phoebe depositing the holdall in the living room. Ginny held aside the beaded curtain to let Phoebe through without a tangle, and Phoebe unbuttoned her coat and gave it to Ginny who hung it on a hook on the back door.

'Darling!' Harriet spun round with arms outstretched and air-kissed her friend on both cheeks. 'Belated happy solstice.'

It was the same every year, a nod of acknowledgement to the pagan festival of a northern-hemisphere winter while partaking in all the trappings of a heavily commercialised Christmas. 'Tis the season to be jolly,' their mantra, and Harriet, fa-la-la-la-la'd as she poured Phoebe a glass of fizz and topped up her own.

Phoebe surveyed the spread. 'Fine fare, Harriet. Fine fare. I've brought along some extras.' And out came pretzels, rice crackers, hummous and baba ganoush, a chocolate orange, after dinner mints and a box of Turkish Delight.

Ginny struggled not to screw up her nose. It occurred to her that her mother and her friend were playing at kitsch, snapping up all the fare that came out at that time of year in every supermarket or grocer, fare crammed on shelves and cluttering the checkouts. Harriet even made use of the packaging, cutting out random shapes of bright colour, stringing them together and pinning them to the shelves of the dresser. She made decorations out of plastic, cardboard and old Christmas cards, using anything with a motif and festooning every available place.

Her zeal for furbelow must have begun soon after they moved to Sassafras, for Ginny had no recollections of adornments at Christmases in Gore Street. In the Sassafras house her mother would set her up with scissors and scraps of packaging that had the shape she was to cut already marked out. Or she would be given the hole punch and told to make a hole on the black dot. She soon lost interest.

To add to the gaiety, Phoebe had put on a dress—she never wore a dress—this time of bright-red silk printed with reindeer. Ginny felt a hankering for paisley at the sight of it and wondered what had possessed her to dress so formally. She was on the outside again, these two women, her mother and her friend, performing an annual ritual they plainly had all figured out.

The kitchen was filled with bonhomie yet Ginny couldn't help noticing there was something missing. There was no fire in the grate, no warm spicy smells, nothing cooking in the oven or on the stove. On that cool December night, they were to feast on nibbles and dips and Ginny saw the subversion, the game they were playing, the mockery, the hearth cold, all on display rendered shallow and soulless. It bore the pretence of Christmas and was at once a critique, at one time cooked up by these conspirators who played life like charades. And they were content to be the only ones to understand their ruse, happy to carry on as if this celebration were real to them, sincerely felt, and she realised she had been conned all along, every year of her life, by a mother so lacking in depth, so pretentious and arty, that she couldn't even be bothered to provide for Ginny an authentic festive time. It was a betrayal, one that revealed her mother's alliance with Phoebe, an alliance that took precedence over her own daughter.

She was a child again, lonely, compliant, never making a fuss, being quiet while mummy did her art, waiting for daddy to come home. Was that how things were? She couldn't recall bedtime stories or outings or birthday parties, just that yearning for her father's presence. Had she been an unhappy child? Neglected? Unloved? Or was that an invention, a projection created by her adult self to justify her resentment towards her mother? All she knew was that forlorn child lumped about inside her, growing more demanding by the day.

There was another rap on the front door. Harriet and Phoebe were squeezing the additional foodstuffs into the crannies on the table. Neither heeded the knock. Ginny put her glass on the dresser and slipped through the beaded curtain.

Veronica and Poppy stood side by side on the path, Poppy holding a sprig of something above their heads. 'Merry Christmas!' they cried in unison.

Ginny opened the door wide and ushered them inside, wanting to ask, 'What is that?' when Poppy planted a full kiss on her lips.

In the hall, they divested themselves of their light summer coats, dumping them on the banister and revealing a pigeon pair of dresses, low cut and waisted with short sleeves and voluminous skirts: polka dots of yellow on black. It was the Andrews Sisters meets Tweedledum and Tweedledee and Ginny stifled a laugh even as she vowed to seize the first opportunity to change into her paisley.

'Party time!' Veronica cried, with a jiggle that set off her bangles. She handed Ginny a small package wrapped in pink paper embossed with red Santas saying, 'From both of us.'

And her friends trooped on through the living room and the beaded curtain, with Ginny following on behind. She swapped her present for her wine and stood, watching.

There were loud, exaggerated greetings and what'll you haves, and with glasses brimming they all arranged themselves around the kitchen table, taking up their usual places, Harriet at the head and Phoebe the foot, Veronica and Poppy together with their backs to the window and Ginny opposite and next to the empty seat beside her mother that was Rosalind's. And the universe shrunk so that there was nothing beyond their table, no other place to be, no other way to celebrate, as if they were trapped inside a bauble suspended from her mother's blouse. Ginny suddenly felt she was suffocating.

The incense smouldering in a brass holder on the dresser didn't help, filling the room with a sweet sickly odour that Ginny presumed was faux frankincense. Its only redeeming quality was that it masked the smell of the Turkish Delight that Phoebe had set down in front of her table setting. She awaited a chance to pass it on.

Scott Joplin played in the background. She listened, following the notes, until the commotion of voices drowned them out. She knocked back her champagne and reached for more. She could see that her mother was already tipsy. She had become demonstrative, trying to hold court with rambling vignettes that no one wished to listen to, mostly because they never reached their destination.

After a lengthy period of polite attention, Phoebe attempted to afford the rest of the party an opportunity to make a diversion, interrupting with 'Harriet, you remember the Diproses.' Harriet paused mid-flow, frowned, nodded, grinned, then launched into another vignette that had nothing whatsoever to do with the Diproses.

The Diproses used to live next door but one, before their sons grew up and left home and they downsized. Ginny had a vague idea that the parents were musical. She might have taken an interest in what Phoebe had to say about them but couldn't bring herself to interrupt her mother's inebriated blather.

Poppy and Veronica listened too, but as their own glasses emptied, filled and emptied again, there rose in them both a buoyant cheer and the courage to converse with Ginny across the table. The Hunnacots had gone skiing in the French Alps with a party of friends ostensibly to escape the silly season, so Veronica was spending Christmas at the Pargiters. And they related in fragments, interrupted by raucous laughter, how they had hidden the turkey from Poppy's mother until she became so frantic she started having palpitations.

Food was nibbled, more wine brought in from outside and the evening wore on, Ginny remaining in her herringbone suit, privately pleased with the sense of separation and superiority it granted her.

Harriet had reached that stage of drunkenness when she would reminisce on the distant past, her sentimentality settling tonight on her one and only pregnancy. Ginny had heard it all before. It was one of the few stories Harriet would tell, although only when drunk. How Wilhelm would talk to Ginny through her mother's skin with soft endearments and tales of his plans for her future. How she had already changed his life and they hadn't even met. Then there were his words of caution to Harriet, and his admonishments. She mustn't drink wine. Mustn't eat sweet foods. Must play Wagner and not Bauhaus, and above all she mustn't paint. The fumes, he'd said. How dare he! Harriet said she had felt oppressed. And during his murmurings to his as yet unborn child he would slip into German and Harriet had no idea what he was saying, but his expression was so gentle and kind it made her recoil with disbelief.

'What sort of man does that?' Harriet said, plonking down her glass.

'I've never heard of one.' Phoebe would always stand in her defence, which only encouraged her.

Harriet turned to Poppy and Veronica, making a show of searching their faces. 'Was Mr Pargiter...was Mr Hunnacot like that?'

'Of course not!' Phoebe said, stepping in to save the young women embarrassment, perhaps regretting her recent remark, for a look of apprehension flitted across her face.

'And your mothers would have been as disturbed as I was if they had.'

'Definitely,' said Phoebe.

'I saw a movie once,' Poppy offered, 'where the pregnant woman had similar thoughts and the father turned out to be really nice.'

'Balderdash!' Harriet said.

'No, I did.' Poppy blushed.

'Which movie was that?' Veronica asked.

'I don't know,' Poppy said, bowing her head. 'Maybe I dreamt it.' She looked up and Ginny caught her eye.

'Take no notice,' Ginny mouthed, plucking an olive from a platter nearby.

Her friends fell into silence.

The music had stopped and Ginny went and put on Fats Waller. As she passed back through the beaded curtain, Phoebe stood up and made for the wine, colliding into Ginny's chair. 'Steady as she goes,' she said and laughed.

'He was consistent. I'll give him that,' Harriet said. She drained her glass and held it out to Phoebe for more. 'When you were born,' she said, addressing Ginny, 'he doted on you as if you were a precious doll. He never paid me that sort of attention.'

'You were just the womb, darling,' said Phoebe, returning to her seat.

'True. It was never me he wanted. It was you.' She pointed an unsteady hand in Ginny's direction and put on one of her confounding smiles. 'Not a daughter. An extension of himself. Like another arm.'

'He must have been disappointed when she turned out to be nothing like him,' said Phoebe.

'You'd think so.' Harriet slugged her wine. 'She's a carbon copy of my mother.'

'A throw back,' Phoebe said, tossing a pretzel into her mouth.

'And here she is, a grown woman, a talented woman, a Brassington-Smythe.' Harriet enunciated her surname with elongated consonants.

Ginny caught Veronica's eye and raised her glass. 'To BS.'

'To BS,' her friends both said at once.

'BS?' said Phoebe.

'Short for Brassington-Smythe,' Ginny said quickly.

'Yes, of course.'

Phoebe leaned forward and rearranged the fare, lining up what there was of all the vegan, vegetarian, gluten and lactose free in front of Poppy and Veronica with a 'There you go gals, tuck in.'

Her friends obeyed, reaching for a dab of this and a dollop of that. Ginny quickly relocated the Turkish Delight. She hadn't thus far seen Harriet eat a thing, but at last her mother arranged on her plate a canapé and some dried fruits, nothing like enough to soak up the booze.

Ginny forked the last of the smoked salmon on the platter in front of her and sat back in her seat, wishing away the evening. When the music stopped she went to change the record, finding in the stillness of the room relief from the atmosphere her mother had created in the kitchen. She took a few moments to listen to Duke Ellington but the music couldn't shake the feeling that all her life she'd been cheated out of a Christmas she had never known.

There was a rap on the front door.

It was Rosalind, all quaint and homey looking. Ginny bent a little and kissed her on her cheek. 'Come on through,' she said and led the way, wondering what effect the old woman's presence would have on the room.

Once through the beaded curtain, Rosalind paused and cast her eye over the others. Then she took up the chair beside Ginny, leaned towards her and said, 'You are looking especially elegant this evening my dear.' Rosalind was in a finely woven dress of demure green.

'Are you enjoying your Christmas, Mrs Spears?' Poppy said politely.

'Indeed, I am, Poppy. Although partaking in a little too much rich food. It's unavoidable, don't you think?'

'It's easy for me. I'm vegan.'

'That makes little difference. I have known vegans who gorge on cake and pie.'

'I'm gluten free too.'

'Celiac? Really? You've been tested?' Rosalind raised her eyebrows at Poppy's blush. 'Well, clearly one must be careful with one's digestive tract.'

Harriet, who appeared miraculously sober, stood and quickly cleared away some empty platters. Then she sat down and reached for the Sauvignon Blanc. 'Rosalind, let me pour you…'

'Tea, I think, Harriet. Yes, a nice pot of tea.'

She turned squarely in her seat to address Ginny, leaving Harriet to the kettle and the teapot. 'The young today here in the

West have allowed themselves to become too suggestible, don't you think?' She paused, searching Ginny's face. 'The mind, you see, Ginny, the mind is the most powerful thing we have, far more powerful than the body. Should we not let it be thus? For if we allow the body supremacy, succumb to its appetites, we weaken the spirit. We in our society today pay far too much attention to false demands, demands imposed on us from beyond our own skins, needled in so to speak, part of a toxic infusion of popular cultural nonsense. Don't you agree?'

'Well, I…'

'You must agree. You are a pianist. A pianist must master her body, train it to play the instrument and in so doing become an instrument herself, of her own soul.'

'Such elevated thoughts, Rosalind,' Phoebe said.

'Possibly, but nevertheless pertinent,' Rosalind said with a quick glance at Poppy, who had averted her gaze.

There was an awkward silence. Poppy remained red cheeked and Harriet had coloured too. More than coloured; her face was glistening.

Ginny sensed that Rosalind had no idea the hurt she had caused. Her sudden condemnation was out of character, even for her. In all likelihood, it was Harriet she was annoyed with for being visibly drunk on Christmas Eve. For Rosalind still treated her as she would one of her child students and rather than risk a confrontation with an inebriate, she had chosen instead to sober the gathering with a barb at the most vulnerable woman present.

An air of unease hung in the room.

Harriet returned with the tea things on a tray and placed Rosalind's china cup and saucer before her, making every effort to pour with a steady hand.

'You'll be leaving for England soon,' Phoebe said lightly, breaking the silence.

'And with much anticipation.'

'Where's the conference?'

'Bournemouth. Doesn't start until the twenty-eighth. But I'm leaving a little earlier to do some sightseeing.'

'Then you must look up Fritz,' Phoebe said.

Ginny stiffened. Fritz had moved to England when she was twelve to take up a post at the university. She had been disappointed at the time. Up until he left he had made some effort to replace her father. In the years after her mother had taken her to live in the Dandenongs, Fritz would visit every so often, take her to the parks and gardens and tearooms nearby and buy her small gifts from a handcrafted toyshop. When he went overseas she had felt abandoned all over again and had resented her mother even more.

Fritz knew Wilhelm. They had grown up in the same German town. Although he never spoke to her of him. As she grew older in those years before he went away, she would ask him and she always got the same reply. 'It's best not to dwell on who he was, Ginny. Best to forget about him.'

The only information she had discovered, overhearing her mother and Phoebe in one of her listening-behind-closed-doors episodes, was they suspected that her father, too, had gone to England. That Fritz had sighted him once at a railway station.

She sat at the Christmas table, holding herself in, making pretence of gaiety, endeavouring to respond with titters of laughter in the right places, watching Rosalind slowly drain her cup and at last take her leave, and then she capitulated, privately, to an unexpected intensity.

When Harriet returned to the room after seeing Rosalind to the door, Ginny was unable to contain herself and she flew at her with, 'I'm going to find him.'

'Who?'

'My father.'

There was an exchange of glances. Veronica and Poppy looked puzzled.

Ginny stood up abruptly, knocking the table and making its

contents quiver. Without the apology she knew was expected of her, she left the room.

Harriet followed her and yelled through the beaded curtain, 'You better do it then! Go and find him. Go and live with him if that's what you want!'

Ginny, who had almost made it across the Kashan rug, turned. 'You know where he is,' she said in a low voice.

'No. But you're old enough and if this is what it takes to get this obsession out of your head then so be it.'

'Harriet,' Phoebe said sharply. 'Have you taken leave of your senses?'

'I've done all I can for this child. Shielded her for long enough. But it's no use. She has to know.'

'Know what?' Ginny hadn't meant to shriek.

'It's Christmas,' Phoebe said, her face appearing beside her friend's. 'Now is not the time.'

That's damn right, Ginny thought. Now is not the time. Now is never the time.

She ran from the room and up the stairs. She slammed her bedroom door behind her, kicked off her boots and flopped down on her back on the bed.

The room seemed small and close, the furniture overbearing. It no longer felt like her room. Everything in it was alien. The half-opened wardrobe, her clothes slung on a chair, the mirror reflecting the gloom. She was adrift, a tiny rudderless boat, too far from calm. She hadn't anticipated that Rosalind's imminent trip would precipitate such a violent outburst. And in front of everyone too. At least she had managed to wait until after Rosalind left. But what of Poppy and Veronica? They must think she had lost her senses. And she hadn't given them their presents. She wanted to go downstairs and apologise but her pride wouldn't let her. Tears welled, tears of confusion, for now that she had burst out with her statement in front of everyone, she wasn't entirely sure she really wanted to go through with it.

Wednesday, 18 January 2017

Bournemouth

The flat was dim, the air stale and sharp and she cursed that she'd agreed to help Madeleine move out her things. She glanced at her watch. Eleven minutes past eleven. Fifteen seconds until eleven twelve. She had been noticing eleven eleven a lot lately. The recurrence of the numbers alarmed her, especially when she saw them on a digital display, four straight lines glowing red at her, four slices of time: we mean something and it's up to you to figure out what. She had no way of deciphering such a thing, if such a thing could be figured out. More likely it was an accident of time. Her eyes drawn to the clock, her brain logging the single number series, isolating that series as a pattern. For some inexplicable reason humans notice patterns. Maybe it's a primal thing, she thought, something to do with survival, with finding our way.

She topped and tailed a zucchini, sliding the knife twice down its length and dicing the segments. Onion rings sizzled in the copper-bottom pan she had gifted Madeleine when she moved to Bournemouth. The pan had hardly been used. Neither had the small saucepan with the glass lid or the sandwich maker. The blender was still in its box. Most of the kitchenware Madeleine had removed from the cupboards and drawers and bundled into a plastic tub without much care. Judith had retrieved the crockery and wrapped it in the copy of yesterday's newspaper that she had brought along.

She turned down the gas, added the zucchini and put on the lid, then she looked over at the monster-sized television at the other end of the room. The camera panned over a desolate cityscape of half-blown-up buildings, makeshift corrugated-iron huts, streets littered with debris and dead bodies, and an oil tanker on its side. Smoke billowed from random hidden sources. And at Zol, who was meant to be at a tattoo convention, kneeling on the floor, engrossed, tense, anticipating the action. He held a controller in both of his belly-white hands. A wireless headset gripped his lank and straggly dyed-black hair like a plastic Alice band. Hair crumpled around the ears, tapering to wisps about the shoulders. His gaze fixed on the screen, he reached for a can of bourbon and Coke perched on the edge of the coffee table between the wrappings of a burger and an ashtray full of butts. He swigged a mouthful and wiped his mouth. Then, with a deft tug of his black jeans he adjusted the lie of his balls and belched.

She watched the screen. There was little action, just a scuffling of hurried steps that came to a halt and all went quiet.

Then a male voice, American, hollered, 'They're closing in.'

A square-jawed, thickset man dressed in a combat uniform hunkered down behind an upturned car, gun in hand.

'Chuggah, chuggah, chuggah. Kaboom. Hut, hut, hut, hut. Chuggah, chuggah, chuggah…Arghh,' and the man fell to the ground.

'Fuck you!' Zol yelled. 'You got me from behind.'

The screen turned blood red and 'Coward's way out: Press X' appeared.

Zol pressed the key and a virtual gun fired straight at the screen. He reloaded the game and took up his console.

She picked up her knife and hacked a carrot into large chunks. The knife thwacked the chopping board and another piece of Zol flew across the bench. Damn Madeleine for not making sure her toad of a boyfriend would be absent when she came to help her move out. Damn her for insisting Judith made lunch while she packed. To use up the vegetables Zol would never eat, Madeleine had said, but Judith would rather have tossed the whole lot in the bin.

Damn her father too, for being away that weekend. On retreat, he had said when she phoned him the night before. Then that he was relieved Madeleine had come to her senses at last and would be in touch. Still, her expectations were low. When Madeleine received her place at Bournemouth University, Zol found a position as piercist in a tattoo parlour in the city, an impressive feat, and Judith had been as thrilled as Madeleine when the parlour offered them the upstairs flat. Peter had been so incensed he cut off all ties with his daughter.

Judith thought his reaction extreme yet she shared his sentiment. Zol was Madeleine's age, the youngest son of a checkout assistant and a furniture-delivery guy. Earlier in their relationship, Madeleine had spent most of her time at his parents' place. Only once did she bring him home. And he had brought with him a storm and a power cut and they had spent the evening by candlelight, Judith struggling to hold a conversation. By morning she was relieved to see him leave and happy never to see him again. Since she had so little influence over Madeleine she was also pleased not to have her in the house. Even birthdays and Christmas Judith had spent alone in those two years before Madeleine moved out.

Christmas without Madeleine was pleasant enough, although the occasion amplified her solitude. She did her best to regard the day itself as a calendar number among all the others in December, the village church bells that sounded out a special service alerting her to the possibility of communion. But she would not be religious, not even for a day.

She put the diced carrots in the small saucepan with a dash of water and lit the gas. She added mushrooms to the other pan and beat four eggs. Suddenly, she was a mother. She would be cooking for two from now on. Her chest tightened at the thought. She hoped that Peter would soften and he would at least speak to his daughter. That he might spend time with her seemed too much to wish for. She poured the eggs in the pan, certain he would always remain disinterested.

He had been an absent presence for the whole of Madeleine's life, there in essence, and sometimes in person, answering to a call of duty always less than enthusiastically, as if his daughter didn't measure up to some standard of his. She was, she never had been, good enough.

Yet Judith had been more than good enough for him until she conceived his child.

They had met on campus. She was at the end of her first year in fine art, still fresh and eager, and he newly arrived, replacing Dr Samson, her lecturer in 'Cherubim and Devas,' an elective she had chosen upon her fascination for the works of Raphael and Hieronymus Bosch. Dr Samson had collapsed midway through a seminar, which was a tragedy and a relief, for he was a crusty old man and his lectures were hard to follow.

Dr Love was enthralling from the first. He was swarthy and dark, thick black hair framing an expressive face, but what drew her most were his suggestive eyes. When he talked of Seraphim in his soft accented voice, a voice she took to be eastern European, she found herself swooning. At the end of his second lecture she waited behind. He lingered too, collating his papers. She made her way down the aisle carrying in her mind the question she had formulated about halfway through the session, and as she approached him the question became gossamer. The moment he greeted her, a warm smile spreading across his face, the question vanished and she felt her cheeks redden. A sympathetic look came into his face and he offered to walk with her, that perhaps a coffee would help her memory.

Things developed quickly from there. It was the month of March in 1995. They met at lunchtime on Mondays, Wednesdays and Fridays. She would walk about half a mile up the road, and he would collect her in his car and take her to his cottage on the outskirts of Exeter, Judith infatuated, Peter ardent. He would tell her how much he was drawn to her. He would hold her tightly. The secrecy was heady. He was seventeen years her senior and while others of her age paired up and walked hand in hand or canoodled in the university bar, she was set apart. Her secret, held fast from her friends and her family, was at once a burden and the conferrer of a creative burst. Her artistic output trebled. She explored her twin passions of style, producing a unique hybrid of Raphael and Bosch on canvas upon canvas. For months, she existed in a cocoon, guarding her hope that one day, perhaps after she graduated, they would marry.

She discovered she was pregnant in the August of that summer.

Apprehensive as she was, she thought he might be pleased. They were lying together in his bed one Wednesday afternoon, sated and drowsy, when she turned on her side and stroked her fingers through the dark wool of his chest. His eyes were closed, arms relaxed, fingers threaded together across his belly, his manhood limp and resting against his thigh. A sudden rush of unease came forth as she spoke the words, three syllables in all, and his fingers clenched before springing free and he sat up and scowled that she should have been more careful.

Tears welled and she pulled away from him, the realisation immediate that an end had been reached, but when he said she must abort and he would pay for it, her guts clenched in rebellion.

There was much commotion in the bedroom. Zol didn't register the yelps and calls. Judith went to help, glancing at the laundry floor on her way past, pausing before the dirty socks and a pair of scrunched jeans, then the cat litter tray bedside the outside door, brim full of litter, the turds on top unburied, presumably because the poor cat couldn't break its way through the crust formed by its own urine. At least that explained the acrid smell that had hit her on her way inside the flat, a smell she had initially attributed to Zol's poor hygiene.

It was Madeleine's cat, a tortoiseshell moggy called Kali, and a much-pampered cat she was. Madeleine had acquired her from a friend in the months before she left for Bournemouth and the thing had been sleeping in her bed ever since. At home, attending to the litter tray had fallen to Judith, as in all likelihood it would again. Madeleine would feed and cuddle and dangle toy mice and Judith assumed she still did all that, but she clearly wasn't dealing with its shit.

Thank heavens Madeleine hadn't fallen pregnant.

Those months of her own pregnancy, when she was not much older than Madeleine was now, were arduous and lonely. She hid the news from her parents for as long as she could and they were oblivious until the bump of her belly became a melon.

One day her mother, Florence, sat her down in the kitchen. Florence had chicken stock on the boil and a fruitcake in the oven and it was as much as Judith could do not to heave. Her mother came right out and asked, and she looked down at her feet in shame as she told her who the father was. Of course, then came, 'He should lose his job over this,' followed by Judith's tears and Florence standing close and stroking her hair and Judith slumping against the warm softness of her mother.

It was decided she must leave university to avoid a scandal. Local gossip, even in the nineties, would be bad enough, without the village finding out she had been having a liaison with her lecturer.

She might have made a fuss and had him sacked but she didn't, not in deference to her parents, although she rarely went against their wishes, but because she believed him when he'd said she should have been more careful.

He visited Fernley cottage once during her term. She was eight months gone when one Saturday in December he arrived unexpectedly, pulling up in the driveway a little after ten. He told her later he'd found her address in the university records, which she found odd since she had already given him her details. She waddled into the kitchen to find him there, with her mother saying, 'You've a visitor,' and putting on the kettle and making it plain she had no intention of leaving the room.

'How are you?' he said, without an apology for his absence all those months.

'Perfectly fine,' she said, unwilling to let down her guard, her gaze trailing her mother as she set about preparing the tea.

'Are you getting plenty of rest?'

'Yes.' What else was she to do but rest? She could no longer bring herself to paint and viewed with disgust at her earlier works of cherubs that she had painted in a passionate frenzy. Her Raphael-Bosch phase was over.

He looked askance at her mother then said without preface, 'Make sure you don't eat pickled fish.' And at her mother's sharp intake of breath, he went on. 'I take it you've been avoiding alcohol, cigarettes and all fumes.'

At that, Florence swung round. 'We don't need your advice,' she said, and he looked taken aback.

'Very well then,' he muttered. Her mother's hostility could not have been more damaging. He maintained a pretence of polite conversation, focusing mainly on the weather, and avoiding all mention of university. It was not long before he finished his tea, made his goodbyes, and left.

Judith went into labour two weeks and two days before her own birthday. Madeleine had looked like him from the first, making her appearance in the world with a crown of thick black hair.

A whole month later, on a cool Sunday afternoon, she pushed the pram through the village and down a narrow lane, waiting at a crossroads about half a mile on. High hedgerows flanking the lanes obscured the fields beyond and allowed the scantest view of oncoming vehicles. She listened, rocking the pram, and waited, anxiety gripping her tight.

A blue car approached and slowed. The driver glanced over then braked suddenly. 'Are you all right?' the woman said through her open window.

'I'm fine,' she said, although she didn't feel it.

'Do you need a lift somewhere?'

'No, really I'm fine.'

She watched the car disappear and glanced back to see Peter pulling up in a narrow lay-by. She pushed the pram to the driver's side door. He was still strapped in his seat. She manoeuvred the pram so he could see their baby's face and he gazed for a while without smiling before releasing the buckle and opening the door. She gathered Madeleine in her arms and passed her to him. He was hesitant. Then he cradled the little baby bundle for a short while before handing her back.

'She's yours,' Judith said.

'No, she's yours.'

'She looks like you. Aren't you pleased?'

'Judith.' And with that he said he had to go. He thrust a twenty-pound bill into her hand and said he would be in touch.

His visits were sporadic. After that first time, she caught the bus to Exeter, struggling with the baby and the pram, and met him in a park or by the river. As the months and years slipped by, Madeleine took on more of his features, and by the time she was seven she was his doppelganger. Yet he remained indifferent and distant.

Judith found Madeleine frantically pulling posters off the bedroom walls. Madeleine's gaze darted at the doorway as she entered, a mix of guilt and apprehension on her face.

'Oh, it's you,' she said and carried on.

'Food's almost ready.'

'Can you zip up my suitcase? I need to get these posters.'

'Why the frenzy?'

'If Zol finds out he'll lose his shit.'

'They're your posters though.'

'He didn't want me to take them so don't say anything. Okay?'

'Okay.'

The posters were large and left a conspicuously blank space of wall. Smudges marked the presence of the adhesive. The wall seemed a touch whiter where they had been.

Judith wrestled with the zipper of the suitcase Madeleine had overstuffed. The zipper had caught in a scarf. Judith eased it free then pressed her forearm along the soft-case lid and drew the zipper round the rim.

'Lunch then?' Madeleine said in lieu of thank you.

They returned to the living room where Zol was still playing his video game. 'Ignore him,' Madeleine said and sat at the bench before an empty bowl. Lowering her voice, she went on. 'At least he's not on the Forum.'

'The Forum?'

'Some weird networking site. He spends half the night posting on conspiracy B S.'

'I don't follow.'

'Conspiracy bullshit. Like the royal family are really alien lizards.'

'That's absurd.'

'Tell me about it. And you know what's even funnier. He calls himself Ashtray Petrolstick.'

Ashtray Petrolstick? Judith shot a look at the oaf across the room surrounded by his detritus, and she couldn't have conceived a more apt appellation. Yet she couldn't imagine he had the wherewithal to string together two coherent sentences, let alone hold his own in a forum.

'I reckon he copies and pastes from other sources,' Madeleine said as if reading her mind.

Judith filled their bowls and took up the stool beside her daughter. She ate quickly, keen to load the car and leave, keen never to have to encounter Madeleine's troll of a boyfriend again.

Variation

Harriet was at work. That was the attitude with which she awoke and how she had remained all day, resolved, now the yuletide festivities had passed, to bring the exhibition to fruition. She stood before one of her easels, eyeing painting number four, the daubs of yellow newly applied, the Prussian blue triangles dry enough for a line or two of an orange hue. Startled by a sudden crash, she turned, brush in hand, to see on the lawn a dead branch of the messmate that grew beside the fence. The weather had turned nasty and a vicious northerly was forcing kiln-hot air across the state. The last rays of the sun backlit the tall and straight mountain ash in the neighbour's garden, their tops keeling in the wind. Glimmers of fiery light stroked the studio's south-facing window. It wouldn't be long before the sun gave up and sank below the mountain. Despite nightfall there was no sign of the wind abating. Inside, the windows still gave forth a glowing heat. A fan on the bench circulated the stale air. It would be much cooler in the house, and a good deal safer off the mountain, but Harriet returned to her painting. She was dressed in a thin singlet and baggy dungarees, her pendulous breasts hanging free, her hair tied up high on her head in a hair band. She ignored the odour of her armpits. The flushing came and went without notice. She was too preoccupied, too focused, too frantic to care.

She surveyed her nine paintings in various stages of completion as a jilted lover would her former beau: critically, unsympa-
thetically, dismissively. They were all variants of the one painting,
her first, propped on her other easel, a painting she disliked a little more each time she viewed it. Her idea of aligning the various
forms with the aspects of the Moon as it made its way around the
zodiac had proven just as uninspiring as her original approach.
She was unable to fathom how a model of profound metaphysical
significance could end in mediocrity. She had become part of Kandinsky's vulgar herd, her work barely more than a mimicry of the
movements of this most feminine of heavenly spheres. There was
no inner meaning. In its place, simple correspondences that meant
nothing and evoked nothing. As far as she could tell, there was no
revelation, no profundity.

Her dissatisfaction provoked a cascade of doubt. It was exco-
riating to admit to herself that she had always been an imitator,
a copyist, a reproducer who added little originality to her works.
She had found modest commercial success only because Phoebe's
assiduous promotion brought undiscriminating clientele to her
door. Here she was in the prime of her life when she should be at
the peak of her career and in full mastery of her powers, a hack.

When she created the Moon model she had secretly hoped the
collaboration would represent a union of her creative and intellectual interests. In the face of her artworks she had to admit she had
been flattering herself, bolstering herself with false pretentions. As
if she had adopted Phoebe's marketing spin and pegged it to her
breast, believing she was indeed a hugely talented and yet to be discovered gem. She had never considered herself vain but perhaps
she was. Perhaps she had been sneaking quick looks in the mirror
and, satisfied, quickly looked away, never once breaking into that
reflection. She felt painfully and decidedly shallow. And if she was
shallow, so must be her paintings.

With a final scathing look at her artistic output she redirected
the fan and went to sit in the club chair, arms hanging over the

armrests, grateful for the wafts of stuffy air. She leaned her head back and closed her eyes.

She must have nodded off, for when she opened them it was dark. She left her seat and flicked on the lights and forced another look at the paintings. The dots and the shapes were static and she could see straight away that her work lacked vitality. There had to be some way of invigorating the works. She was about to open a window when it occurred to her imperative that she found a place deep within herself, immanence commensurate with the transcendence of the model. It was in those depths that she would find the sense of the whole composition and so find a way to breathe life into the works. This was why she had been thwarted, her imagination dry. She had placed too much emphasis on the cosmology without. She needed to look at the cosmology within. And an idea came to her like a sudden rush of rejuvenating air.

Rather than tracking the Moon as it went on its monthly amble around the heavens, she would superimpose her own horoscope, taking note of all the aspects the Moon made with the planetary positions at the very moment of her birth. It would be subversion but Ginny would never know unless she confessed.

She rushed out of the studio and across the garden to the kitchen, where she rifled through the dresser's bottom drawer that contained all things pertaining to the occult, along with a ball of string, last year's Christmas cards and some packing tape.

She returned to the studio with her horoscope, her ephemeris and the calculator Ginny had given her. She had had it drawn up years before by an associate of Rosalind: an erudite Jungian therapist who went by the name Cosmo. She wasn't sure she entirely believed in the significances astrologers ascribe to planets, their locations and various interactions. She was a Leo and therefore above such naval gazing, yet like her zodiacal lion, she felt at once elevated, bolstered, lent an almost regal sense of grandeur, and she was fine with that. Cosmo had gone on to tell her she had a drifty Moon in Pisces and a preponderance of off-kilter quincunxes. She had been struggling with her quincunxes ever since.

She placed her horoscope on the table, opened her ephemeris, switched on the calculator and, with less attention to mathematical precision than she had applied to the original scrolls, she charted the Moon's movements in her own universe, noting the angles of significance.

Several days' labour and the result was another series of coloured dots strung out on nine timelines. The order was different, the colours and their frequency the same. She had anticipated upon her gaze an inner resonance, some sort of deep knowing. Instead, her creative senses were mute. And another hot and windy evening turned to darkness.

She went to the studio's south-facing window and looked back at the house, noticing a warm glow through the curtains of Ginny's bedroom. She had been spending a lot of time up there these last weeks, whenever she was home. They had been avoiding each other since Ginny's outburst on Christmas Eve. As far as Harriet could glean, Ginny was holding fast to her desire to go off in search of her father. She had taken to wearing her paisley jacket around the house no matter what the weather. Harriet never saw her in anything else. It was her armour, and perhaps too, a demonstration of her alliance with Wilhelm. Not that he wore paisley. Heavens no! Colours to him were white, grey and black. On this he was intractable. What father and daughter shared was stubbornness when it came to their apparel. Come to think of it, they were both intractable about many things. It was a discomforting thought that the child one parent nurtures, turns out to be more like the other.

Perhaps it was the seed that matters, she thought, and not the soil it grew in. Bad seed. Although she couldn't be quite so emphatic that Ginny was the product of bad seed. She had to resist allowing the hurt and the apprehension she felt to colour her view of Ginny, despite her infuriating quest. A quest that had become no longer a demand on Harriet to search her memory and reveal the past, but a real present-tense endeavour, all because Harriet had been too tight-lipped. Yet for all her reticence, it was as though Ginny's probing had cracked open Harriet's psyche, rendering her at the mercy of her inner gravedigger bent on exhuming memories.

Those last years with Wilhelm from when Ginny had been about four, had been intolerable: Wilhelm Schmid, with his doctorate in the occult, always dressed in a vintage fifties suit and plain white shirt, rarely home and when he was, he only took an interest in Ginny. A brooding man, and as the years at Gore Street slipped by, he became more distant and more disinterested, yet always critical, when he did address Harriet, of all she did or didn't do for their daughter. There was no doubt in his mind that he was the better parent. By then their relationship, which had never amounted to much once the initial frenzy of love making had passed, had deteriorated beyond redemption. Although they rarely argued, which was largely because she never defended her mothering.

Not normally given to self-criticism, Harriet had awoken each morning gripped by guilt. A self-admonishing narrative unfolded in her by the day, taking over her confidence, a narrative told by an amalgam of Wilhelm's reprobation and her own shame. For he was right, her mothering was wanting. The more dominant the narrative became, the stronger the shame she felt. She was a failure and everyone could see it. She could no longer meet people in the eye. Too often she hung her head, stared down at the floor when she walked, and her shoulders had begun to hunch.

Her life contracted until she saw only Phoebe and her parents who, while judging Harriet with eyes filled with disappointment, adored their only granddaughter.

Her parents were old. They had been in their forties when Harriet came along and by the time Ginny was born they were both seventy. They lived a very quiet life in Mont Albert. Having no car, it was an effort from Gore Street to visit, negotiating, with Ginny in a pushchair, the tram, the train, and the fifteen-minute walk, a journey she was only prepared to make every second week. Shortly after Ginny's seventh birthday, when they were both seventy-seven, Harriet was freed of the obligation.

Their age was a fact that Harriet had forgotten and she wondered if the number seven had been lucky for her after all, although it would depend on how she interpreted the events that followed, for it was undeniably the most critical time of her life, at once devastating and liberating.

Her parents had gone for their morning walk to the park, following their usual route along a stretch of road they traversed so often they would surely have known the chips and scuffs of the kerbstones where they crossed to the other side. That morning, as they stepped from the kerb, a truck cornering a side street slammed into them both before driving off. A brutal happenstance, an accident, a wayward truck barrelling into them on that particular day. An ordinary day, and nothing could have altered the moment when habit had chanced to end their lives.

It was such a shock: the knock on the door, the police on the doorstep, that look in their eyes. They wore about them the colour of death. Standing in the doorway with Ginny somewhere behind, her mind pitched. It might have been Wilhelm. She would have handled it better if it had been. In fact, she probably would have felt nothing but relief. Instead both her parents were whacked to their deaths by a speeding truck.

There were no witnesses and the driver was never found, facts that made the event all the more distressing, and there were times that Harriet doubted the accident, but the police would not have lied. Besides, she had identified their bodies.

Thirty-four was no age to lose both parents at once. She was thrust unwillingly into a thick despair. She went hollow. Sometimes she wept. Sometimes she felt as if her mind were on a tilt, all her thoughts sliding into oblivion. Her despair thickened further by a new measure of guilt. She should have been there. She had planned to be there. She had cancelled her scheduled visit that morning on a fabricated pretext of stomach ache, for really, she couldn't be bothered. Ginny was having a sulk and she didn't fancy the tram and the train and the walk with a sulky Ginny. Especially with the weather turning inclement. Yes, it had been an inclement day.

The inheritance had proven straightforward. Yet when the family solicitor had told her the amount she could expect, and she found herself a woman of ample means, she was stunned. The deaths, the inheritance, yes, that was surely the one significant turning point in her life.

She thought back to that day she had sat in the Brassington-Smythe's solicitor's offices in Clifton Hill, watching the corpulent Mr Gamble read the will to discover that she, the only beneficiary, was set to inherit a fortune. She had sat there in disbelief. She knew her parents had been wealthy, their Mont Albert home alone of considerable value. Then there was the weekender in Sassafras, but she'd had no idea the investments, the trusts. At one time, she had even speculated that she might have been disinherited after going against their wishes over her career and then her union with Wilhelm, which they had always considered inopportune.

And there she was, living in Gore Street, that sorry little terraced house of remarkable ugliness, with its tawdry veranda and misaligned window in the façade. Where there should have been a balcony with a nice lacework railing, should have been and was in all the other houses in the street, there was nothing. A house smaller than the rest, stunted, stuck on as an afterthought and erected with no care. For seven years, almost eight years—and she found she was counting the months—she had endured the hovel, all the while Wilhelm, despite his income, refusing to move, refusing to buy, refusing them both a foothold in an escalating property market.

Leaving him sooner would have meant moving back with her parents, or facing deprivation as a struggling single mother in shared rental accommodation, dependent on the sale of her art. The boom times were over. Phoebe was lucky to sell a piece of hers a month. Was that why she had stayed, kidded herself that he was a good man despite their loveless union, used her own reprehensible disinterestedness in motherhood as an excuse to accommodate him?

All these thoughts sped through her mind as she listened to Mr Gamble.

'Only,' he said and paused.

'Yes?'

'There's a caveat.'

'A caveat?'

He cleared his throat and told her she would only receive her inheritance if she cut off all ties with Wilhelm.

His words smashed through her grief with the force of revelation, scattering the constructions of her reality like so many timbers of a poorly built edifice, replacing her immobilising guilt with an upwelling power.

She had cycled back to Gore Street in a daze.

Wilhelm had been astonishingly unsympathetic about the deaths, even for him. Soon after hearing the news his disinterested yet critical demeanour shifted and he became almost sly. About that time, he had been engaging Ginny in long private chats. She had become his ally and on more than one occasion they had sat together, observing Harriet as she set about doing the daily chores. They observed her quietly, knowingly, conspiratorially. It was as if he knew about the caveat and was plotting some sort of countermeasure. Although he couldn't have known. She hadn't told him and she had hidden her copy of the will in the bottom of her tin of pencils, somewhere he would never look. Yet paranoia grew beside her grief until she, too, became watchful and suspicious.

Phoebe, who had disliked Wilhelm from the first, told her on one of her regular visits that if she thought him to be in any way dodgy she should leave him. But then, that was exactly what Harriet had expected Phoebe to say. She'd refrained from divulging the details of the will, knowing that would only have sealed things for Phoebe, which would not have helped her make up her mind.

She had to be clear in her heart that it was a well-founded suspicion and not her imminent wealth that would motivate her to leave. The caveat had given her a choice and it was a choice that seemed to have lifted a veil on Wilhelm. But still, she wasn't sure.

She told no one, for she had no idea where to look for clarification. Rosalind was away on holiday in India and Fritz, whom she had met for coffee a few weeks after the accident, was reticent when it came to Wilhelm and his dubious past.

He had looked at her sympathetically and told her that she should give herself time. 'Be easy on yourself,' he said. Then he diverted the conversation towards topics of an artistic nature. He was writing a paper on Tim Storrier and wanted to talk about the Australian landscape. She suspected he didn't want to involve himself in her affairs, a stance understandable when she considered he was still her jilted lover.

Alone and feeling unsupported, she had floundered, until one day a few months later, when she found a letter folded into the dust jacket of Wilhelm's tome on the Rosicrucians. Oh, the letter! More likely it was that letter that had turned her circumstances. How was one to know the root cause of anything? How, when events tumbled one upon another? It was like sifting through sand when all of the grains formed the dune. All she could be sure of was that when happenstances do coincide, the actor becomes the victim of their fate. Life had a higher order to it and it revealed itself in those moments like a yank: she was no longer the arbiter of her choices.

The wind showed no sign of abating. In the dark of the moonless night, its roar was all the more menacing and in the area illumed by the studio window, gum leaves littered the lawn. A figure emerged from the black into the reach of the studio's light. Harriet pulled away, quickly sliding her horoscope under some scrap paper on the bench as the studio door opened and Phoebe stepped inside.

'Ginny told me you were out here,' she said matter-of-factly. 'Sulking.'

She stood in her trench coat, hands on hips, and gave Harriet and her artworks an appraising stare.

Harriet was immediately defensive. 'She said that?'

'No. I did. Or rather, have. Just now in fact. Look at you!' She flicked a hand in Harriet's direction.

She was instantly annoyed that anyone, especially Phoebe, should accuse her of a sulk, and the heat rose and this time she was acutely attuned to the discomfort, which left her no choice but to relinquish her ire.

'Tea?' she said lightly.

'I don't want tea. I didn't come out here for tea!' Phoebe sounded furious yet Harriet saw in her face a familiar camaraderie.

'What *are* you here for?'

'We've been friends a long time, Harriet.'

'Since high school.'

'I've known you longer than anyone else, even your parents as it happens.'

'You've always been good at maths,' Harriet said wryly.

'And this isn't you.' She walked forward and swept her arm wide.

'The studio?'

'The grumpy retreat.'

'I'm at work.'

'No, you're not. You've made no progress since I was last here. You're avoiding Ginny.'

'That's not true. I have a deadline to meet. *We* have a deadline.'

'There's plenty of time.'

'Nine paintings!'

'Each one a variation. Once you've nailed the idea. Besides, you've always been a fast worker. Remember that Cezanne you knocked out in two days. We had to blow dry the paint!'

'For a Japanese tourist, wasn't it?'

'Korean, but never mind. The client was ecstatic. That was the pace of things. And never a complaint. You've always had the knack.'

'For imitation Phoebe,' she said with a forlorn grimace. 'For derivation.'

'You're an interpreter.'

'I'm a copyist.'

'This isn't like you, Harriet.' Phoebe sounded exasperated.

'I haven't produced a satisfactory work since the Wessex series,' Harriet said, fingering her paintbrushes neatly lined up on the bench. 'Which I am beginning to see as a harbinger.' She paused. 'A death knell.'

'You sold one.'

'To Rosalind. Not exactly an appreciator of fine art.'

'Who knows who has taste?'

'You. And you don't like those works.'

'They're accomplished. Just not marketable in today's climate. England is not popular in the zeitgeist at present. No one I know likes bucolic scenes of the mother country.'

They were hardly bucolic but she made no comment. Instead she said, 'If my works had merit, they'd resonate regardless, and sell.'

'Rubbish. Most buyers are no more than the great unwashed with Porsches.'

'So, I'm right. My work suits the unenlightened many. Or not, as the case may be.'

'Harriet, I simply meant that the market overrides quality. People don't have the wherewithal to decide for themselves. They have to be told what to like.'

'Even Rosalind.'

'What do you mean?'

'Perhaps not like that. But she no more resonated spiritually or aesthetically with the painting than the average Joe.'

'You can't know that.'

'I can. She told me. She bought it as a memento to commemorate her trip to Bournemouth. A Union Jack may have done just as well, but where do you buy such a thing in Sassafras?'

They were silent for a while. Harriet went and sat down in the club chair. Phoebe took up one of the wooden chairs in the centre of the room, angled in Harriet's direction.

'I've known you for forty years, Harriet,' she said reflectively.

'You've already said that.'

'Well, it's worth restating. I've known you long enough to know that this is bullshit.'

Harriet avoided her gaze.

'You're upset,' Phoebe said, her manner softening. 'About Ginny. You haven't been yourself since she moved back in.'

'She's unbearable.'

'She's your daughter and you love her.' Phoebe watched her steadily. Then she took a quick breath and exhaled sharply. 'And, she's a mess.'

At that Harriet's thoughts tumbled from her and she stood and paced the studio floor.

'She's wallowing as far as I can tell. Mooching about the house in that god-awful paisley. Over Garth.' She thrust her hands skyward. 'How could anyone mooch over Garth?' She stopped beside her easels. 'Frankly, Phoebe, I'm getting desperate. The exhibition was meant to be her salvation. Turns out at a great personal sacrifice.'

'You're exaggerating.'

'Am I? This collaboration has been a disaster from the start. She opposes everything I suggest and when I finally get her to agree on the Moon model she goes off and composes nine works in as many days, at great personal triumph no doubt.' She paused then said beneath her breath, 'I wonder too whether also out of spite.'

She went to the west-facing window and made a pretence of looking out into the dark, before swinging back and directing her perambulations around the table where Phoebe sat.

'And now she's still morose. No, not morose. Livid with me for some inexplicable reason. All because of Rosalind and that ruddy conference.'

'You can't blame Rosalind.'

'No? No, of course not. It's just that it has her all stirred up about that Lemurian turd. I feel like shredding the Wessex series; then I'd be done with it. Those paintings mock me every time I enter the gallery. I can't bear to look at them. It's as if I had brought all of this into being in the act of every brush stroke.'

Phoebe smiled. Harriet stopped her pacing and stared at her blankly. 'You don't see it, do you?' Phoebe said.

'I don't see what?'

'She blames you. She's always blamed you.'

Harriet was silent as she ran through her recent divulgences and Ginny's reactions. She had to admit, if only privately, that Phoebe was right.

'You have to tell her.'

'Tell her? Tell her what?'

'All of it. The whole bang lot.'

'I have no proof,' she said weakly, yet she knew the time she had dreaded for two decades had finally arrived.

It was Fritz who had kindled her suspicions. A few weeks after they had met at Mario's upon the death of her parents and he had allayed her apprehensions, he had invited her to his farewell dinner. He was due to leave for Berlin to take up a post as senior lecturer, although days later, the position unexpectedly fell through. She hadn't wished to attend, uncharacteristically preferring the confines of Gore Street to any sort of outing, but Phoebe insisted, encouraging her to dress up for the occasion and enjoy herself.

The dinner was a strange affair. They were a party of twenty at La Travera, an Italian restaurant in Southgate, seated round a table overlooking the Yarra river. For a fine art lecturer, he had very con-servative-looking friends. All had adopted the straight hair and austere attire of the Nineties. Harriet's untamed black hair alone was enough to make her feel out of place. She had on a vintage flapper dress of shimmering red, thick black tights and flat leather shoes. She felt like a relic, but defiant with it, since it was she, and not they, who displayed originality. She who, in point of fact, portrayed to the world the artist that she was.

As the evening wore on, upon the strain of being in such staid company, she drank a little more Sauvignon Blanc than she was used to. Dessert was still to arrive. The boor on her left put his hand on her thigh and she promptly removed it, turning her face to the shrew on her right, who had pecked at her food all evening and interjected in conversations around the table in a high-pitched chirrup, espousing some obtuse opinion on whatever it was being discussed.

The woman unexpectedly directed the same haughty manner at Harriet. 'You'll have heard about the scandal, I take it?'

Harriet had no idea what she was talking about. She scanned the table in search of Fritz, thinking the woman must be referring to him.

'Who would have thought that a satanic death cult could thrive in Mont Albert.'

'Mont Albert?'

'Don't you read the newspapers, dear?'

'Not recently.'

'Multiple arrests. One or two high profile types. Speculation that the daughter of a former professor had a narrow escape.'

She felt the world that was the table close in on her. She was struggling to think of an excuse to leave when she felt a tap on her shoulder. It was Fritz inviting her outside with a smile and a 'Cigarette?' She stood without hesitation.

Once outside he said, 'I thought you needed rescuing.'

She laughed and went to lean on the wall beside the river, taking in the buildings on the other bank, solid and proud, the shimmying reflections of the city lights on the water, the watery gloom beneath the arches of Princes Bridge. The evening was cool and a soft breeze blew.

'I'll miss you,' she said, caught in the moment.

'Me too.'

'Halfway round the world...' She caught his expression and let the sentence slide away. He seemed urgent, the concern in his eyes unnerving.

'There's something I must tell you before I leave.'

'Fritz, I don't…'

'About Wilhelm.'

'Oh?'

She made to turn away when he said, 'I think you were right to be paranoid.'

'What do you mean?'

He hesitated. 'He's got himself mixed up in something.' He glanced at his watch then back at the restaurant and she wondered if that was all he would say.

'Fritz,' she said, 'just tell me.'

'They're called the Order of Shannon,' he said quietly.

'And they are?' she asked.

'I would describe them as an occult sect of the lowest order. Purported to be involved in the abduction of a minor. Just allegations, mind. A body was never found.'

'When was this?' she said with sudden alarm, thinking back to the scandal in the newspaper.

'About a year ago.'

She felt relieved. She took a sideways step but he reached for her arm.

'Look, it's only a rumour,' he said quickly. 'But I know Wilhelm. I mean, I knew Wilhelm. No, that isn't true. I knew of Wilhelm. Back in Munich. Even then, in his teens, he had some weird interests.'

'Lots of boys have weird interests,' she said doubtfully.

'Perhaps,' he said then he went on in earnest. 'But when an interest becomes a belief, is given credence by a set of apparent truths, is enshrined in dogma and ritual.' He shrugged. 'Well, I thought you should know.'

Yet it was all conjecture. Conjecture perhaps motivated by an enduring resentment, Fritz having never transcended being usurped. Standing there while he finished his cigarette she hadn't the heart to tell him that things would never have worked between them, Wilhelm or no Wilhelm. That he had been a dalliance, nothing more. From that first encounter at the Bauhaus concert she had found him as she did now, a little comical and far too serious.

Besides, she already knew Wilhelm's occult interests were far reaching. He had made matters esoteric the centre of his doctoral inquiry and had been writing papers and contributing chapters to books on the subject ever since. His ambition was to see established in Melbourne a graduate school of esoteric studies, an ambition thus far showing no promise of success. While the history of the occult was a growing specialism in Europe, funding for things in any manner religious in Australian universities was being funnelled, he said, into indigenous areas. He complained of this so often it was practically the only thing he did say in her presence other than criticisms of her mothering. It made sense that he would join an occult society. It might be part of his research. She could imagine him critiquing the society in a lengthy piece in some journal of esotericism. In this light, Fritz's insinuations seemed preposterous and she reassured herself that in all likelihood Wilhelm had joined that occult group of ill repute simply out of scholarly interest.

For all her justifications, a claw of suspicion anchored in her mind on her way home on the tram and she began to wonder if there was any substance to Fritz's claims. If his occult interests extended beyond the academic, would he then allow himself to be drawn into whatever rituals the group performed?

She took a deep breath, attributing her thoughts to the dark of the night and the company on the tram: the brooding man standing near the driver sneaking glances at the young woman seated nearby; the louts at the back eyeing the other passengers with contempt.

Then again, Wilhelm was too doting, too indulgent and too furtive. Those whispered conversations across the kitchen table less than innocent.

They were all impossible thoughts. She had allowed her

misgivings to grow like ghouls and haunt her imagination and it had to stop. And when she alighted the tram at the corner of Gore Street she sent them on their way.

Even so, after that night she was watchful.

Before her parents' deaths, she had accepted that Wilhelm was one of those men over-zealous with affection for his daughter, as if he had fathered Aphrodite herself, and was forever beholden to the glory of his creation. It was a love that was an extension of self-love. His attachment had always been exclusive: Harriet the unwanted. Yet she had never questioned his motives before that night with Fritz, never seriously considered, not for the seven years of Ginny's life, that he was in any way untoward. She had been ignoring for months the black lights that would flicker at the corners of her eyes whenever he sat with Ginny in the kitchen. It was counterintuitive that a man who loved his daughter so much would then wish to do her harm.

The weeks that followed were a tumult of inner wrangling. It was hard to admit, even to herself, that she had never enjoyed Ginny. Not in the way other parents do. Games, outings, parties, sleepovers, she viewed them as impingements. Caring for Ginny had always competed with her creativity, her attention at best half on her daughter. And her poor attitude to her mothering allowed her to assuage her misgivings about Wilhelm. She would reassure herself that Wilhelm was undoubtedly the better parent. That was certainly what Ginny had thought, and was still thinking, despite that he had never been at home anywhere near as much as she. He gave Ginny quality time. Whenever he was home she had his undivided attention. Harriet had been an absent presence, filled as she was with her own creative preoccupations. Fritz's disclosure couldn't change her view of herself. Certainly not enough to take the drastic action she later did.

It was the letter that finally changed her attitude.

One Saturday evening, about two months after Fritz's fare-well dinner, she had on her Bauhaus album, loud, to draw some synaesthetic inspiration for her derivation of a Hirschfeld-Mack. Ginny was in bed and Wilhelm at the university putting the final touches on a conference paper. It had been a wild week of storms and although the sun had begun to shine, gale force winds still blew. Doing her best to ignore the rattling of the front door, she went to the kitchen to replenish a jar of murky water before cleaning a brush and as she passed by the table on her way to the sink, a book fell to the floor. It was his copy of *The Rosicrucian Cosmo-Conception*. She must have knocked it. She went to put it back on the table when the letter slipped from the dust jacket.

The content of the letter appeared harmless. Formal in tone, it welcomed Wilhelm into the Order of Shannon. A privilege to have someone of his calibre, the letter going on to mention that with initial formalities successfully completed they were looking forward to his attendance at their next meeting, which seemed to imply that he had passed some sort of test. And at that point 'Kick in the Eye' began, triggering her synaesthesia, but the lights weren't the pastel hues she normally saw when hearing Bauhaus; these were black, iridescent and black. She stood still, watching. Then she slipped the letter back inside the dust jacket and placed the book on the table. Suddenly she found Bauhaus overwhelming and she turned off the record player. The front door's rattle was joined by an insistent juddering of the sash window, taking up the silence.

She heard movement upstairs and thought Ginny might have awoken. She climbed the treads in twos, flicked on the landing light and peered into Ginny's room. She was asleep.

Then she went and stood in the doorway of the main bedroom. The room felt cold. The curtains were drawn against the night. She thought she saw them billow slightly. She stared into the dimness and noticed his bulging suitcase on the floor. She again saw in the centre of her vision the flickering black lights. Only this time the lights were not triggered by sound. Her first thought was that Wilhelm had packed too many clothes. He always packed at the last minute, but this time he had done it early. He was due to depart for his conference in Amsterdam the following Monday, catching a Sunday afternoon flight.

He knew that she had planned to meet Rosalind for lunch on Sunday and return before he was due to leave.

In a sudden rush it occurred to her that he was planning to leave sooner and take Ginny with him.

Her world cleaved at the thought. She was no longer who she was. She had just lost both her parents. She was not about to lose her daughter.

She had no idea what to do. Her mind was a whirligig. Then she realised with something like relief that if Wilhelm was planning to bolt with his daughter, then she would beat him to it.

She paced the three strides between the bed and the wardrobe and devised a plan.

Then she stood on the threshold of their bedroom, eyeing his packed suitcase, wondering at all the other women who stay, women who compromise truth and reality for false security. Poor or rich it didn't seem to matter, yet she was a little self-disgusted that the inheritance had given her the impetus. It seemed to be that simple. And that material. She suspected that other women put comfort high on their list of criteria for staying. Though she could hardly call Gore Street comfort. She puzzled over what had been keeping her there when she was that unhappy. Not love. She didn't love him. Loyalty perhaps, tradition, or shame.

On that Saturday, as night drew in and Ginny was alone in her bedroom along the hall, Harriet went downstairs and took the letter from the dust jacket of Wilhelm's tome on the Rosicrucians and she found his camera and took several photos, removing the film and slipping it inside her clutch bag. She left the letter open on the table.

Phoebe was due in an hour to give her verdict on the Hirschfeld-Mack. An hour to pack.

She had taken Ginny to her parents' weekender in Sassafras. Wilhelm could easily have found out where she was but not immediately, not unless he went to the police. And she had suspected he wouldn't do that. It turned out fortuitous that in nine years he had never once visited that weekender or her parent's house in Mont Albert. It seemed that he had despised them as much as they him.

The one time they were forced into each other's company was shortly after Ginny was born. Claudia and James Brassington-Smythe would never understand their daughter's predilections. That she had gone against their wishes and pursued a life as an artist was beyond their comprehension. She knew she had disappointed them, suspected they held out hope that she would grow up and come to her senses, but when she moved into Gore Street at the age of twenty-six to live with a German-born student doing a doctorate in the occult they were mortified.

Claudia and James were the sort of practicing Christians who thought the occult was devil worship. A fact that had caused Rosalind to keep from them her own views on the matter, only revealing them to Harriet when she was sure she could be trusted.

Harriet did not share Rosalind's discretion. Outspoken and rebellious, she had made no secret of her dalliance into the realms of Theosophy. She did have the prudence not to betray Rosalind, so her parents had always suspected she had been influenced by Phoebe. A misconception reinforced when she had explained upon her parents' inquiry that she had met Wilhelm at one of Phoebe's functions. And why, when her parents visited Gore Street that one and only time to see the baby and Wilhelm brushed past them on his way out the door, they had shuddered.

'So, that's him.'

In the recollecting, it occurred to Harriet she might have stayed with him all those years out of spite.

The thought of explaining the story to Ginny made her heart palpitate. She turned to Phoebe, who looked impatient to leave the studio.

'You owe her an explanation, Harriet.'

'What could I possibly tell her?'

'The truth,' she said as she made for the door.

'What woman would want to know such a thing? Her entire perception of her father would be shattered.'

'I can't believe you think that.'

'Better she hate me. At least it's the status quo.'

'Just tell her.' And she left.

Harriet went to the window. The light was still shining in Ginny's room. The canopy high above was silhouetted against a haze of moonlight. The wind had finally dropped. She heard the throaty growl of a possum, saw next door's cat darting across the lawn, then all was still.

Perhaps Phoebe was right. Ginny ought to know the whole truth before she went off in pursuit of her father. It might even stop her, but Harriet doubted that. Ginny was too headstrong. Besides, what Harriet had to offer by way of explanation might help Ginny understand her motives but would do nothing to quash her curiosity. If anything, it would give it strength.

Damn the past and the ugly way it crept up on you from behind.

Tuesday, 4 April 2017

Fernley Cottage

Judith was drawn into the desolation. The felled iron bark. The black stubble. The sanguine sap. She thought about adding new growth. Perhaps a touch of green about the stump base. But she couldn't bring herself to put it there. Besides, some scenes were best left to express themselves uninhibited by the artist's manipulations. The work would sell, she was sure of it. She would take it to the Aussie bistro in the morning.

She thrust her hands in her trouser pockets. Twilight, and outside all was still. She looked out at the silent scene, trees dark presences, the sky a pale glow. A shadow swept behind the wood shed and into a nearby tree. She thought it might be an owl.

She knew she should eat but she wasn't hungry. Listless, she left the studio and went to the living room.

There was a nip in the air but she couldn't be bothered to light the fire. Instead she opened her laptop and scrolled through the Forum's threads, stopping to read a post of Franken Form's on the Order of Shannon. Her flesh broke out in cold tingles.

Celestial Petal called the Order 'grovers' and when Fred Spice asked for elucidation, Fagbutt Oilcan came in with a link to a Bohemian Grove exposé by none other than Lawrence Pike.

She didn't follow it.

'They're a cabal,' Fagbutt said.

Celestial Petal followed with a brief outline of a ritual, all black robes and owls, centred around the burning of an effigy. 'It's called the Cremation of Care.'

'And what do these grovers do?' Fred Spice asked with what she gleaned was a touch of irony.

Fagbutt answered with a string of links she didn't bother with.

The insinuations were grim and she didn't want to believe that those conspiracy theorists with all their gullibility and whacky ideas were right about anything. She wanted to believe that satanic rituals were the stuff of horror novels, that cults of that type were rare and revolved around a megalomaniacal psychopath with enough charisma to draw in the undiscerning and the weak. She wanted to believe that judges and politicians and academics were too educated, too rational, too decent for such vile interests.

Then Ashtray Petrolstick commented that the Templars were running the joint and anyone who says otherwise is a nonce.

Ashtray Petrolstick? Could that be Zol? Madeleine had mentioned Zol was obsessed with a forum filled with conspiracy nuts. That was his username. No one else would call themselves Ashtray Petrolstick, surely?

The knowledge of his presence right there on her laptop was so repellent she logged out of the Forum straight away. It was fourteen minutes past six and she was left wondering how else to fill her evening.

She went to her inbox. There were no new emails. Bethany's sat about halfway down the list.

Bethany had meant well. She was a concerned friend. Her email was filled with love heart emoticons. No mention of Hannah. An open invitation to lunch at the Aussie bistro. That perhaps Judith would consider a session with Viv the clairvoyant who might have messages from the other side. No, she wouldn't. Not ever. She wasn't ready for any of it. She wanted to be alone, although she knew, dimly, that alone was not the best way to be.

She filed the email in a folder marked Bethany and noticed

another, sent about six months after the opening, when Viv had made those strange remarks about the triptych. In the email, Bethany said she felt compelled to let Judith know that regrettably she had had to part ways with the silver birches. Viv had warned her a number of times that she would do well not to have that energy hanging in her rooms so she had sold the works to a passerby from Australia, who had gazed at them through the window for an age before entering the rooms, having just had lunch at the Aussie bistro. The gentleman in question enthused for so long that Bethany had been concerned he was a touch insane. And when he asked if they were for sale, explaining that they were just the thing for his wife for their wedding anniversary, Bethany had taken the opportunity to rid herself of the man and the works. Bethany said she thought Judith would at least be pleased to know they had been rehomed, and she was very sorry to have to tell her, but she didn't want her to receive a shock if she popped in and was confronted by a blank wall.

It felt strange knowing those paintings had been shipped to Australia and she wondered where they had ended up. Not in the Wimmera, for surely no one living in a landscape like that would want hanging on their wall a triptych of silver birches depicted in sterile black and white, with the merest hint of grey.

She let her imagination drift in the land she loved, even though she knew she would never go there, and she returned to her studio and replaced the ironbark scene with another canvas: a stricken scene with a dam bereft of water, its base of clay cracked, tessellated. A stand of dead river gums. A thirsty dog. An old fibro cement hut falling on its stumps. And a cattleman on a horse. All that, beneath a dome of blue and cloudless sky.

Dynamic Intensification

The stumps of old growth mountain ash stood like head stones bearing dates centuries old: the dead at rest; the tree ferns at their base green bouquets. The soft grass in the shade still bore last night's dew and a cool wind blew from the south. Ginny drew her cotton scarf up around her neck. She was taking a walk along the lane by the creek, ignoring Harriet's bid of appeasement earlier that morning, when she suggested Ginny join her in the gallery to help hang Phoebe's latest finds. Ginny had no idea what use she would be and didn't much feel like her mother's company.

More than a month had passed since Christmas Eve and her announcement that she planned to find her father. Then Rosalind had gone off to her conference in Bournemouth, leaving Ginny consumed by questions. She had applied for a visa, which had arrived in the morning's post. She could, she should book a flight and go and see Fritz, demand he tell her what he knew. Yet she was hesitant.

The sun broke free of a cloud and shone through the canopy. A plump woman wearing a wide brim hat that obscured her face approached with a black dog straining on its leash. 'Morning,' the woman said cheerily as she passed and Ginny realised she was Veronica's mother, Mrs Hunnacot. She smiled and returned the greeting.

It occurred to her she hadn't seen Veronica or Poppy since Christmas, turning down their invitations on the pretext of gigs, sometimes real, other times fake. She knew her reactions were childish but in the days following her outburst her friends had taken sides with her mother, which she thought they had no right to do. What then, of their loyalty to her?

'We think you might be obsessing,' Veronica said when Ginny had swung by with their presents.

They were standing in the Pargiters' doorway, dressed in onesies and matching bandanas.

'You need to let it go,' Veronica said sagely.

'We're worried about you,' Poppy said.

'Ginny.' Veronica folded her arms beneath her ample breasts. 'You've gone all strange.'

Ginny observed their outfits and made no comment.

'Come round for a pamper,' Poppy said, her eyes filled with concern. 'I can do your hair.'

'And I'll do your nails.'

'Thanks,' was all Ginny could think to say. A part of her wanted to confide, craved the release of the unburdening, but Veronica and Poppy wouldn't understand, they couldn't possibly, and then she would be stuck offering clarifying remarks and fielding wellmeaning advice.

She could only imagine what they would have come up with had she mentioned her dream. Out would come the dream dictionaries and the comparisons with their own dreams, and those contents residing in her depths that kept breaking through the surface of her awareness, demanding to be known, screaming for her attention and offering up no recognisable explanation in their wake, would be rendered meaningless. She would rather not know and be puzzled than invest belief in a falsehood. There was something sacred about the unconscious, of that she was certain, a greater self existing out of reach of her lesser self, which was stuck in a state of perpetual bewilderment, bumbling through life forever looking in the wrong direction. If you want to look out, look in, she thought, and if you want to look in, look out, but first you have to learn how to look.

She was having the dream with greater frequency. It was more or less the same each time. The cave, the dark, the looming presence, the flickering lights, the down draught stroking her back and the slow realisation that she was naked. Always, she was unable to move. In last night's episode, something had passed before her, or someone. There was a smell, aromatic but not incense. She heard low murmurs in deep voices, rhythmic and repetitive. She had no idea what was being said. A smouldering dark-red five-pointed star appeared in her near vision and she knew it was a branding iron, sensed the searing heat of it.

She had awoken to Count Basie playing downstairs. Her mother had taken to commandeering the record player. She would turn up the volume and play old school jazz from daybreak until she took off to her studio. They were barely speaking and only civilities. Ginny spent most of her days in her room, practising on her Roland.

There were few gigs to occupy her or indeed to earn her money, which she used to justify the delay in her travel plans despite having enough for the airfare in her savings. That morning, like every other morning for the whole of the last six weeks, she had slipped out of bed wondering why she was still in her mother's house. Harriet clearly didn't want her there. Probably had never wanted her. And the same narrative of the sad young Ginny ran through her mind, a Ginny little loved by a mother who had snatched her from a doting father. Every morning as the narrative played itself out, she searched for clues, insights, understanding. None came. Just an incessant questioning of her mother's motives.

Her grandparents had died suddenly in a terrible accident. That accounted for a mind filled with grief. A certain irrationality. That she had inherited the entire estate on the condition that she leave Wilhelm was motive enough only for a woman who put wealth before love, which in her mother's case was not hard to imagine. Obviously, she didn't love him. It was remarkable that she hadn't left him sooner. And she might have left her daughter behind as well since she clearly didn't love her either. The sudden and dramatic nature of the event demanded justification. And most troubling of all was the inexplicable fact that her father had failed to come and find her.

She heard a rustle in the bushes beside the lane. She stopped and listened. A bird burst into song. She followed its melody until it fell silent and she continued on.

She thought she remembered music in her dream. Maybe not. Remembering a dream was a dubious process. So easily and quickly the mind adds and deletes in a frantic effort to reconstruct the ephemeral. Perhaps she thought there was music because she wanted it there. What music? Her own?

She had been practising her nine new songs every day since she wrote them. She was growing into them, giving them shape, colour, embellishments. She was pleased with the way they had turned out and the one thing out of the collaboration she was looking forward to was the recording.

Phoebe had contacted Tommo the Tank, who had a recording studio in Bayswater, and passed on his details to Ginny. Phoebe was a remarkable woman: practical, organised and generous with it. Yet it was impossible to fathom what motivated her. She never let down her guard. She was unwavering in her affection for Harriet too, who must at times be a burden. She knew Harriet confided in her friend and wondered how much Phoebe knew. Yet there was no point in asking. She would never betray her friend. Besides, it would be counterproductive. And there would be no prising the truth from Harriet once she discovered that her daughter had quizzed her friend.

She kept walking until she reached the intersection of Nobles Lane, the place where Poppy had wanted to turn back upon surveying the incline. Ginny headed up the lane undeterred. She pictured her mother in the gallery, alone with her Wessex series. Nothing spoke more of an artist at the base of a decline. Not even Phoebe could shift them.

Something about the steep rise spurred her to adopt a brisker pace, despite the ache in her thighs, the quickness of her breath. A hill surmounted was an accomplishment of its own, the reward simple, and satisfying.

Her mother had her own hill to climb but she remained stuck somewhere at the bottom. Ginny knew she was struggling to create the nine paintings, although she was banned from the studio so there was no way of assessing progress. She felt a curious pity for her mother, constrained as she was by her adherence to Kandinsky's absolutes.

Kandinsky, it seemed to her, was nothing more than a born-again, an evangelist on a mission to impose his views on others. One synaesthetic experience and a soupçon of theosophical thought and he was off rationalising his experience and turning synaesthesia into a bunch of rules, as if he alone were the conduit for this revelation, a revelation that must thenceforth be transmitted to others, clothed in *his*, the great Kandinsky's, special formulation. Like so many born agains, he turned knowing into knowledge. He was an adherent who sought literal representations of the abstract, his insights fixed, absolute. Her mother, an acolyte, would never transcend that locked-in reality. Thence she was doomed to regurgitate.

Ginny feared that Harriet would never understand the extraordinary mysteriousness of creativity and inspiration. That ineffable drawing forth from within, that immersion in the process, fluid, loose, free. A process in which truth was no longer the goal, and reality became metaphoric and fecund.

What mattered to Ginny was immediate knowing and she held fast to it with the conviction of the scholar carrying forth the passion of a new idea. These were her thesis findings and nothing could have more greatly sharpened her understanding than those three doctoral years. Three years spent proving Kandinsky's ilk wrong, although that was not what she had set out to do at the time.

Ginny felt adamant that once the extraordinary mysteriousness of creativity was cast as knowledge, no matter how spiritually profound the insight, it would attract adherents like a wasp trap. It baffled her that any and every artist didn't share her understanding. It was so obvious. The artist, like the composer, needed flow and flexibility, not rules. Artistic composition, like musical composition, was a transformative experience. Hadn't she been transformed a little each time she wrote something new? The process of composition offered fresh insights into who she was, cultivating poise, reflection.

She stopped at a bend and looked up into the cathedral of trees and thought of its human interpretation—a church. That home of religious music and of inflexibility, at once glorious and pristine and intended to bewitch the masses. Composers, like architects, strove for godly heights. There was something undeniably exquisite and hauntingly evocative in the works of Christian mystics like Hildegard von Bingen and Thomas Tallis, composers whose quests were revealed so perfectly in a church, itself a custom-built performance space. She heard voices rising to meet vaulted ceilings and descending again; disembodied voices, invoking awe and wonder in listeners, yet constraining composers, who were forced to merge each phrase with the descending echo of the last.

She continued on her way, giving a wide berth to the blowflies that were gathered around a pile of dog mess.

Blowflies. Dog mess.

She laughed inwardly. Composers used anything as a source of inspiration, but their works would be hollow imitations had the composer not been able to invoke some sort of mystical awareness, which might be hard to achieve if flies and dog mess were the source, but still.

As far as Ginny was concerned, works of mystical inspiration were timeless, revered to this day by wannabe mystics and admirers of the divine. Poppy played Tallis on her way to work each day. She said it put her in the right mood for fantasy fiction. Music moves the listener, touches the emotions, fills and swells, elevates or depresses. Lost in his born-again wonderment after his synaesthetic episode at a Wagner concert, Kandinsky wanted art to emulate music. Wanted a painting to move the viewer as much as a song moved the listener. How often had her mother opined this in one of her many unsolicited Kandinsky lectures, usually after her third glass of Sauvignon Blanc and therefore never that coherent.

Ginny knew Kandinsky had set himself an impossible task. No painting could ever have the power to consume the emotions the way music does. Sound envelops. Of the senses, it is our hearing that is the pathway between our emotional state of being and the world outside ourselves; a sharp sound startles, bird song awakens, a babbling brook soothes.

Her stride lengthened. Sweat broke out on her brow. She found she was panting. She forged ahead at a determined pace, her thoughts wrestling with synaesthesia, that blurring confusion of the senses. Synaesthesia, she decided, was an altered state of awareness and not of itself a mystical experience, and therefore belonged to the mundane and not the spiritual. Although she knew that it was the individual's response to an experience that made it mystical and not the experience itself. A bell might ring a thousand times a day, then someone happens by and has a unique engagement with the bell ring. Light shining through trees, a certain song, anything can trigger a mystical experience in one person on one occasion and never again. Upon repetition, the awe recedes and the exceptional becomes ordinary. And this was Kandinsky's and Harriet's mistake. The episode that evoked a response of awe and wonderment was merely something experienced in a mystical manner. Kandinsky mistakenly believed he had touched the divine and he thenceforth became a missionary, capturing the hearts and minds of his followers and filling them up with contrivances and arbitrary correspondences.

But what riled her most was the elitism that came with it. As if Kandinsky and his ilk were privy to superior knowledge, that he was part of an elect, at odds with and out to convert the art scene of his day. Springing to her mind the ornately framed portraits on her mother's dresser and mantelpiece, in which Kandinsky's righteousness blazed out of him, Ginny easily imagined him looking down from his lofty heights at all representational art, just as the academics at her university scorned popular music as trash for the masses.

It was the sort of elitism in the art world that caused a Rothko to sell at auction for over forty-six million American dollars. Or was that another sort of elitism altogether—the elitism of the grotesquely rich? The work in question essentially a plain blue stripe on a plain yellow background. To put that kind of dollar value on a stripe; Phoebe would be incensed. Perhaps Rothko was drawing on Kandinsky's colour theory. Ginny knew the colour theory well. Harriet once had a chart pinned above the bench in her studio and Ginny had attended a lecture on the correspondences of music and colour in her third year. Maybe Rothko intended for the viewer to hear flutes and cellos playing across a fanfare of trumpets. Or viewers were to feel a deep blue mourning in the face of an attack of blind yellow rage. Since Rothko was a Russian Jew, it could even be said that his work depicted, in the most abstract way possible, the Holocaust. Although she had no idea if Rothko was a fan of Kandinsky, and she sensed that he wasn't. In fact, it was hard to imagine an artist as independently minded as Rothko adhering to a set of silly rules. From what she had seen of the work in the news on her laptop, it was as if his vast fields of colour were meant to mesmerise the viewer. Maybe that's all Rothko intended. For spectators to lose themselves in his work.

And who, save the chosen few, the inner circle of the art world, would know any of that. To the ordinary viewer, the painting remained a single blue stripe on a plain yellow background.

She stopped and struggled to hold her breath as a ute screamed past her in second gear, whorls of dust billowing in its wake. Before the word 'bogan' had fully formed she rejected it. Who was she to judge? She felt a moment of self-disgust, knowing she had succumbed to the same elitism, isolated in her North Melbourne flat. And she had instinctively rebelled against her own prejudices, shunning that very same elitism rooted in her heart, in that moment when she paused to watch Garth busk. Perhaps some moral part of her propelled her to Garth so that she might learn the value of humility. And not, as she had previously justified to herself, a reactive and somewhat desperate need to balance the seclusion of her doctoral years.

She reached the crest, panting hard, and she stopped until her heart and her breathing slowed. Then she followed the lane to the intersection, regretting her earlier decision not to take the footpath along the creek bank that would have led to an entrance to the Alfred Nicholas Gardens down by the lake. She could have wended her way up to the top and exited about where she stood and avoided the dust kicked up by that ute.

Once she had cornered the next bend she changed her mind. On the opposite side of Sherbrooke Road, the parking area was full of cars, and sightseers were crossing the road in both directions, entering and leaving the gardens through their stately wrought iron gates. It was Saturday, the gardens at that time of year full of day trippers eager to walk through the shrubberies, the plantings of majestic trees, the ornamental lake, an entire hillside of native ash and ferns given over to acres of the exotic and the picturesque.

She passed by the gates and pressed on, the walk no longer the pleasant isolation of a little used lane, although the footpath was set back from the road.

She supposed she would always set herself apart from the throng. Her preference for solitude less an attitude of mind, more an inner need. In retrospect, the isolation of her North Melbourne flat suited her well. She wasn't a herd animal. Neither, she told herself sternly, was she a snob. Although she knew that the academics in the school of music had formed their exclusive group as a shield. She had done the same in her own fashion: a club of one.

It was a family trait. Her mother lived not in a club but a bubble blown up and maintained by Phoebe, Rosalind, and a fat inheritance. If she had to fend for herself in the art world she wouldn't survive. She had barely evolved since the eighties, her heyday, her homage to Matisse heyday. Although she had been living not in the Eighties but in the Twenties, oblivious to the trends and paradigm shifts ever since. She was scathing of postmodernism and technology. She didn't own a mobile or a computer. The Internet was to her something abnormal. Yet Ginny was sure this stuck fast attitude of mind had ossified Harriet's muse.

She came to an intersection and turned towards Sassafras and her mother's gallery. Now she walked beside the main road that divided the mountain in two and traffic whizzed by en route to the foothills and the vast suburban sprawl of Melbourne's east. The wind gusted, pushing her along. Feeling the unseasonal chill of it she tightened her cotton scarf round her neck.

There were other reasons for her mother's thwarted artistic flow. Not least that the whole collaboration served a selfish purpose. It had been a corrupt desire from the start. Harriet had claimed from the inception that the exhibition would help Ginny, that it would take her mind off Garth and lift her spirits, when in truth Harriet was motivated by self-gain. She had even admitted it herself as a means of persuasion. 'Good for the gallery,' she had said. Since Ginny had moved back, Harriet had not sold one painting other than the piece Rosalind had bought, and Phoebe had provided not one commission. Ginny might have felt pity for her, were it not that she felt thoroughly used.

She rounded a long arc of road where The Crescent veered off to the right and wended its way down the mountain. Past The Crescent, the footpath was cut into an overgrown slope below the road. She entered the tunnel of green. On her right, houses clung to the incline, their driveways impossibly steep, the forest unfolding beneath them like a blanket thrown over a sleeping body.

She emerged at an intersection and the beginning of the small parades of shops that was Sassafras. She slowed her pace to a stroll, pausing outside a boutique that sold fine woollen clothing ideal for the cooler mountain weather. A woman in a silk suit and matching hat stepped out onto the pavement, purchases in hand, wearing the self-satisfied look of the happy shopper. Ahead, clientele trickled in and out of Agatha's tearooms. If her mother was a relic then she was in good company up here in the ranges that abounded in dabblers of the quaint.

She found Harriet in the back room. The walls were bare and paintings, lined up shoulder to shoulder, skirted the floor. A 'You took your time' look appeared in her mother's face but she said, 'There you are.'

'I took a detour along the creek.'

'To clear your mind, I suppose.' She sounded uncharacteristically grim.

'Not at all,' Ginny said, thinking the silence between them better than the carping. Whenever one of them made an effort to be nice, the other swiped it aside. And she hadn't cleared her mind. She had filled it with uncharitable thoughts and was chastened at the sight of Harriet, still her mother after all, hurt and trying not to show it.

'I think this one would go well in the centre of the wall.' Harriet gestured at the painting that held her gaze. 'Eye-catching as people walk through from the main room.'

Ginny viewed the painting. 'I prefer the one beside it. The one on the left.'

'Really?' Harriet seemed about to go on then changed her mind.

The painting Harriet favoured was a lively expressionist beach scene. A sun lounger, a large umbrella, a sand castle, a bucket and spade, an assortment of beach balls, and a few boats on the water, all rendered in a shivaree of blues, yellows and reds. Her mother was right; it did catch the eye.

194 ~ Isobel Blackthorn

The one Ginny favoured depicted a woman and a child in a forest, the child looking up at the canopy, the woman's gaze off away, her expression expectant. Pre-Raphaelite in style and Ginny found herself drawn into the scene, imagined herself the person the woman was waiting for, then she gazed up into the canopy as if she were the child. She preferred the style, the intricate detail, its play on her imagination.

Without a word, her mother took the beach scene and hung it in the centre of the wall. Then she took Ginny's preference and hung it on the opposite wall, almost but not quite facing the beach scene. 'There,' she said, still avoiding Ginny's gaze. 'We can each build a display around them.' It was her way of resolving their differences. Since they would never agree on anything, it seemed they were to hang their individualities on separate walls.

They began to select from the other works, the silence broken by occasional murmurs of 'This would do better on your wall I think.' And sharing the space, as he had done since she moved back home, was the spectre of Wilhelm.

Eventually, Ginny could endure the atmosphere no longer. 'Something's been puzzling me,' she said tentatively.

'What is it?' Harriet said, nudging the bottom corner of the beach scene.

'When did you find out Wilhelm was in England?'

Harriet sighed. 'Fritz told me. But I've no idea how long Wilhelm had been there.' She remained where she stood, facing the beach scene. 'Now, when was that?' she said, with a surprising willingness to talk. 'Around the millennium, I think.'

'So, he could have been there a while.'

'Yes.'

'Almost from when you abducted me.'

Harriet swung round. 'Must you be so inflammatory? I didn't abduct you!'

'That's what it felt like. Still feels like.'

She stood squarely, hands on hips. 'Sit down,' she said.

'I don't feel like sitting down.'

'Sit down.'

She sat.

Harriet remained standing, her hands now clasped together, her eyes imperious beneath her voluminous black hair, yet Ginny detected apprehension in her manner. 'I did what I thought was right,' she said. 'I knew it would hurt you. But he left me no choice.'

'Of course you had a choice.'

'Will you listen?'

'I'm listening.'

'You're being snide.'

'Just tell me.'

'That weekend he was leaving for a conference in Amsterdam.'

'And?'

'I was to be out the day of the flight, returning to you before he left.'

'That tells me nothing.'

'That was the Sunday. On the Saturday, he went to his office to work, leaving me alone with you. I saw that he'd already started packing. He never packed the day before. He always, without exception, packed at the last minute. And there was his suitcase, all packed and ready. A very heavy suitcase. Far too much for just a few days.'

'He might have wanted options,' Ginny said sarcastically. 'The weather might have been variable.'

'Wilhelm was not the sort to care about such things. He was a habitual dresser. Always the same suit and shirts no matter what the weather or season.'

'That is hardly a reason to do what you did.' Was this the best she could manage? A suitcase?

'It was a combination of things. Fritz tried to warn me about him. I thought he was jealous so I didn't take him seriously. But he insisted that Wilhelm had deviant interests. That when he was a teenager, he was mixed up with some sect.'

'No wonder you dismissed the rumours. That's ridiculous. Heaps of teenagers get mixed up with all sorts. Drugs, alcohol, petty crime.'

'This was different apparently.'

'Even so.'

'Ginny, I assumed his interest in the occult was purely intellectual. It was something we had in common. And I never thought of him as a practitioner. Then I found the letter.'

'What letter?'

'It was tucked in the dust jacket of a book. I found it when I knocked the book.'

'What did it say?'

'It was from the Order of Shannon, welcoming him into the fold. I knew nothing of the Order, but Fritz said they'd been implicated in a scandal involving a small child. A girl. About seven she was, your age at the time. I don't know the details.'

Ginny was astonished that after nearly two decades all her mother offered up were scant excuses. 'But you decided the sect was culpable,' she said.

'It reminded me of something Rosalind had said.' She hesitated. 'About Lemurians.'

'For god's sake!' Ginny said, scarcely able to believe her ears.

Harriet ignored her and went on. 'She said some Lemurians were sadistic occultists bent on inflicting pain and suffering on others to stimulate their spiritual growth.'

'And you put two and two together, and made ten thousand.'

'I was mad with grief.'

'Is that right?'

'What do you mean?'

'Don't forget the caveat,' Ginny said in a low voice.

Harriet seemed shocked. 'You know about that?'

'That's what this is really about, isn't it? Your inheritance.' Ginny stood up. 'You're unbelievable. All that talk of suitcases and letters and you were just looking for an excuse to claim what was yours. I was just a pawn.'

'I was trying to protect you.'

'Rubbish!'

'Then why didn't I leave you with him?' Harriet snapped.

'I wish you had.'

Harriet took a backward step. Her face glowed red and her brow was slimy with sweat. 'And why, pray tell, didn't he try to find you?' she said, her voice shrill. 'Have you thought about that? He could have called the police. Tracked me down. But he didn't. Instead he disappeared. So much for your close bond. Frankly I think he realised I was on to him and he didn't want a scandal.'

'More supposition,' Ginny said, not moving, not allowing her mother to walk away.

'No. Not supposition,' Harriet said, regaining her poise. 'I left the letter on the kitchen table before I left.'

'He may not have noticed.'

'He would have noticed.' She was emphatic.

'He was probably stricken,' Ginny cried, not quite believing it. 'My poor father. No wonder you didn't tell me.' She went to the doorway, turning back to glower. 'I'm going to find him. I have a visa and now I'm going to book a flight. And if I do find him, be prepared, as I might well not come back.'

She marched through the gallery, slamming the door behind her on her way outside. She headed up the street in a haze and almost knocked over Rosalind, who had stepped out from the tea-rooms as she passed by.

'I'm sorry,' she said quickly, eyeing the pavement.

'What on Earth is the matter?'

Ginny lifted her gaze. 'Go in there,' she said, pointing back at the gallery. 'She'll tell you all about it, I'm sure. About my father the Lemurian.'

'Oh dear.'

'You knew! Not you as well. It's a conspiracy of silence. How could you?'

'You don't understand.'

'I think I understand very well.' And she left Rosalind and strode on, taking the quick way back to the house.

Harriet pulled her handkerchief from the pocket of her dress and dabbed her brow, then set about straightening each painting in the room. She felt by turns confused, infuriated and stung. Phoebe had been wrong to urge her to reveal what little truth she knew. Telling that story to hostile ears, doubt stepped in from all sides. The story did sound lame, and even though at the time she had in a fashion abducted her daughter to prevent another imminent abduction, she had no idea if he really would have taken her. What right had she to have done such a thing? Her grief had blinded her. She had been hysterical. It was a dramatic time calling for dramatic action. She had had the same thoughts a thousand times. But the fact remained that he never made an effort to find them. For years she had wondered whether he had jumped off the Westgate bridge, or driven the Great Ocean Road and hurled himself to a watery death, but he wasn't the suicidal type, if there was such a type. Besides, he hadn't taken his own life. As far as she knew, he was alive and well and living in England. Fritz swore he had seen him at a London railway station one time. Which raised the unanswerable question again: why didn't he track her down?

Perhaps Ginny should go and find out. At least then this could all be put to rest. Although more likely it would open up all sorts of problems. She had kept the truth hidden for years to deter Ginny from going in search of him. Despite what Ginny thought, this had nothing to do with shattering her idealised view of her father and everything to do with wanting to protect her. And as for the base motive Ginny held so tightly, there was not a granule of truth to it.

She stood before the pre-Raphaelite that Ginny had favoured: the child gazing heavenward, the mother looking off. It was a sensory overload. There was far too much detail. She thought sourly that they didn't even share an aesthetic temperament. Their perceptions of reality so distinct they might as well have been born of different root races.

She was suddenly, violently hot, her heart aflutter. Feeling breathless and weak, she sat down on the sofa to ride it out.

She would have to cancel the exhibition. How could she ever have imagined that a collaboration between them would work, that Ginny's music would have any sympathy at all with her paintings? It would be discord from go to whoa. They had struggled even to agree on a number. And it had been a descent from there. As for the Moon model, she preferred not to think about it. Easier to cancel. It would save her the aggravation of coming up with something.

Succumbing to an urge to move and flex her body, she heaved herself to her feet and went through to the main room, casting around as a steel-blue cloche hat appeared in the window, skirting a Masonite screen. She opened the door before the knock and Rosalind entered the gallery, daintily dressed in a skirt suit of fawn and blue twill, grey curls of hair all in their place.

'There you are, Harriet,' she said with a bland smile.

'You're back,' Harriet said, gathering herself together. 'How was the conference?'

'Tremendous of course,' she said, following Harriet to the back room. 'Fine speakers. Remarkable insight. And thankfully in a well-heated venue.' She scanned the paintings. 'These are all new, Harriet.'

'Phoebe has been doing well.'

She nodded, her gaze fixed on first one painting then another, as if she had no intention of looking at Harriet.

'Bournemouth was suffering a cold snap,' she said without preface. 'I might as well have been in Reykjavik. So, I spent most of my free time with Fritz.'

Harriet's heart made a small jolt. 'How is he?' she said.

'Fine. He has a blessedly warm house. And he's an interesting man.'

'I always thought so.'

Rosalind stood before the beach scene for some moments before continuing to move on around the collection. Harriet watched her, envying her assurance, the way she tilted her head to the side before taking a few short steps to view the next work.

'We had much to talk about, which I found surprising,' she said, standing before a portrait of a Great Dane in pen and ink. 'He's never married, you know.'

'I know.' They had been corresponding by letter and postcard since he left.

'I suspect he's still in love with you,' Rosalind said, at last turning to Harriet.

'That's absurd,' Harriet said with a short laugh.

'Is it? He speaks of you with much fondness.'

'Sentimental fool.'

'Perhaps. Still, it must be of comfort to have an admirer across the miles. I quite like this,' she said, pausing before the pre-Raphaelite woman and child.

'Rosalind.'

'What is it dear?' she said without shifting her gaze. 'You seem out of sorts.'

'Ginny.'

'I met her on my way here,' Rosalind said sedately. 'She seemed troubled.'

'We had a terrible row.'

'Children can be trying sometimes. She'll come round.'

'I doubt it. She's gone off to book a flight to England. She's bent on tracking down her father.'

'She's upset,' Rosalind said gently. 'Shall we have tea?'

'I only have bags.'

'Ah. Then never mind. Do you think she's still in love with Garth?'

Harriet hesitated, confused and not sure what to say. Then, before she could stop herself she blurted, 'I think she bears me the most awful grudge and this is my punishment.'

'Come now,' Rosalind said with a sympathetic smile. 'She loves you dearly. You're about to put on a wonderful exhibition together. She'll change her mind.'

'I really wish that were so. She accuses me of leaving Wilhelm to claim my inheritance.'

Rosalind looked thoughtful for a moment. 'They are the words of immaturity,' she said. 'She's irrational.'

'Rosalind,' Harriet said. 'I'm beside myself.'

'Try not to worry. I shall have a word with her.'

'I'm not sure it will do any good.'

'Leave it with me, Harriet,' she said firmly. 'Sometimes it takes a third party to mediate. She'll see reason. I'm certain of it.'

Rosalind made to leave. Harriet sensed she was holding something back. It was uncharacteristic of her to intercede. Those three days with Fritz. Had Wilhelm been there too? Not in person, for he was no friend of Fritz, but in their conversations, awkwardly, reluctantly, tossed back and forth like a bar of radium neither party was keen to handle for long.

She returned to the back room and the pre-Raphaelite, following the woman's gaze beyond the frame.

Tuesday, 4 April 2017

She had vowed to herself never to do it again. Earlier that evening, when she had given into compulsion and for the second time seen his Ashtray Petrolstick nom de plume on the Forum, it was as if Zol had entered her being as she read. She had sat in a trance and an unknown number of minutes passed by, minutes of unaccountable time. Why ever would she wish to invoke a repetition? Yet here she was, scrolling through that labyrinthine world of misinformation, false flags and secret plots. Every second profile picture, a *V for Vendetta* mask.

On one thread, Fagbutt Oilcan was insisting the banksters were the puppet masters, and Celestial Petal was there chiming in with references to the Rothschilds. Franken Form wanted to know if anyone had watched the footage of Lawrence Pike filming outside Bohemia Grove. No mention of the Order of Shannon, but Fagbutt made reference to the Freemasons. He always made reference to some secret order or other. She struggled not to take it seriously. Told herself she was a voyeur, that was all. It was something she did to occupy her restless mind. Stay in the present. Look ahead and not behind her. It had worked until Ashtray Petrolstick appeared on the scene, or rather Zol, and disturbed the respite the Forum afforded her.

It was an ugly coincidence that Bethany suggested she check

out the Forum. Judith thought it likely that Hannah had put her onto it, for Bethany was not a social media user. Bethany could not have known that out of all the people who used the site Judith would encounter Zol, any more than she would have known that her daughter Hannah had betrayed her best friend. A betrayal that had caused Madeleine to walk out on Zol, and leave her degree and Bournemouth and move back home. Hannah was the catalyst and thus somehow culpable in the events that followed. Her mother inadvertently complicit, complicit by her very existence in Judith's life, right down to her rooms next door to the tattoo parlour where Zol had worked. She felt a sudden hatred for them both. And then there was the triptych and that clairvoyant Viv with her ominous allusions. What to make of that she had no idea, unless the entire course of events was preordained. Which would also mean she had unwittingly foreshadowed the future with every brushstroke. It was farfetched. She could make no connection between those silver birches rendered in black, white and grey and what happened to her daughter. Bethany, Hannah, Viv, it was useless to point fingers. Except at Zol. It was easy and satisfying to point at him. He deserved to be singled out. He was repulsive.

She wouldn't move. She felt a weak impulse to stand up, walk about the house, go outside, occupy herself in some other way. She could paint, watch television, garden, take a walk. Instead, despite Zol, she continued to scroll through the posts on the Forum. It was familiar, comforting; the real world disappeared. Her body with its deep ache disappeared.

Taking refuge in virtual realities was a habit she had formed fourteen years earlier. Back then she had a taste for video games. Not the virtual killing sprees that the boys Madeleine's age played. Judith went for games that were a little educational. While the boys were running through city scapes, gun to the ready, Judith and Madeleine would click their way around a castle or an island, collecting clues and solving puzzles. Madeleine would sit on her lap and press the arrow keys, and together they would spend hours in a maze, the day outside sliding into night, another day done.

It was a manner of coping after the death of her parents.

With Peter's lack of involvement, she had been forced to rely on her parents in those early years. After the initial shock at finding their only daughter with child, Florence and Bernard had rallied. Her mother had held her hand during the birth. They had fussed and doted on Madeleine, who could always be seen in the warm attentive company of one or other of them. Judith even managed to complete a few paintings. But her life had shrunk. Her college friends forgot about her, the village gossiped, and only Bethany remained loyal. Bethany, happily married with a daughter of her own, ground into Judith's lonely narrow life like salt. Yet Judith reciprocated the loyalty. She felt she had no choice. Perhaps Madeleine had come to expect too much, for when her parents both died, Judith was left to fulfil all her needs. And she had done that, dutifully given her life over to it, for surely the girl always had food in her belly and clothes on her back. But it was never enough. She was no replacement for Florence and Bernard. She was forced to heed her daughter's demands through a fog of despair.

No one could have anticipated their deaths. Florence and Bernard both in their fifties, too young to be struck down by the same cancer in the same year. Too much sodium nitrite, Bethany had surmised in one of her more callous moments, in reference to Judith's parents' affection for bacon.

In Bethany, with her obliging husband and obliging daughter, self-satisfaction seemed to have replaced whatever empathy was in her. Judith wondered if human nature was hardwired in such a way that only affliction fostered empathy: suffering, that most essential of human experiences; grief its inevitable, universal form.

Her parents died seven months apart, to the day. Her father passed first, on the third of January, the anniversary of Judith's grandfather Stanley's death: Stanley, the haberdasher of Sidwell Street. Her mother passed on the third day of August that year.

It hadn't seemed normal, possible or fair to lose both parents that way. A long year of pain and failed treatments. The steady decline of her father then of her mother, the nursing, the forced brave face, the waiting and the bedside vigils—she had been too young for all of it. And all the while Madeleine had demanded her attention, her explanations. 'They've gone to heaven,' she would hear herself say in the days after the funeral, when they were alone in the house, when she was haunted by every crack and creak and speck of dust.

Over time Judith packed up her parents' things and gave them to charity. She gradually made the house her own. And looming in her, clicking along with every footstep up and down the stairs, was time, and its curious fatalism.

She reflected that her parents had passed at the same hour on the third day of the month and for all she knew the very minute, for both had gone in the early afternoon. And she would have known had she been paying attention and not been distracted by Madeleine, who, at Bernard's passing had a feverish cold and was fractious, and when Florence went she was outside pinching all the flower buds off a hollyhock.

All Judith knew was that she had lost her parents at the age of twenty-six and found she was entirely alone and left to cope with Madeleine. She desperately needed Peter's participation in her upbringing, but he had already accepted a post at Oxford.

The day he telephoned with the news she was working on a landscape, a commission for a birthday, and she held a wet paintbrush in one hand and pressed the receiver to her ear with the other. Madeleine was watching cartoons.

'I'll keep in touch,' he'd said and she knew he wouldn't.

She faced an uncertain future, surviving on benefits, his maintenance payments, garden produce and the occasional private sale. Commissions were rare. She exhibited when she could, which wasn't often. She felt her will slither out of her and often she would stare at Madeleine staring at the television, wishing the cartoons would go on forever and she would never have to deal with a pestering child.

She forgave his absence, accommodated the demands of his career, and reminded herself to be grateful for that portion of his income.

Seven years passed and Peter returned, telephoning to tell her he had taken up a post at Exeter university. By then Madeleine had grown into a teenage version of her belligerent self. Gone the temper tantrums, the obstinate will, the incessant I-wanting. She became withdrawn, moody, brooding and driven by the basest wants. She had acquired a hateful sneering attitude that would spread across her face, narrowing her eyes to slits. The burden that was her daughter relocated from Judith's shoulders and took up residence in her mind, leaving Judith convinced that Madeleine needed a father's guidance, moral and strong.

They arranged that Madeleine would meet him in Fore Street outside Nicholas Priory at half-past eleven on the fifth of August 2010, and he would take her to lunch. Madeleine hadn't wanted to go. Judith had to bribe her with mobile phone credit and once the front door had closed she stood by the living room window and watched her amble up the lane to the bus stop as if she were intent on missing the eleven o'clock bus. Judith would then be forced to drive her in. The imposition, the loss of time, the necessity of an exchange with Peter, the presence of a sullen Madeleine in the car, and she waited by the window until she saw the bus chug by, heard its idle rumble and the revving engine as it went on its way. With no sign of Madeleine, she left her post and went outside to garden.

She picked beans, a spring onion, the ripest of her tomatoes and a small Cos lettuce. She thinned out a few carrots, brushing them free of soil. She enjoyed the cool damp soil on her skin, the sun on her back, the hum of bumble bees feasting on the lavender and marjoram flowers nearby. And the soft folds of hope enveloped her. She pinched a few sprigs of parsley on her way back to the house.

She steamed the beans then tossed them in olive oil, black pepper and crushed garlic. She made a salad, adding diced avocado and sunflower seeds and a drizzle of balsamic vinaigrette, serving herself a generous helping before taking her bowl outside to sit at the wrought iron table in the courtyard.

She ate slowly, listening to the slow hum of summer, taking in the scene. The herbs on the terraces that fringed the courtyard were lush and proud, the lawn a swathe of cadmium green, the meadow on the rise beyond the garden a dance of Naples yellow, the leaves of the oak veering towards a viridian hue that augured the browning of autumn.

She went inside with her empty plate and returned with her copy of *Dracula*, chosen a week before from her row of to-be-read second-hand books. She was two pages past halfway and finding the story predictable. That Lucy and Mina should fall foul of the Count, that it was the men that Bram Stoker saw fit to save the day, that Dracula himself was a villain to his core—it was all so obvious from the first. Dracula, with his supernatural powers, his command of the elements, whipping up storms at will. She told herself it was fantasy. In real life there were no vampires mesmerising, grooming, seducing young women for the kill.

Upon completing the latest of Dr Seward's diary, Judith went up the garden and knelt on the soft grass and pulled a few weeds with her bare hands, feeling the resistance of their roots, then the release, shaking off the cool moist soil. Then she returned to the house and to her studio.

Madeleine arrived home late in the afternoon. When Judith heard the front door close she went to ask how things went. All she received in reply was a shrug and a muttered, 'All right, I guess,' Madeleine's words trailing behind her as she slumped up to her room.

Madeleine went to Exeter for an outing with her father every second Saturday after that. But it made no difference to her behaviour. She remained taciturn about the visits and Judith didn't probe, happy to assume that things were as fine as she could expect.

Feeling thirsty, she left her laptop and made for the kitchen, stopping in the hall by the landline. The chunky white phone was a symbol, not of her connection to the world beyond the house, but of her isolation. Often, she would find herself in the hall, waiting by the phone, wavering. This time, rather than lifting the receiver to call the only person she had left, Bethany, she unplugged the phone and disentangled the lead, metres and metres of thin white tape that allowed, when the tape was untangled, the phone to be carried as far as her bedroom upstairs. She untwisted and straightened until her fingers ached.

The respite lasted no longer than the labour.

In the kitchen, her mind was back sniffing over the past.

Two years went by and Judith had begun to notice the ten-pound notes missing from her purse, the sour odour of cheap wine on her daughter's breath, the elements of a home-made bong stuffed in a bedroom drawer. Then Madeleine met Zol and Judith could only assume she had been happy with him. They had shared that dismal flat above the tattoo parlour in Bournemouth for two years and five months. She thought back to the date and added three days.

It had been her duty to help move her daughter in and her duty to help move her out. She had been called, and she had answered.

Yet she suspected it wasn't the fulfilment of her maternal obligations that Madeleine had been seeking since her grandparents died. It was Judith's attention. Her exclusive, undivided attention, all eyes and all ears with more empathy and understanding than could be found in the universe; attention not one single hang-on-a-minute later.

Were all mothers so burdened? All children so self-centred?

So, it was her fault after all. For dissatisfied, Madeleine had sought attention elsewhere. In the hairy arms of Zol. Although she couldn't have found much satisfaction; she would have been competing with his Xbox.

And then she had returned, unchanged, still carrying the echoes of the ill-tempered child that she was, a child sure to exert her dominating influence on the house as she always had. It was self-preservation and looming desperation that had driven Judith to suggest Madeleine reconnect with her father. It had been the right thing to do. The obvious thing. No one could blame her for that. Although she blamed herself. She never stopped blaming herself. Yet she couldn't have known how things would turn out.

It was ten forty-five on Wednesday the eighteenth of January when Madeleine had made the call. They had returned from Bournemouth and unloaded the car, Madeleine piling all of her belongings in her room. Judith heard her voice, muffled and soft, then a pause, a shout and a loud crash as she slammed down the receiver.

'Bastard!'

Judith left the studio and went through the kitchen to the hall. 'What is it?'

'He says he doesn't want to see me.'

And she had run up the stairs, hiding her tears behind her hair, leaving Judith nonplussed. It was a reversal of the cordial Peter she had spoken to the day before.

She should never have tried to shunt her daughter in his direction. She should have taken responsibility, sacrificed a little more of her time, hidden that wretched business card and pretended to Madeleine that he wanted nothing whatsoever to do with her ever again. Yes, there could be no doubt she was to blame. For she was being punished in exact measure.

She took four long deep breaths, exhaling slowly, steering herself back to the present. Desperate to block out the memories, she clicked on another thread, then another and another, until her eyes settled on Franken Form's latest discussion on the Order of Shannon. He accused the Order of being behind the rise to prominence of a conservative show pony that had swung voters in the last general election. Celestial Petal claimed members of the Order were funding an anti-immigration party that wanted to keep the 'scroungers' out.

Fred Spice said that the two claims were ludicrous and contradictory. No one argued with him. Then Fagbutt Oilcan posted a list of names, none of whom she recognised, and their various positions on boards of directors of investment banks, and said they had all been accused of dodgy deals, fraud and corruption at one time or other. Follow the money, a faceless commentator called Lemony Aide said. Franken Form claimed the whole situation was a ruse to keep the Left out of power and continue the shift of wealth from the poor to the super rich. Ashtray Petrolstick posted a link to the Templars, which the others ignored and so did Judith, for she found she agreed with Madeleine—Zol aka Ashtray had to be pasting from other sources. Her whole being lurched in the realisation that she was in concord with her daughter, and she forced her attention back to the Forum.

The comments were predictable and she began to lose interest, when Franken Form claimed that the Order of Shannon was so secret that if it hadn't been for his discovery of a letter that his uncle had kept concealed in the heel of his shoe, no one would be any the wiser. Judith laughed out loud. A *shoe*? It was the closest she came to participating. Those people had let paranoia drive them into collective insanity.

She remained fixed on her laptop screen regardless. She followed links to blogs that claimed insider knowledge. There was a lot of speculation and dot joining.

But as the night drew in and the room grew cold the Forum couldn't hold her attention.

She went to the only other source of solace she had: the Wimmera. Even in formation, there was an enormous weight of stillness in the painting, a sense of timelessness, and a deep knowing that emanated from the land and the cattleman on horseback, who seemed to stare at her inquiringly through wise, soulful eyes. She took a brush and set about adding texture and highlights to a length of barbed-wire fence, an oil drum on its side, and the dilapidated fibro shack.

Dimunition

Ginny's suitcase was packed. Three days before, Ginny had lugged it downstairs and deposited it in the hall not two strides from the front door. Whenever she passed it by Harriet felt ragged. She took pride in considering herself an upright woman of much fortitude and here she was, all asunder, pacing the studio floor.

Before the sun had tickled the day, she had tidied her bench and collated all her brushes into bristle, sable and synthetic, and round, pointed, flat, filbert and fan. And her paint: acrylic with acrylic and gouache with gouache. Then she had swept the floor and rolled up the scatter rugs, taking them outside for a thorough beating. She had even thought of cleaning the windows then changed her mind. Instead she stacked her nine artworks, face to the wall. They were complete, more or less, and she loathed each and every one of them. Phoebe had not been impressed either, upon viewing them the other day, her single 'Mmm' more telling than any critique. Harriet was about ready to toss in the bin her eighteen scrolls of coloured dots but she couldn't bring herself to such a destructive act, not after all the effort it took to produce them. She rolled them up and shoved them in a box under the bench.

A hazy light filtered through the windows. The worst of the summer heat had passed, the days were shortening and the maple leaves on the turn. Despite the cool, Harriet was flushing in intervals of about twenty minutes, which only added to her fluster. She knew a shower would soothe her inner thermostat but that meant entering the house. She made another black cohosh tea and sat down in the club chair, clutching her cup. Without a reason for remaining in the studio she was restless.

Lately, inside her own skin was not a pleasant place to be. Ginny was too quick to blame her for trying to protect her, too quick to condemn. Harriet owed her nothing. She had done her very best in rearing her daughter. She hadn't left her on a stranger's doorstep, or dumped her in a storm water drain. She would never hit her, rarely yelled, as far as she could recall, and had provided her with a comfortable and stable life. Harriet was not so arrogant as to consider her mothering perfect. She still carried a tinge of guilt over what she considered to be a half-hearted engagement in Ginny's early childhood. But no woman was perfect. If she wanted to, she could conjure a long list of complaints against her own mother, but she wouldn't, not because she didn't want to asperse the dead, but because there was no purpose to it. Nothing would resolve because things were the way they were. Time cannot unravel. The past is already knitted up and fit to wear and that's all any daughter can do. Learn to be comfortable whatever the weave might be. But there was no explaining this to Ginny. She had to discover it for herself.

She sipped her tea with grimaces as she stared blankly out the far window at the trees and the creamy sky, when the door unexpectedly opened and Phoebe appeared clutching a large parcel. She leaned it against the near wall and disappeared outside, returning with two more. Once inside she closed the door, tossed her satchel on the table and turned on her heels without bothering to remove her hat or her trench coat. There was a look of triumph in her face.

'A safe passage through no woman's land then,' she said.

'Phoebe,' Harriet said, her tone deflated. 'What on Earth do you mean?'

'You in here and Ginny in there.' She pointed.

'Not for long. She's leaving.'

'I saw the suitcase. So, she's going through with it?'

'Determined as ever.'

'Did you tell her?'

'I told her.'

'Didn't help then. Oh well.'

'Oh well?' Harriet leaned forward and put her cup beside her on the floor lest she threw it before she went on. 'She knows about the caveat.'

'Ah,'

'And that's her interpretation of why I left. You know what, Phoebe?' she said bitterly. 'I'm beginning to wonder if she's right. I was and I am an unscrupulous woman.'

'Nonsense,' Phoebe said. 'The argument lacks logic. Firstly, if you had loved Wilhelm you would have contested the will and had the caveat lifted. If you loved him you might even have foregone the inheritance. There are women out there stupid enough to do such a thing. Secondly, it's too simplistic. You were distraught. You'd lost both parents. And thirdly,' she said, lowering her tone, 'Wilhelm was an arsehole.'

'Ginny idolised him,' Harriet said, sinking down in her seat. 'She still does.'

'Of course she does. He was all over her.'

'Then what am I to do?' she said haplessly.

Phoebe outstretched her arms. 'Paint.'

'I can't possibly paint.'

'You can. It'll do you good. Put Ginny out of your mind. Let her go. She'll be back for the exhibition. She's promised.'

Harriet opened her mouth to speak but Phoebe raised a censorious hand and said, 'I persuaded.'

'How?'

'Never mind. She's written nine glorious songs and now we need from you nine glorious artworks.'

She went to the door and levered free an end of tape on one of the parcels and ripped. A few moments later Harriet was staring at nine blank canvases.

'There you go,' Phoebe said. 'Nothing like a fresh start.'

'Phoebe.' She paused. 'There isn't time.'

'Of course there's time. Nine weeks in fact, thanks to March being a long month.'

'Nine weeks.'

'That's a painting a week. Just like the old days.'

'That was different. I had another artist to inspire me.'

'So, now you have a Moon model.'

'It isn't the same. It's just a series of coloured dots. No matter how hard I try I can't do a thing with it.'

'You can.' Phoebe reached into her satchel and pulled out two rolled up posters.

'Moon planting guides,' she said. 'For this year and last.'

'What use will I make of those?' she said doubtfully.

'Visual, Harriet. Now you have something visual. You can transpose a few of your dots from the scrolls if you wish.'

Harriet paused. 'From a line to a circle,' she murmured.

'I thought you'd prefer it. And to help, I've brought you this.' She reached in her satchel and pulled out a CD. 'Bauhaus,' she said. 'First two albums. Tommo the Tank burnt them from the vinyl.'

Harriet stood. 'Bauhaus?'

'Make sure you play them loud. Now, I must get on.'

'Phoebe,' she said, reaching out her hand. 'Thank you.'

'Don't thank me,' Phoebe said on her way out the door. 'I have a party of eager goddesses coming to your exhibition. Call it a vested interest.'

Harriet was touched. It was true that Phoebe would want the exhibition to proceed, but she was a capable woman who could easily have arranged an alternative. This was much more than protecting an investment. Phoebe cared.

She tacked the planting guides to the wall and placed a blank canvas on an easel. She pulled out the box beneath the bench and rummaged for the original nine scrolls with their long bands of coloured dots. Shoving aside her paints and her brushes, she laid out the scrolls in sequence, pinning them down on the bench with Ginny's painted rocks.

In the course of the nine months the Moon made a hundred and thirty-five aspects with each planet. There was simply no room on the Moon-planting guides for all that information. She would have to pick a planet or two. The Sun moved a degree a day, in one month passing through a Zodiacal sign. The Moon whizzed round the whole zodiac in as many days: the result, the Moon's phases. There was something rhythmic, natural, and obvious about it. After the Sun, the first aspect the Moon made was with gloomy old Saturn, and she recoiled at the thought of starting there.

Instead, she was drawn to Pluto, or Hades, Lord of the Underworld: a compact icy rock barely large enough to warrant the appellation planet, and not according to many. Yet to deny its existence would be to pretend that our darkest passions lacked transformative possibility. Rosalind would often allude to its potency, describing as plutonic any and all the dark rumblings in our souls. Harriet knew that the planets were not simply spinning balls orbiting the Sun; they were named after the gods and in that very naming took on the nature of those gods. There was nothing incidental about that moment when some astronomer chose a planet's name, unwittingly tuning in to the cosmos and drawing down a correspondence. To embrace the symbol of Pluto was to acknowledge the archetype and allow its power for spiritual renewal. She decided she would help to restore the little ice ball to its rightful status in the cosmos.

She studied the scrolls. Each month the New Moon conjoined the Sun in a different sign. The first month was Virgo. From there the New Moon made a harmonious trine with Pluto and for Harriet this formed the initiatory pulse for the aspects that followed.

In the next month, the first contact the New Moon made with Pluto was stressful. The month following, exciting.

She set about transposing the lunar aspects. Then she went to put on the Bauhaus CD, turning up the volume, letting the haunting tones, the bass, the rich vocals infuse her.

She drew the curtains on the windows, shut out the garden, the trees, the sky.

Two bars into 'Bela Lugosi's Dead', she saw in colour the notes she heard: iridescent, kaleidoscopic, intense. And she gazed at the initiatory month of Virgo on the planting guide, and let her synaesthesia and the coloured dots interplay, and synthesise. She chose a wide, hog bristle brush, squeezed cadmium yellow gouache onto her palette and turned to the blank canvas on her easel. She was her old self again, back in Moor Street knocking out Matisses. Her best years, before Ginny, before Wilhelm, when she would meet Fritz for coffee at Mario's, or go with Phoebe to the Evelyn, or meet Rosalind at the Theosophical Society bookshop and wander down to South Bank for afternoon tea.

The summer heat had at last given way to cooler days, mist filled mornings and freshening rain. A downpour last week had spurred lush new shoots in the undergrowth. The maples in next door's garden were turning a tawny red. The golden elms were shedding leaves. Seasonal sensitivities ensconced in the majesty of the mountain ash. She ignored her mother's studio, pretended it wasn't there, and ran her left hand lightly down the keys, sensing each note, the grooves between, the cool smoothness that was her instrument. She didn't look down, enjoying the calm on the other side of the window. For she was a prisoner of her own making whenever she was home, which was more often than not, installing herself in her room, waiting until she saw Harriet slink off to the studio before heading to the kitchen for food. For the last two days, she had to pass her suitcase at the bottom of the stairs, which she had packed and plonked in the hall in a moment of rage and later found too heavy to move.

She was due to leave for London in three days, allowing about a month to interrogate Fritz and track down her father. She would be back in time for the exhibition, although if she found him, if they got on, if he wanted to see more of her, she might apply for another visa and return, find work, a place to stay. Perhaps move there permanently. She was half English after all.

A small part of her sensed it was fantasy. That her quest would be fruitless. She was in the grip of a childish fixation fuelled by her anger towards her mother. She wanted to punish Harriet, clench her by the nape of her neck and rub her nose in the mess she had made of her daughter's life. A fatherless daughter was adrift, rudderless. The perfect man, the moral exemplar of whatever it is to be good in male skin, absent. We all need models to guide us, she thought, templates to afford comparisons. She was twenty-eight and her life was rubble. Garth had stripped her of a promising career, rendered her jobless and homeless. It was a simple logic, cause and effect, one she adhered to with the tenacity of a crab.

There was a knock on the front door. At first Ginny didn't respond. Then, knowing she was alone in the house she went downstairs to answer it and was surprised to find Rosalind on the doorstep.

'Harriet's in her studio,' she said blandly.

'It's you I've come to see,' Rosalind said, holding her gaze with a closed mouth smile.

Ginny ushered her inside. She couldn't help noticing Rosalind glance at her suitcase as she crossed the threshold. Rosalind made no comment. She went through to the living room, Ginny following on behind.

There were a few moments of hesitation as they both stood, some feet apart, Ginny on the Kashan rug, Rosalind closer to the sofas. Rosalind cast an eye about the room and seemed about to sit down when she changed her mind and pointed to the kitchen. 'Shall we go through?' she said.

Ginny parted the beaded curtain.

'Tea?'

'No thank you. I'm on my way to Agatha's to meet a friend and thought I'd pop in. Are you keeping well?'

'I'm fine.'

'Good. Shall we sit in the sun?' She didn't wait for an answer.

They sat on two of the deep wooden chairs arranged around a low table on a small area of paving. The garden looked splendid. Herbs in large pots were dotted here and there. The vegetable beds in the far top corner sported a jumble of leafy greens, tomatoes and runner beans. Purple flowering plants grew in clumps around the trunks of the golden elms. The lawn lightly dusted in golden leaves. A mild sun warmed their faces. It was idyllic save for the steady bass throbbing inside the studio.

'She must be at work,' Ginny murmured, her gaze wandering in the opposite direction, until it reached the grey-blue worsted skirt suit of her guest.

'I've been meaning to talk to you since I returned from Bournemouth,' Rosalind said. 'I understand you're planning a trip there yourself.'

'I am.'

'To discover your father.' She didn't say it as a question.

'That's right.'

'What I have to say may change your mind.'

'You met him?' Ginny said quickly, her heart picking up a beat.

'No. I stayed with Fritz. Bournemouth was experiencing a dreadful cold snap so we sheltered inside his house for the duration. You can imagine we had much time to dispose of.'

'How is Fritz?' she said in as casual a tone as she could manage.

'He is well. I'm sure he would enjoy seeing you. But perhaps not if your purpose concerns Wilhelm.'

'He doesn't care for my father. My mother supposes it is because he was gazumped.'

'Funny way to put it. And that might play a part. I know he was very fond of your mother. Still is. I told him about your exhibition by the way. He was delighted by the idea and wanted me to convey his best wishes to you both.' She glanced down at her watch then cleared her throat. 'I better come straight out with it. Your father is not the man you think he is.'

Ginny had suspected Rosalind would say something of the sort. She sat back in her seat and folded her arms across her chest.

Rosalind shooed away a wasp that was buzzing around the table, then she went on. 'Fritz stumbled on the revelation in a newspaper report. He said he doesn't normally follow such reportage but it was impossible to avoid. Every paper was running the story. He said he couldn't fail to recognise Wilhelm on the front page.'

'What do you mean?'

'There's no easy way to put this. He's been arrested.'

'Arrested?' She made to stand and changed her mind.

'On suspicion.'

'On suspicion of what?'

Rosalind was evasive. 'There's been rather a lot of this sort of thing lately,' she said. 'High profile celebrities, priests.'

'What sort of thing?'

Rosalind didn't speak. They both stared out at the garden.

'You mean child abuse?' Ginny said.

'I find it a strange truth that with some people, one only finds out how evil they are after the fact. They hide themselves so well.'

She could scarcely believe she was hearing this from Rosalind. 'It can't be true,' she said, keeping her voice quiet. 'It isn't true. My father would never harm anyone.'

Rosalind gave her a sidelong glance. 'No, especially not his own daughter. I quite agree the whole thing seems unusual.'

'He never hurt me,' Ginny said, puzzled.

'Not you. He fathered another, it seems. Not long after he settled in England.'

It was impossible to take in. Her thoughts whirled. She jammed her hands between her arms and chest and pushed at her cuticles with her fingertips. The music stopped. She heard the rumble of a car going past in the lane. All fell quiet until the music started again.

'He replaced me?' she said, her disbelief fading.

'Perhaps.'

'Then I have a sister.'

It was an odd thought, hard to fathom, that there was a young woman whom she had never met, with whom she might share confidences, develop a kinship bond, and she wanted to fly to England that minute. But her brief musing was crushed when Rosalind said, 'Had, Ginny. She was found in a quarry.'

'Found in a quarry? Where?'

'On the edge of Dartmoor. Somewhere to the southwest of Exeter, where your father was a lecturer. Fascinating part of the country. Quite remote too.'

'Found in a quarry?' she said again. Perhaps she had jumped. Ginny had heard of people taking their lives that way.

'Not exactly a quarry,' Rosalind said. 'She was found in a cave nearby. The quarry leads to a riddle of caves, apparently. Not many are open to the public.'

Ginny realised with something like horror that the image of her father that she held so dear she had fabricated over the years out of skerricks of memory and a craven wish. An image designed to plaster over an empty space, like Pollyfilla, one now fast crumbling.

'How old?'

'Coming up to her twenty-first birthday, I believe.'

Ginny did a quick calculation. Eight years her junior meant Wilhelm had wasted no time fathering her replacement. 'Did Fritz know her?' she said, catching Rosalind's gaze.

'I think I've said enough.'

Ginny leaned forward. 'Don't go. There's more. There has to be more.'

'There's always more but I'm sure I've covered the main points.' She rose to leave, looking down at Ginny, at once firm and pitying.

'Please don't go.'

'I'll be late.' She paused. 'You'll be fine. You have your mother's strength.'

She walked away, cornered the house and disappeared. Ginny stayed in the garden with her thoughts, straining in vain to block out the insistent bass spilling from the studio.

She had a sister, a sister murdered in a cave. It was her dream, the dream she had been having for months. Perhaps coincidental, yet its repetition seemed to undermine that view. The dream had been so vague, surreal, and lacking in meaning that each time she awoke she made every effort to dismiss it by the swiftest of means, associating the symbology with her mother or with Garth.

Most likely the dream had been a warning. Yet there could be no point to a dream if the dreamer couldn't possibly heed that warning. When it concerns not themselves but someone they don't know, would never know. A dream with relevance to her now that she could align it with real events, only ascribe it significance with hindsight.

She remained seated in the garden, squinting into the sun, resisting the demands of her mother's music bellowing from the studio.

Perhaps none of Rosalind's report was true. Yet if the man in the newspaper was her father then that she also had a sister seemed undeniable. The newspaper would surely not have been mistaken and Fritz had no reason to lie.

There must be evidence, confirmation, the mother, whoever she was, having identified the body. Had her sister really been murdered? Again, the usually cautious police would not have claimed such a thing had there been any doubt. But the perpetrator, that had to be an unknown, awaiting irrefutable proof and a verdict in a court of law. It may not have been Wilhelm. He was only under suspicion. That didn't mean he was culpable. She could go to Exeter and find out. Ask him herself. Visit the mother. Get to know the sister that she had gained and lost in a second.

But her dream was shackled to her, a dead weight thwarting her every move, as if it alone were proof that her father had committed that act. A dream of a naked girl surrounded by shadows, flickering lights, low incanting voices. It was a ritual, a sacrifice, just like the one her mother had mentioned in connection with a sect. A sect Wilhelm had joined.

She wondered if she had been dreaming the wrong dream, one that belonged to her sister. Her inner dream catcher mistakenly believing it was meant for her. She emitted a sharp laugh at the thought.

All she could be sure of was that the dream had saved her from a harrowing journey. No one would want to travel halfway round the world to confront a father turned murderer. It occurred to her that Harriet had been right in her suspicions. And Fritz.

Remorse slowly replaced the horror she felt. That she had treated her mother with disregard all these years, held on to her resentment, her blame. Even if Harriet had left to fulfil the demands of the caveat, perhaps deep inside there had been another honest and true motive, an impulse to protect her daughter.

The music stopped. There was a long silent pause and Ginny anticipated her mother exiting the studio. She watched the door but it didn't open. Instead the music started up once more and Ginny went inside and upstairs, leaving the bedroom door open behind her.

She stood in the centre of the room, taking in the little sanctuary of it: the scruffily made bed, her Roland beneath the window, her laptop on the chest of drawers, the old wooden wardrobe.

She felt numb and resolute all at once.

She peeled off her paisley jacket, her paisley shirt and her paisley skirt, tossing the apparel on her bed. She took the plain grey dress she had slung on the back of a wooden chair and put it on. Then she opened the wardrobe and pulled out every paisley-printed shirt, dress, skirt and pair of pants. She went through the chest of drawers and did the same. Before long she was staring at a pile of paisley on her bed: her childhood.

She ought to burn the lot. Isn't that what people do to mark an ending? Make a pyre? Instead she went downstairs and came back with a large black plastic bin liner.

By the time she had finished, she had a sack of apparel destined for the charity shop. She dragged it downstairs and dumped it by the front door. She grabbed the handle of her suitcase with both hands and heaved it tread by tread up the stairs. Then she grabbed her keys and left the house.

The Crescent was quiet. Grassy verges, neatly mown, fringed by clumps of agapanthus, silver birches, maples and elms, all enjoying the shade of the mountain ash that were dotted everywhere, the well-to-do living in expensively renovated houses in acres of secluded gardens behind neat blue stone walls. The less well-off squeezed away long ago to the less quaint, less historical parts of Melbourne's outer fringe, living beyond the foothills on the flat land of the suburbs, where no one she knew lived. Veronica had grown up in Gwenneth Crescent and Poppy in Wilton Grove. It was Sunday afternoon, and most likely they were both visiting their parents. Ginny walked slowly down the hill, taking her time.

Too soon she found herself in Wilton Grove, standing on the nature strip outside the Pargiters'. Mr Pargiter was a curator at the Melbourne museum and Mrs Pargiter a librarian at the state library, both integral to the functioning of the archives and the art collections of the city. Poppy was their only child, their pride, their joy, and never their disappointment. Or did they, too, find her dotty? What sort of expectations of her did they have, if any? Ginny suspected they were unconditional types, accepting their daughter for who she was, final. Poppy hadn't been molly coddled or pushed. An average girl of average aspirations and now she had a promising career in publishing. And she, Ginny, the high achiever destined for greatness, here she was scratching a living playing Gershwin to grannies. She envied Poppy the regularity and the conventionality of her nine-to-five work, and the security of two good parents still together.

Poppy hadn't suffered what she had, and neither had Veronica: the tragic death of her grandparents precipitating the dramatic upheaval of her childhood. Brought up thereafter by her mother alone. To discover after years of unknowing that the father she adored and ached for was a murderer. She couldn't imagine anything worse.

A queasy feeling swept through her as she realised she had half his genes.

Perhaps he had acted on impulse and not a long-harboured urge. She pieced together the fragments; the occult interests—he undeniably had those, if only as an academic and not a practitioner. But then there was the letter. One day the other week Harriet had left a photograph of it on the kitchen table for her to read, just as she had left the original for her father to see, to know he had been found out. The Order of Shannon—it was probably just a bunch of sleazy old men filled with an inflated sense of their own importance, happily engaged in silly rituals away from the scorning eyes of their wives. A sect wasn't necessarily of sinister intent. She had known friends into Wicca and all they did was hold new and full Moon dances and garden blessings.

She opened the Pargiters' gate and walked up the path to the front door. She hesitated, not ready to confide, to shock, but need overrode reticence and she rang the doorbell, heard the tinny tune of 'Greensleeves', and waited.

Before long the door opened and Mrs Pargiter greeted her with a smile and a hello, turning her head with, 'Poppy, it's for you.' And she headed back down the hall and disappeared, leaving Ginny wondering if already the word was out and everyone in the village knew she was the daughter of a murderer. She at once dismissed the thought. A strong smell of frying garlic and onions wafted outside.

Poppy appeared and gave her a lingering hug, until Ginny pulled away and said, 'Let's go for a walk.'

She waited for Poppy to grab her jacket and change her shoes then they headed down to Gwenneth Crescent and the Hunnacots', Ginny listening to Poppy's enthusiastic account of a play she had seen the other night at the Butterfly Club. It was yet another take on *Romeo and Juliet*. Poppy explained that the woman seated beside her in the audience had on the same dress as the lead actress, and they both had long blonde hair. As she watched, she couldn't help imagining the woman as Claire Danes in the movie. Which woman? Before long Ginny had no idea who Poppy was referring to, the woman in the audience seemed to fuse with the actresses on stage and film and Juliet herself was entirely lost.

At the Hunnacots', they were forced to wait while Veronica changed out of her onesie, then the three of them strolled down to the creek, the neat frontages of The Crescent giving way to tree ferns and native shrubs, houses on large properties well hidden behind dense foliage, a driveway or a path the only evidence of a residence.

Veronica and Poppy were all giggles and 'Isn't this nice? We should do this more often.' Eventually, Veronica noticed Ginny's manner and said, 'You're quiet.'

'Been playing any good gigs?' Poppy asked.

'A few.'

'You don't seem happy,' Veronica said with a look of concern.

'I'm all right.' She found she couldn't confide, no matter how desperate she felt. She laughed and turned the conversation back to Poppy's play.

They stopped under a stand of silver birches planted on a nature strip, the foliage turning gold. Poppy looked up into the fine web of branches of the tallest then ran her hand down its cracked white bark.

'The lady of the woods,' she said. 'This tree symbolises the maiden phase of the Moon.'

'Is that right?' said Veronica.

Poppy giggled and raised a hand to cover her mouth. 'Do I sound all pagan?'

'Not at all,' Ginny said dryly.

'I've been editing a manuscript. *The Witches of Birchwood*. Part of the *Celtic Lakes* series. It's got me all clued up.'

Ginny shivered.

'Are you okay?' Veronica said, putting an arm around Ginny's waist.

'Perfectly fine,' Ginny said, pulling away with a short laugh. 'It's getting cold. Shall we turn back?'

The wind had picked up, rustling the fallen leaves and lifting Poppy's skirt. They walked even slower on the ascent, twice standing aside for a passing car.

As they neared the Hunnacots', Poppy said, 'Mum's been cooking a slab of dead meat. Let's head back to Brunswick for tempeh.'

'Yeah,' said Veronica with sudden enthusiasm. 'Want to come?' she added, addressing Ginny. 'You can stay over.'

'Love to but I've things to do,' Ginny said evasively.

'Like what?' said Veronica.

'Yes, what could be so pressing?'

Unpacking a suitcase, she thought but didn't say.

'Come and hang with your besties,' Poppy said.

'Another time,' she said with as much warmth as she could muster.

For Ginny knew it would be a long time before she told them, if ever. She needed solitude, time to make sense of things.

Her friends seemed disappointed, but not for long. They headed back to Sassafras listening to Veronica enthuse about a forthcoming lipstick launch.

Wednesday 5 April 2017

The scene from the studio window was bleak. Spring's swollen buds and tender new leaves were shocked frozen by a dusting of unseasonal snow. The meadow on the rise was a mottle of brown and white. The sky was heavy, the wind freshening from the west, and Judith knew that in her garden the vegetables that she planted during last week's heat wave would be dying or already dead.

She felt cold, too cold to paint. She left the studio and went through to the living room where a meagre fire burned in the grate. She poked and stoked and waited for the blaze, then stood and warmed her back.

On the edge of the hearthrug her laptop flashed at her its tiny sharp light. The lid was down. She picked it up and sat with it in the chair closest to the fire and opened the screen to the Forum.

Franken Form was again up in arms about the Order of Shannon, this time their involvement with The Five Eyes. Fred Spice wanted to know what he meant.

'The WASP nations,' writes Celestial Petal. 'They're a secret surveillance network.'

'They're probably reading this,' Fagbutt Oilcan says.

'Bring it on,' says Franken Form. 'No accident that there's five eyes either.'

'The pentagram,' says Lemony Aide.

'The Freemasons are everywhere,' says Fagbutt.

'Is the Order of Shannon a sub group, do you think?' asks Celestial Petal.

'More likely of the Rosy Cross,' says Franken Form.

'What's with fives?' asks Fred Spice.

'Symbol of power. It's everywhere. Flags, corporate logos...'

'Yeah, well V is five too,' says Fagbutt.

'Victory will be ours!' says Franken Form.

The others follow on with thumbs ups, smiley faces and love hearts.

Judith thought of the five-pointed star on Madeleine's tattered shoulder bag and decided victory unlikely. With irritation she closed her laptop, knowing even as she did that she was opening the door on memory.

By the morning of Thursday the nineteenth of January, Madeleine's rage at her father's rejection of her the night before was replaced with a brooding darkness. Judith clutched a cup of tea in both hands and leaned with her back to the sink, eyeing her daughter seated at the kitchen bench, her cereal bowl pushed aside to make way for the Exeter bus timetable. Judith watched her run a finger down a column.

They didn't speak. Judith's mind was blank, no thoughts gaining purchase in the presence of the emotion moiling in her daughter.

Madeleine glanced up at the clock on the wall above the fridge. Judith followed her gaze. Eight past eight. So she was catching the eight twenty-two that would get her into Exeter at five to nine.

Judith suspected she was on her way to confront Hannah, or more likely Bethany, for Hannah would be in Bournemouth. And Bethany would be mortified at the news of Hannah and Zol. It was the sort of vindictive act commensurate with Madeleine's mood.

She watched, waited, hoped Madeleine's plotting didn't involve her friend.

Relief replaced concern when Madeleine left the house. Once

the front door closed she let out a long sigh and went to the studio and stood by the window. The snow was beginning to thaw, revealing patches of brown and green, the drifts in the hollows and by the walls still banked high. The sky was pale and close, rashers of pale pink cloud streaked above the horizon. The trees were black, their twiggy branches like upturned besoms, and she half-expected a lone figure in rough clothes, hat and staff, to appear at the hillcrest as if from *The Mayor of Casterbridge*.

She stilled her mind in the labours of her new work. A Wimmera derivative, for she was fixated with the Outback: the haunting sense of space, infinite and sparse, the dam bereft of water, its clay base cracked, the fibro hut falling on its stumps, the scraggy dog and the cattleman on horseback, his face full of character. The soulful eyes, the broad nose and mouth, a cattleman who seemed to her as she rendered him in paint to know far more than she.

It was five minutes to four when she heard a door slam and knew that Madeleine was back. She put down her brush, still full of paint, and went and found her in the living room. She was standing in the middle of the floor, sobbing angrily. Her cat, Kali, slunk past Judith and on down the hall.

'Madeleine,' she said softly, reaching for her.

'Don't.'

She backed away.

She felt something like sympathy despite a mounting sense that Madeleine had done something dreadful to cause her current state.

The tears eased. She waited.

'The bastard. The total bastard,' Madeleine said.

'Zol?'

'Not Zol,' she said between clenched teeth. 'Why would I be talking about Zol?'

And she made to leave the room, knocking into Judith's arm on her way past, leaving her standing there nonplussed.

About five minutes later the phone rang.

It was Peter.

'You better do something about your daughter,' he said in a low, even voice.

'What do you mean?' she said, hesitant.

'Just that. You deal with it.'

And he hung up before she had a chance to draw a breath.

She thought of Madeleine upstairs in her room, hesitated, and went back to her painting.

The cattleman stared off at her and over her shoulder all at once. He was at peace and she dared not add a single brush stroke to him; she was too distracted. She cleaned her brush and went upstairs.

Madeleine was slumped on the floor beside her bed.

'What do you want?' she said at the sight of her mother.

'Your father phoned.'

'Yeah, I thought he would.' She looked down at her phone in her lap.

Judith stood in the doorway. Another mother might have sat down beside her daughter, put an arm around her shoulder, another daughter might have accepted the comfort, but Judith had learned a long time before to keep her distance. Even as a baby, Madeleine pinched.

There was a long pause. Judith's gaze flitted around the room, taking in the chaos of Bournemouth piled all over the floor, then alighting on Madeleine's face, obscured behind her curtain of hair.

'So, I disturbed his lecture,' Madeleine said without looking up. Then she laughed. 'You should have seen him. There must have been a hundred students in the room. And they all heard me, too.'

'What did you say?' Judith said cautiously.

'I told him he had no right to slam the phone down on me last night. No right at all.' She looked up and held Judith's gaze, her red, swollen eyes defiant. 'I have every right to see him, I said. Even if he doesn't want to see me.'

'In front of all those students?'

She didn't answer, her gaze sliding back down to her phone.

'Is that all you said?'

'Kinda.'

'What else, Madeleine?' she asked, although she wasn't sure she wanted to hear the answer.

'I asked the students if they knew he was a member of an occult order. The Order of Shannon, in fact.'

'The Order of Shannon? How could you know such a thing?'

'Zol found out on the Forum. Some guy posted a list.'

'And you believe that?'

'Why not? But the students just laughed.'

Judith suppressed an inward smile as she pictured the scene, Peter's outrage, the incredulous looks on the faces of his students. It was a moment of triumph and she thought to congratulate Madeleine on a successful execution. For it seemed to her then that his occult interests, academic as they were, had always lain between him and his filial responsibilities.

She observed her daughter with sudden pity, her stout, squat stature, the tangled black mass of hair, the wild air, a callous youth little loved by one parent, an encumbrance for the other. Yet Madeleine was hard to have around. There were few points of intersection where mother and daughter might share soft times. Her daughter seemed to occupy the whole house, even when she was quiet. The habits and rhythm of Judith's solitary life disrupted, to shift in line with Madeleine. She would phone Peter. Explain Madeleine's hurt. That she could do with his help in encouraging Madeleine back to university for her last semester. Then she would talk to Madeleine.

At a quarter to nine on Saturday the twenty-first of January, Judith was at work in her studio. She had slept well the night before, her first long sleep since Madeleine had appeared on her doorstep last Monday. Four nights of restlessness and she was relieved to have awoken refreshed.

It had taken Judith the whole of the previous day to soothe the squealing pig that was Madeleine's relationship with her father. Much coaxing and preening and reassurances and promises. By the end of the day, despite the exhaustion from the strain, so successful had been her efforts that she felt like a prize winner at an agricultural show, her mediation skills worthy of a badge of excellence: father appeased, daughter contrite, both willing to start again.

They had arranged to meet for lunch, and that morning Madeleine was transformed. Gone the petulant child. She stood in the doorway of the studio and chatted about her plans. How she would find a job in Exeter, a waitress in a café maybe, although Judith found it hard to imagine a café taking her on. Madeleine enthused about how good it was to be back home and that she would help around the house and even mow the lawn if Judith wanted her to. Judith had no idea what to make of this miraculous spurt of conviviality.

'Will you be meeting outside the Priory?' she said.

'He says for me to get off the bus at Pocombe Bridge.'

Judith put down her brush. 'There's nothing there.'

'He's taking me somewhere else. Somewhere special.' She grinned as she swung round and went upstairs to her room.

Judith allowed herself a private smile. Her negotiations had been more successful than she could have hoped. She turned from the cracked clay dam of her painting and let her gaze settle on the wintry scene outside. The snow was gone from the meadow except in patches by stone walls where the sun couldn't reach. All was still in the muted low light of winter.

Madeleine set off for the five past ten bus, leaving Judith optimistic that she would return with her sanity restored, Peter having persuaded her back to Bournemouth. She waved to Madeleine, something she hadn't done since Madeleine was a child, and she closed the front door and watched from the living room window as her only child disappeared from her view.

The house, blessedly empty, relaxed. Even the fire in the grate seemed to emit a long sigh. She tidied the kitchen, stacked dishes in the sink, fed the cat, went outside for more firewood, then returned to her studio.

All day she worked painstakingly on the tessellations of the clay in the dam. Hours squinting, and standing back and easing forward with her brush passed her by before she realised it was four o'clock.

Madeleine seemed late. In the past it had been unusual for Peter to want to spend longer than two hours in his daughter's company. At three minutes past four she called Madeleine's mobile.

Madeleine didn't answer. Judith felt a flutter of anxiety in her belly. It was not a feeling she could ignore. She waited a full eight minutes before again trying Madeleine's phone.

Nothing.

Quarter past. Twenty past. Half past.

No response.

She sent Madeleine a short text message: Call me. Mum.

She went out to the garden in time to catch the last of the light. Already it was almost dark. She pulled on her Wellington boots and picked her way up the garden path, avoiding glassy patches where puddles had frozen. She picked turnips and kale, and returned to the kitchen where she left them on the bench, then she took the wheelbarrow to the woodshed for more firewood.

Back in the courtyard she kicked off her boots and ferried the wood inside. In the living room, she prodded the coals and added a log. Once aflame, she went to the studio and stared out the window at the dark shapes in the gloaming.

Minutes ticked by.

She ignored the cattleman, whose eyes stared right into her, and she closed the studio door.

In the kitchen, she thought about preparing dinner. She glanced at the clock, paused, and again she reached for her phone. It was five o'clock. Still no answer.

She fought away her unease and went to the living room, coaxing aside the cat to warm her legs by the fire.

What time was the last bus? She couldn't recall. She went to the kitchen for the timetable but Madeleine must have taken it.

Back in the living room she sat beside the cat on the hearthrug, clutching her knees, gazing at the licks of amber flame. Night drew

234 ~ Isobel Blackthorn

a dark cloak around her and she felt its cold on her back. She stood and went to the window, looking out at the black before drawing the curtains.

She returned to the fire and again tried Madeleine's number. Nothing. She kept telling herself she had no reason to be concerned. Madeleine was safe. She was with her father and she was safe.

She left the fire. In the kitchen, she went through the motions of chopping, frying, stirring and grating, and at half past five she put in the oven a turnip bake. It was not an imaginative repast but she could think of nothing else.

Back by the fire she gazed at the flames. Time crept by like a stalker.

She looked at her watch. Six o'clock. Madeleine would have to walk home from the bus stop in pitch darkness. Surely Peter would bring her home?

At half past six she served a small portion of the turnip bake and sat by the fire, nibbling at the melted cheese. The cat ignored her.

As evening became night, her anxiety grew into raw fear. She was nauseous. She stared into the fire as if in a trance, until her legs grew stiff and she roused herself to stand.

She paced back and forth to release the tension in her calves, her thighs, her knees, before parting the curtains and peering out the window at the night.

She phoned Madeleine again.

No answer.

She phoned Peter's mobile.

No answer.

If there'd been an accident she would have heard. No news was definitely better than bad news and she spent the following two hours holding onto the thought and dreading a knock on the door.

Eventually she took herself to bed.

The following morning, she rose upon little sleep.

She went straight to the phone. One last try. Still nothing.

She resisted an impulse to throw her phone at the wall, suddenly angry at both of them for not having the presence of mind to make contact. She told herself not to be ridiculous. Peter had no doubt dropped Madeleine off at a friend's house on their way home and Madeleine's phone had run out of charge. That would be the logical course of events. But by the time she had filled the kettle she was unbearably anxious. No news was not good news. It could never be good news. The not knowing was immobilising.

She left the kettle to its rumbling and its hiss and went to the landline to call the police.

'With the father, you say?' a man said indifferently. 'Have you tried his home phone?'

She hadn't thought to do that.

When she heard Peter's voice she caught her breath.

'Is Madeleine with you?' she said, putting on a casual tone.

'No,' he said slowly. 'I dropped her at Pocombe's Bridge.'

'When?'

'Yesterday afternoon.'

'When?'

'In time for the bus, of course.'

Her stomach lurched. 'And you didn't wait with her until the bus came?' she said, trying not to sound hysterical.

'Of course not. She isn't a child.'

'She isn't here either.'

'What do you mean?'

'She didn't come home last night.'

'Then she's probably met up with a friend. You know what she's like.'

His rationalisations, spoken in that familiar accented voice, became her rationalisations. It would be just like Madeleine to take off and not inform her mother. Besides, she was nearly twenty-one, old enough to make her own decisions. Judith had no need for concern. She had let herself get too overwrought, Madeleine consuming her, even in her absence.

She made coffee, toast, convinced herself Madeleine was fine.

She went to her studio and set to work on the riverbank scene, determined to finish it. Gradually she smoothed out its flaws, teased out the hints of light on the surface of the water, worked her way into the deeper reaches.

She worked on the painting all day, sometimes pausing to gaze out the window at the bleak wintry sky and the frosted branches, tracking the shadows cast by the sun's low arc, long fingers of dark. Twice giving in to an urge to try Madeleine's number.

The light began to fade. She didn't think she could endure another night of not knowing. She forced herself to keep working.

It was four sixteen when she heard a knock on the door. At last! She put down her brush and rushed to answer.

Madeleine should have been standing there, all sullen and dishevelled, pushing her way past her mother into the house. Instead she faced two uniformed police officers who asked if they might come inside.

Dread bolted through her, a single violent pulse.

She sat down in the chair farthest from the fire. Her hands were trembling. She clenched them together in her lap. The officers remained standing. One of them cleared her throat. The other's gaze drifted around the room.

They were both terribly sorry.

Judith found it hard to focus on the words.

A body had been found in Baker's Pit. A young woman with Madeleine's phone. Would she be prepared to identify the body?

At first she couldn't take it in. Then she thought there had to be a mistake. Baker's Pit was near Higher Kiln Quarry in Buckfastleigh to the southwest, the bus stop at Pocombe Bridge was to the east. How did Madeleine get from the bridge to the cave after Peter had dropped her at the bus stop?

She told them. She told them that someone must have snatched her as she stood there waiting. The officers exchanged glances. She told them they should get out there.

One of the officers produced a notepad and pen.

She explained as clearly and succinctly as she could the lunch date, and the arrangement to meet at Pocombe Bridge. Then the unanswered phone calls. What times were those calls made? She listed the times. Then she mentioned the conversation with Peter at his home that morning, made on the advice of their colleague. Can you remember exactly what was said? She tried.

And she privately cursed Peter for not staying with Madeleine until the bus came.

The police asked if there was someone they could call. She told them no. There was no one. Although in the days that followed she lost her solitude to the police and, what seemed like nanoseconds later, the media.

She identified the body. She could barely look at the white cold flesh on the slab, eyes closed, hair neatly arranged about the face. Hair that had never looked so tidy.

The truth unravelled quickly after that. Madeleine never did stand alone at the bus stop at Pocombe Bridge. There had been a memorial service that afternoon for two lads whose motorbike had slammed into an abutment the week before. The bus stop was not twenty metres away. People would have noticed a girl matching Madeleine's description waiting there. The bus driver confirmed this fact.

Peter was taken in for questioning. In the interview, he was arrested and charged. The police thought others were involved. Peter wouldn't say. Judith was warned things could turn ugly, especially for her. The media scrummed as the scandal broke.

She kept the curtains drawn. She told Bethany to stay away after she visited one afternoon filled with dubious concern and shovelfuls of advice. She had spent most of a long hour preoccupied with Hannah's devastating guilt. Something like malice unfurled in Judith as she listened, at last suggesting Bethany take the cat, which had been rubbing up against her friend's leg. To her surprise, Bethany agreed without hesitation, saying it would be of tremendous therapeutic help for her daughter.

Once she had closed the door on her friend, it was only the police who came and went. They searched Madeleine's room. Interviewed Judith. Interviewed her again. Just a few questions each time. And with kind looks and sympathetic smiles they left her alone and pressed their way through the vigil outside.

The cameras and eager faced women and men were not outside Fernley cottage for long. A mass of cold air rolled down from the north and the wind chill fell well below freezing. The street emptied.

Then the police stopped coming. Her life resumed its regular quiet.

A few weeks later she discovered the fuller story. The police informed her that a seventeen-year-old girl had come forward with allegations that she had been passed around a sex ring based in the area, but that the men in question had found a replacement. The police told Judith that the girl was in fear of her life, convinced she had escaped her own death. About the same time, a sleuth of a journalist, clearly hungry to make her mark in the media world, had unearthed the backstory of Dr Peter Love, his close ties to the Order of Shannon, a sect implicated in a ritual killing of a minor in Australia some time before. Of his associations in Munich. She made him sound like a deviant from the first, and certainly not the Peter Love she had known.

The worst she could have said about him was his absence, his lack of interest in his daughter.

Franken Form, Celestial Petal, Fagbutt Oilcan, even Ashtray Petrolstick are preferable to recalling Madeleine walking down the garden path on her way to the bus stop.

Two months and two days since her death, and Celestial Petal starts a thread entitled The Three P's—Paedophilia, Politics and Power. And within seconds Franken Form makes reference to the Order of Shannon. He claims that the Order engages in ritual sacrifices to enhance the evolution of mankind. That only the lowest order human beings are used in the sacrifices.

'How could they tell?' asks Lemony Aide.

'It's like Lebensborn,' says Fagbutt Oilcan.

'A superior inferior race thing,' says Celestial Petal.

'We're all equal,' says Fred Spice.

'Not according to them. They say some humans are barely more than animals,' answers Franken Form.

'Like sacrificing a chicken.'

She closes the laptop before she sees his name.

She goes upstairs to Madeleine's bedroom, opens the door for the first time since the twenty-first of January. The belongings she collected from Bournemouth are scattered across the floor. The police haven't disturbed a thing. No one thought to tidy up. Fold her clothes maybe. Judith takes a gasp of air. Her throat aches. Tears blind her sight. She opens the suitcase and stuffs it full and struggles with the zipper that catches in a scarf. She doesn't stop until the room is emptied, the car loaded for the charity shop.

She keeps a teddy bear Madeleine's grandmother gave her when she was a baby and her old shoulder bag with the tattered logo of a five-pointed star.

In the studio, her sorrow recedes. She takes in at a glance the felled ironbark in its paddock of stubble, and, beside it, the cattle-man looking ponderous as ever. They'll look fine in the bistro. Lend a greater authenticity to the space. She stands by the window. A tangle of clouds muddles the sky. The forecast is rain but she leaves the studio, leaves the house and takes a long and slow walk down the lane.

Part Three

The Inner Need

The Inner Need

The day was bright and warm, the maples dotted about around Sassafras putting on a fine show of reds. The equinox had passed and despite the turning of the season towards winter's cool and damp, the mood in the village on that Easter weekend was one of optimism and vigour. Even the gallery, a dull space where sunlight strained to reach, felt cheery: a gallery poised for its exhibition opening. A gratifying prospect and Phoebe put a zing in her stride as she went about making fine adjustments to the setting: three rows of chairs in an arc facing the far corner of the room where a small amplifier, a piano stool, and a standard lamp marked the stage.

Harriet's nine paintings hung in a row along the two walls that formed the stage corner, the five on the longer wall that included the chimney breast replacing the Wessex series that Phoebe had relegated to the back room, insisting that Harriet remove her finds to make space. There the series hung, at odds with the triptych of silver birches that had found its way back to the gallery when the buyer, Mr Fitzsimmons, phoned her one day last month and said he was sorry but his wife couldn't abide them. Put an icy chill through her, he had said. Phoebe obligingly refunded the cost, less twenty per cent for her trouble.

She went through to the back room wondering if, at least for the opening, she should replace the triptych with something more convivial, for she shared Mrs Fitzsimmons's sentiment, if not her icy chill. It had been part of an auction lot at a deceased estate. She had had her eye on one or two other paintings in the lot, which she had sold almost immediately.

She eyed the triptych critically, with the sharp knowledge that of all her acquisitions, it was the least inspiring. Despite the skilful execution, there was something stilted, almost manufactured about the works. They lacked emotion and it was emotion that drew Phoebe to a work. She wanted to be moved and for that to occur a work had to be vital, almost visceral, as if the artist had bled her own blood in the making.

Her gaze drifted over Harriet's Wessex series, which, for all the vibrancy, belonged in a curious way in here with the triptych, for those works also lacked something vital. Phoebe suspected that Harriet had let her intellect get the better of her in their execution. They were a confusing layering of conceptual technique, as if Harriet were straining to release her creative constipation. She had thought too much and an over-thought piece showed itself to be just that. If the triptych suggested the artist were somehow constrained or holding back, then the Wessex works were over-cooked, stewed to buggery, as her aunt would say.

Phoebe would keep silent on her thoughts. She heard Harriet moving about in the kitchenette and smiled inwardly. It was less hurtful to blame market forces and the zeitgeist than criticise her friend's artistic direction. Besides, Harriet was stubborn. She had been sinking into the land of the abstract for decades, spawned from her intellectual love affair with Kandinsky. Phoebe found it a matter of enormous frustration, for Harriet's talent and her potential were being buried with it. Still, Harriet was her oldest and would always be her closest friend and she would never threaten that bond, especially today, when Harriet was a lather of apprehension.

She nudged to the vertical one of the Wessex paintings and went to leave the room when Harriet appeared in the doorway, wiping her hands on her apron and muttering about the need to get on.

The diffidence of her friend touched her. 'I'll take care of things from here, Harriet,' she said and swept forward her arms as if to scoop up a breeze to assist her friend's passage out the door.

On her way by, her friend shot her a look of harried gratitude. Phoebe followed her to the front door and closed it behind her, turning to again survey the arrangements. The pier table, moved from the back room, was positioned against the window partition on her right and draped in white linen. Upturned wine glasses stood in neat rows. Beside them was a stack of Ginny's new, her very first, CDs. Phoebe felt an upsurge of vicarious pride in the viewing.

She went through to the kitchenette and cast her eye over the platters of canapés and nibbles.

She wandered around, enjoying the emptiness, the sense of anticipation, the gallery soon to be filled, an audience set to experience something unique, a mother and daughter collaborating on a multimedia event, both drawing inspiration from the same source and, she suspected, as only a mother and daughter could do.

It was her own triumph, too, for without her involvement she was sure Harriet would have crumbled.

And to do it she had had to dismiss her familiar envy the moment the feeling appeared. She knew she must never wish upon her own life the comfort and security Harriet and Ginny had, albeit one marred by a tragedy. She was who she was, a survivor of playground thuggery, pleased with the knowledge that many of her former foes had been her clients at one time or another. She had put on their functions, sold them art.

She was, she thought with some satisfaction, a prized convener and arbiter of taste. Especially now she had stumbled on paintings from women of Middle Eastern backgrounds. That Suhair Subai piece she acquired had sold in a week and now she had a few Laila Shawwa's from Palestine as well. Many of her collectors were able to feel much sympathy for the displaced upon hearing Phoebe's well-honed speech, a twist on the poor-beleaguered-artist spin that she had crafted in the Eighties to shift Harriet's works. Part sales banter, part conviction, for she considered herself a survivor and a battler who identified with all the survivors and battlers the world over. She decided that she had in fact had much to do with her clients' enlightened concern. And now she couldn't lay her hands on enough Arab artworks to satisfy the niche she had created in the market.

Harriet was her one and only bygone artist. Poor Harriet. She couldn't move with the times. Even without its overladen conceptualisations, her Wessex series would never sell in today's marketplace. For all the harkening back to the motherland that abounded in the Dandenongs, when it came to art, Britain was out of favour. Harriet wouldn't sell the works unless she were prepared to ship them and exhibit over there, for only the British were buying British art. At least in her networks. No doubt the occasional British piece would fetch a good price at auction but she wasn't in that league. She occupied the middling ground, her pieces selling at figures with three, not five zeros, prices grand for the emerging and the struggling female artist. She had made one or two discoveries over the decades too, and helped foster the careers of many. She once had high hopes for Harriet back in the Eighties, when she would knock out artworks at an astonishing rate. That she had talent was undeniable. Phoebe had even been prepared to overlook her predilection for her beloved Kandinsky, along with the fact that all her revered painters were men who were dead.

Wilhelm had done them both a favour when he came along and occupied all of Harriet's attention. Although Phoebe couldn't have known it at the time, any more than she could have known that Harriet would stay forevermore stuck in the past. Then again, perhaps without him she might have adapted, in which case it was Wilhelm who had served to freeze her in time.

She ran through the speech she would make to the gallery. She would make sure all in attendance viewed the pieces in the back room. Suggest to Harriet a buy one get one half-price deal. Perhaps she might flog the triptych too. And if one of those moneyed-up priestesses didn't take it, she would give it to the charity shop in Prahran.

She thought it about time she made her way to Maryvale's to collect her guests.

Before she left she passed a purveyor's eye over Harriet's new works. Harriet had surpassed herself. A nine-week deadline had seen a resurgence of her old passion. By the look of them she had managed to bypass her own artistic foibles and prejudices and go with whatever came out of her imagination, capturing that moment of pure artistic impulse. And for once, that she was at odds with the times didn't matter. These paintings contained a purpose, an inner meaning, and a subtle coherence. She had pulled it off, just as she had pulled off her homages series all those years before. Perhaps this should be known as her Homage to the Moon series, and she thought of including the phrase in her speech.

In keeping with her Moon model, the pieces were cosmic. Each painting framed by gossamer threads and translucent striations; not following the exact form of the square, instead curvy, subversive, distinctly feminine and mystical in feel. She had used three main colours, and in each painting the colours—milky white, bluish grey and pale gold—were aligned differently. It was a reference too, to Kandinsky's 'Squares with Concentric Circles'. Silvery triangles ascending to deep violet heavens or descending to indigo depths. Not the two-dimensional triangles of the hack fantasy artist, these shapes stretched to vanishing points, receding into the canvas at odd angles, juxtaposed with other shapes cast on differing trajectories. The result was static movement, a sense of something caught in a moment and fixed in place. They were pure Kandinsky in his Bauhaus phase and despite her dislike of his style, she was pleased she had given her that CD. These works would not easily sell in today's market, not in her circles, but she knew her priestesses were relics too, and it was a perfect match.

Harriet had arrived on the doorstep breathless and flustered as Ginny was about to make her way to the gallery. Leaving her mother to decide which frock would best complement her artwork,

Ginny strapped her keyboard to her furniture trolley and, with her music stand under one arm, negotiated gravel, pavement and kerb. She was garbed in her grey dress and matching jacket that she had worn on Christmas Eve. Then she had worn the outfit with discomfort, the straight woman in a vaudeville scene. This time she would be on stage and the colour and the cut were in keeping with her performer image. She had treated herself to a haircut at O Linda's of Olinda—an impeccably neat crop—and made up her face with a light touch of colour about lips and eyes. She walked with confidence and anticipation, attracting as she neared the gallery the quick gazes of pedestrians drawn to the incongruity of the image: a carefully dressed woman wheeling a large long case on a trolley as if she were a removalist.

She was well acquainted with those sorts of looks. The puzzlement, the figuring out, then the smiles of realisation that the case contained a keyboard. Then there were the appraising looks as if the woman beheld was surely not the pianist. Puzzlement returning to faces as the onlookers asked inwardly, or to each other, why a well-dressed woman would be wheeling a keyboard-laden trolley behind her. Must be the girlfriend.

Where was she going? What's the occasion? Can anyone attend?

She appreciated Phoebe, who would collect her and her instrument and drive her to whatever function they had on, then insist on carrying the gear and helping set up. Ginny suspected she enjoyed the role of roadie, displaying disappointment whenever the venue of the day had its own baby grand.

She unlocked the gallery door with the key Harriet had given her and pulled the trolley inside, closing and locking the door behind her.

Chairs fanned in rows from the far corner where stood a chair, her amp, piano stool and the standard lamp Phoebe had insisted on. She went and set up her stand and returned to the trolley to release the occy straps, easing her keyboard to the ground. She unzipped the case, lifted the instrument and carried it down past her mother's paintings. She put it on the stand and went back to the case for the lead and her peddle.

With the keyboard ready, she took in her mother's paintings, one to four on her right and five to nine on her left.

The paintings looked different in a row. For her CD cover she had arranged photos of the works to form a perfect square. She thought back to last Monday and the moment Harriet swept into the kitchen and declared her paintings finished. After the congratulatory hug and celebratory talk, Ginny had gone to the studio with her camera to photograph each one, then on to the printers, returning an hour later with nine neatly guillotined prints.

By then it was lunchtime and Harriet busy making coffee and bruschetta. Ginny laid out the prints on the table and asked her to take a look. Her mother was always more amenable in the middle of the day, or rather, more easily inveigled. Harriet had wanted a simple linear series from one to nine. Ginny pointed out the other patterns, ones that were non-sequential. 'You can't jumble up the months,' Harriet had complained. But they were not months. They were paintings. The Moon model had stimulated the imagination and that was all.

'More than that, Ginny. The model depicted the movement of the spheres and the corresponding significances. Everything has a correct order.'

'Mum, the planets, the root races, all the correspondences of theosophy aren't literal truths.'

'If not then there's no merit in my reality and I might as well give up.'

'I didn't mean there's no merit. What I'm saying is if you treat theosophical knowledge as metaphor then it still has the power to explain the universe, just not at the expense of other explanations. Metaphoric ways of knowing don't bind us and turn us into slaves. Your paintings work because you stopped being an adherent and allowed yourself creative freedom. And look at the result. These works came from inside of you and they're fabulous.'

A sharp smell of burning toast had halted the exchange as Harriet swung round to rescue the bruschetta.

Ginny glided a hand down the keys and smiled inwardly. It was only after her mother's approval that she had loaded the images onto her laptop and repeated the design.

The arrangement had come up well and, stacked beside the glasses on the pier table in the opposite corner of the room, there was the product, her product, her first CD.

The recording had been a breeze. With just one instrument to mix and master the producer, Tommo the Tank, a middle-aged folkie sporting a full beard and a beer gut, had put his boots on the sound desk, hands behind his head and, leaning back in his swivel chair, he had listened through his headphones, letting her play without interference. Later he called her one-take Ginny. She was flattered.

In her mother's gallery, surrounded by all the elements of their collaboration, mother and daughter exhibiting and performing together, presenting to the audience a perfect harmony, as if they had an enduring rapport—if only they knew, she thought with a soft laugh.

She ran through the songs in the order she would later perform them, then she stood and stretched her hands behind her back and rolled her shoulders. She found she was more nervous than she had anticipated. Those songs were her own material. Other than end of year recitals she hadn't performed her compositions to a listening audience. She was to be judged, not by academics with checkpoints on a clipboard, not by her peers more concerned with how their work measured up to hers and hers to theirs, and not with all of their acutely attuned ears turned to every nuance of tone and interval. This audience would expect to be entertained.

Were her songs entertaining? Tommo the Tank said he liked them. And so far that was all the feedback she had received. For she hadn't let Phoebe or Harriet listen to her CD. This opening was to be her unveiling.

She left her corner stage, unlocked the front door and looked up and down the street. Agatha's was closed and the lights went off in the bric-a-brac shop across the street as she watched. There was a nip in the air so she left the door ajar. She had hoped her mother would arrive before the guests but before long the door swung open and two couples, strangers, filtered inside and she was forced to meet and greet. Thankfully, soon after, Phoebe arrived with her party of goddesses in flowing frocks, along with a young woman dressed in the black and white garb of the waitress.

Within minutes the gallery was a hubbub of voices and laughter. Wine was sipped, nibbles and canapés eaten. Ginny stood aside and tuned into the mood music playing quietly in the background.

Her merchandise attracted much interest, and she was forced to the pier table as a woman in a brightly coloured sari extracted her purse to buy a CD. 'To beat the rush,' she said. Ginny offered to sign it, feeling a buzz as she extracted her pen.

Then came the Pargiters, the Hunnacots, some parents of other old school friends, and several former teachers.

Still no Harriet.

Poppy and Veronica arrived together arm in arm, Poppy sporting a lurid purple shawl over a dress smothered in pansies, and Veronica in her usual copious layers obscuring no doubt much percussive potential about her wrists. As they approached, Ginny hoped that for the concert her friend would have the presence of mind to keep motionless her bangled arms.

She stood with her friends and made small talk, ignoring the queasy feeling in her belly. And the room kept on filling. She noticed Rosalind slip in and take up a seat in the middle of the back row, from where she could observe all the paintings.

Phoebe, who had foregone her beloved trench coat in favour of a silk trouser suit of iridescent sapphire, emerged out of the throng and drew Ginny aside.

'It's time.'

'What about Mum?'

'Can't keep an audience waiting.'

Ginny proceeded to her stage and sat down before her keyboard. Phoebe switched on the standard lamp and disappeared. As the background music faded and died the guests took up their seats. When Phoebe returned and stood beside Ginny's keyboard the room quieted.

Ginny observed her audience in one quick sweep. The rows of faces were so close. Those standing behind formed a thicket near the front door, others lining the far wall. There was little room by the pier table. Little room to enter the gallery from the street.

She felt a surface thrill, her skin alive, yet a deeper part of her remained poised and calm. The exhibition was already a success and as she listened to Phoebe's long and elaborate introduction, for the first time she was happy to be back in Sassafras. Her former peers might be on international tours, recording with the greats, scoring lucrative television and film contracts, but it didn't matter. As Phoebe rounded off her speech and the applause rang out, Ginny was awash with gratitude.

She stood and bowed and sat back down and the audience hushed. She had no idea what they would make of her music, or if they would notice any connections between song and painting, but as she played the first song, eyes wandered discretely in search of the corresponding artwork.

Her fingers worked the keys, her left hand maintaining an ostinato rhythm, her right ringing out a melody centred around the ninth, infusing the music with sweet melancholy, instilling in the listener a creeping, lingering sadness that spoke of poignant loss, as if time itself had paused. And when the last notes rang out the room fell into a complete silence before an uproar of applause broke out and there were cheers from the back. She ran her hands down her thighs that were suddenly cold, quickly scanning the room but it seemed her mother still hadn't arrived.

She quelled her disappointment.

Her second piece was dramatic, heavy, and dark. There were

pauses, unexpected changes in time signature, rippling tones in the B-section, to hold the interest. When she could she glanced at the faces of her audience. Their expressions were surprising. Some had closed their eyes. Others were nodding slowly in time with the music. There was a serious air in the room and she hoped she hadn't overdone the intensity, but the audience looked prepared to be taken on a journey, a journey with lows and highs: life.

Again, the applause was strong. As she smiled she searched the audience for her mother. Disappointment grew into dismay but she dare not show it. She proceeded with her next piece.

The gallery door opened when she was about halfway through the B section. It was Harriet. She pushed through the crowd and took up a spot at the back. Ginny wondered what could possibly have kept her. Then a man entered the gallery. He made his way around the back of the thicket by the door. She barely caught a glimpse and she hadn't seen him for years but she knew who it was.

Black was slimming but perhaps a little funereal for the occasion. The cream, although complementary, too formal. The red might clash and besides, she didn't want to draw that much attention to herself. She thought of going to the studio to play her Bauhaus CD for inspiration when there was a sharp rap on the front door. Standing in her undergarments she had no time but to throw on a voluminous robe of Thai silk before heading downstairs.

She adjusted the fall of her robe, clasping the lapels together against her chest as she opened the door just a crack to peer out.

At the sight of him, her heartbeat quickened.

There is a chasm of age in the life of a human between the decade of the forties and that of the fifties, but he was faring well. Lean as ever. His hair, receding but still his own colour, made him appear learned as did his rimless glasses. He smiled his familiar smile and said, '*Guten Tag.*'

She welcomed him inside and they stood together in the hall, Harriet still clasping the lapels of her robe.

'This is a surprise,' she said with a short laugh, cursing her internal furnace that had chosen that moment to roar. 'I'm in the middle of getting changed.'

'Bad timing,' he said apologetically.

'No, I think you have helped me make up my mind.'

At the foot of the stairs, one hand on the banister, she hesitated.

'Go on,' he said. 'You'll catch a chill.'

'I won't be a moment.'

She gestured for him to go through to the living room and scurried upstairs.

The moment she entered her bedroom she threw off her robe and flung open the window, letting the fresh air cool her skin. Thoughts shot through her mind like darts. His appearance on her doorstep, confusing and fortuitous, was a coincidence of the highest order, the intersecting of the exhibition and his presence a synchronicity, that wondrous perfecting of time. Synchronicity was always about time, she thought, time that made those concerned raise themselves up and take notice.

Feeling a little cooler, she pulled away from the window and changed quickly into the red.

When she entered the living room he was standing by the fireplace viewing her Kandinsky.

'Admirable,' he said without shifting his gaze. 'I think I remember this.'

She blushed at the memory of that one time he came to her rooms in Moor Street. A memory intensified when he turned his gaze to her and, after a lingering pause, said, 'Ravishing.'

'I hardly think so,' she said, embarrassed.

'You haven't changed a bit.'

His comments, flattering as they were and spontaneously uttered, met her ears with a thwack as if they had been lifted straight from Mills and Boon, and she wondered at Fritz for resorting to such commonplace turns of phrase. Perhaps there had been nothing to read on the flight.

'What brings you back?' she said lightly.

'Your exhibition of course. Rosalind told me.'

'Don't be absurd,' she said with a self-deprecating smile, for she couldn't imagine Fritz making that enormous journey for a local art exhibition.

'And a conference,' he admitted. 'I'm presenting a paper at Monash next week. Couldn't come to Melbourne without seeing you.'

'You might have warned me.'

'I wanted to surprise you.'

'You did that,' she said and made to go through the beaded curtain.

He followed and she held the curtain aside for him to pass through.

'Drink?'

'Sure.'

'This calls for gin. You still drink gin?'

'Of course.'

He sat down at the table and she could feel him watching her as she moved about the kitchen.

'My apologies,' he said as she proffered a glass. 'I was heading straight to the gallery when I saw you walking down the street. I thought I must have been early so I followed. I waited in the garden for a while and when you didn't appear, I knocked.'

'I was choosing a dress,' she said, taking the chair opposite and slugging her gin.

Their eyes locked for a few moments. Then he gripped his glass and lowered his gaze to the table. She sensed he was holding things in, things he wanted to tell her, propriety and her short responses rendering him guarded. Yet he looked ready to burst with impatience.

'There is no conference,' she said gently.

'No.' His face reddened. 'I've taken up a position at La Trobe.' He cleared his throat. 'Rosalind, has she spoken to you?'

'About Wilhelm you mean? Yes.' She had found Harriet at the gallery one afternoon and explained that she had spoken to Ginny.

Harriet presumed she had made an identical divulgence. She had been meaning to broach the matter with Ginny ever since but had thought better of it.

'And Ginny?'

'She knows.'

'That he was arrested. That's all I told Rosalind. There's been a development.'

'He's been charged?'

He took a deep breath. 'Harriet, he's dead. Suicide they believe.'

'Wilhelm? Suicide? Never.'

'It looks that way.'

'It doesn't seem possible.'

'Perhaps it was inevitable. The murder made front-page news. Then the usual mud raking began. And his associations were beginning to emerge.'

'The sect.'

'No. Well perhaps, but only obliquely. No one really knows. But he was well-connected. It turns out that behind the scenes, he was much in favour with the government of the day.'

'The poor girl.'

'Yes. The poor girl. Thus far there's no suggestion it was a ritual killing.'

'Even so. The poor mother too. She must be beside herself.' And Harriet couldn't help an upwelling of relief. That mother would never gain the justice of a trial and Ginny would never again meet her father, but his suicide revealed his guilt and Harriet found herself vindicated.

She drained her glass and stood. 'We better go,' she said.

With Fritz behind her, Harriet pushed open the gallery door to a glissando on the piano. She paused, not wanting to interrupt, then she squeezed as discretely as she could through the crowd. Heads turned. A few looks of acknowledgement from those she knew. She joined Phoebe standing near the door to the back room. A look of mild reproach slid from Phoebe's face when she saw Fritz.

Ginny's music was mesmerising, mellifluous, rich. It was nothing like McCoy Tyner and nothing like Count Basie. It wasn't even jazz. She had been anticipating jazz. She had been anticipating music she wouldn't like. She had not been anticipating compositions so intricate, delicate, fragile, yet controlled. It was Bach meets the Cocteau Twins and, staring into that corner where Ginny sat, all demure in her much-favoured grey, Harriet saw flashes and streaks and shards of light in pale colours: pinks, yellows, blues, greens. It was her private show and one so delightful she knew she might as well have conceived all of her paintings by listening to her daughter's works. Bauhaus had had their day. She felt a delicious tingle at the thought of future collaborations, ones in which Ginny composed and Harriet, the imitator, would listen and paint.

At the end of the song, Ginny looked into the crowd, pausing as their eyes met, the beginnings of a smile appearing at the corners of her mouth.

At the concert's end Phoebe came to the stage and over the applause thanked the audience. She introduced Harriet and heads turned and her mother smiled and bowed. Phoebe headed down an aisle and the audience dispersed and there was a rush to the CD table. Ginny left her keyboard and was cornered by enthusiastic fans and she saw that her mother was also trapped. There was no sign of Fritz.

After an hour of banter and CD signing her jaw ached from the grinning. Her mind buzzed yet she felt exhaustion waiting to swallow her.

She saw with relief that Phoebe had gathered her party of women and was preparing to leave. She looked exultant. Catching Ginny's gaze, she walked over and leaned in close, whispering conspiratorially, 'Even shifted the triptych.'

The room quickly emptied and when there were few people remaining, Veronica and Poppy, who must have been waiting and waiting, approached, each holding a CD.

'Team squeeze,' Veronica said, and her friends gathered her up in their arms.

'You were a sensation.'

'No more Thomas Tallis for me,' said Poppy.

'You must perform at the next lipstick convention!'

'And did my parents tell you? They want you to do a house concert for their fortieth wedding anniversary.'

It was hard to absorb. Perhaps one or two of the numerous offers she had received in the last hour would translate into something real. Wine talked grand in the aftermath of a performance, everyone high and exuberant. But she wouldn't let realism dampen her euphoria.

She was keen to find Fritz, but when Veronica and Poppy said their goodbyes Rosalind crossed the room.

'Well worth persevering, wasn't it my dear?' she said with much warmth.

'Thank you, Rosalind.'

'Excellent use of the ninth too.'

'That's high praise.'

'Well deserved. It's a mystical interval. And you handled it beautifully.'

She wasn't sure how to respond. She grinned the grin she had been wearing for so long it felt stuck fast on her face and as a thought occurred to her and she breathed in to speak, Rosalind went on.

'It's as if your mother has given birth to you a second time, Ginny.' She searched Ginny's face. As if pleased with what she saw she left the gallery.

Ginny scanned the room. With all the guests gone there was just one remaining CD on the table and a red dot beside all of her mother's paintings. Harriet appeared and met her gaze and they both laughed.

'We did it,' Ginny said and followed her mother to the back room, where Fritz was sitting on the sofa, gazing at one of the Wessex series.

He stood and shook Ginny's hand. 'Sensational,' he said warmly. 'Thank you.'

'My, how you've grown,' he said, with an appreciative sweep of his gaze. 'Yet somehow you seem no different to when I knew you.'

No, that couldn't be, although she supposed in some respects she was the same.

It was her mother who seemed different. She glowed a different sort of glow to the discomforting one of the previous months.

She had a barrage of questions but gave voice to none. The look that came into his face, into her mother's face, confirmation enough.

'I'm sorry,' Fritz said.

For weeks, she had been caught in a hiatus of disbelief. She had searched through the news reports online until she met with his face but not his name. But it was him. She knew it was him. She had quickly dismissed as implausible the notion that he had a doppelganger. And suicide was his admission of guilt.

'We should go back to the house,' she said, craving a change of setting.

And it was obvious to her then that a circle was completing, that there was a return to a point before her own story had begun and as she walked behind her mother, watching the bounce in her gait, and Fritz, who had turned his torso a little in her mother's direction, his stride somewhat laboured as a result, Ginny was surprised to find herself pleased.

Acknowledgements

I'd like to thank Kathryn Coughran, Jasmina Brankovich, and Rod Beecham for taking the trouble to read my words and give valuable feedback. Suzanne Diprose for taking me for walks and drives in the Dandenong Ranges east of Melbourne and for furnishing me with all sorts of nuggets. And my publisher, Michelle Lovi, whose unwavering support continues to inspire me and spur me on.

And my heartfelt thanks and deepest gratitude to my daughter Elizabeth Blackthorn, who travelled with me from the beginning. *A Perfect Square* is based on her Honours thesis in Music Improvisation, for which she received a 1st at the Victorian College of the Arts/University of Melbourne in 2014. Her interest, dedication and insights have been profound, and are highly prized.

About the Author

A Londoner originally, Isobel Blackthorn currently resides in Melbourne, Australia. She received her BA in Social Studies from the Open University, and has a PhD in Western Esotericism. She has worked as a high school teacher, market trader and PA to a literary agent. Her writing has appeared in *Backhand Stories*, *The Mused Literary Review*, *On Line Opinion* and *Paranoia Magazine*. Other works include the novels, *Asylum* and *The Drago Tree*, and the short story collection, *All Because of You*.

www.isobelblackthorn.com

@IBlackthorn

To accompany *A Perfect Square*, Isobel's daughter and pianist Elizabeth Blackthorn has composed an EP of the same name. To download her work, follow one of the following options:

http://elizabethblackthorn.bandcamp.com

iTunes/Elizabeth Blackthorn/A Perfect Square

'The author, like an artist slowly dabbing paint upon a canvas, methodically yet tauntingly brings to life complex, damaged characters, their pasts, their struggles to relate to each other and the paths they are set upon. I strongly recommend it.'
— Michelle Saftich, author of *Port of No Return*

'*A Perfect Square* is a clever, thoughtful literary novel which still manages to have a cracking plot and complex characters. It should appeal to lovers of psychological thrillers too—think artistic *Gone Girl*.'
— Kate Braithwaite, author of *Charlatan*

'Isobel Blackthorn is a clever author, I very much enjoyed her biting wit.'
— Lolly K Dandeneau

'Isobel Blackthorn is a gifted and insightful writer who has penned this slow burning and intellectually demanding literary read.'
— Paromjit, Goodreads

'Some books haunt you. You rarely know this will happen when you are reading them—the sensation creeps up on you after the last page. With *A Perfect Square* there was a moment as I read where my heart dropped and I knew this book would stay with me.'
— Rachel Nightingale, author of *Harlequin's Riddle* and *Columbine's Tale*

'Flawless'
— Jasmina Brankovich, writer

'Blackthorn is an exceptionally skillful writer, not only at the technical level (characterisation, description, structure and so on) but at the thematic level. As she writes about the power of art, she evokes a range of emotional responses in the reader. The beautiful language in the book inspired me to create, while at one point I felt heart pounding anxiety and at the end, when I realised how few pages were left, I felt bereft because I didn't want to leave the characters whose lives I had become absorbed in. The descriptions of art and the creative process are a reminder that there is much more below the surface than we often notice. I don't keep many books anymore because I've run out of shelf space, but this is one that I will keep and return to. A marvellous work.'

— Goodreads reviewer

.

Lightning Source UK Ltd.
Milton Keynes UK
UKHW040613241219
355963UK00002B/434/P